Stack would have to move fast and take out everyone in the house. It would mean making a lot of noise and alerting others that an intruder was inside Vista Royale. But that was what separated the men from the boys.

The door just ahead jerked open and two bikers advanced toward Stack. One was going for the gun in his belt. Stack let him have a round in the upper chest. Stack then swung his rifle and pumped a round into the head of the second man. The bullet plowed through hard bone, then into softer brain tissue underneath. Stack wheeled around the corner to confront the biker who had raced from the room into the hall. The biker got off a wild shot, which chewed into the wall three feet above Stack's head. A second later, almost as if in slow motion, Stack pumped round number four into the running hoodlum. As the biker began to fall, a grimace of pain on his lips, Stack heard feet racing down the stairs at the front of the house. . . .

HELL RIDE
Paul Hofrichter

LEISURE BOOKS   NEW YORK CITY

I dedicate this story to Dan and Faith Fliegler and Dr. M. Halperin, who read and commented on the book. And last, but not least, to Abe Horowitz, who repaired the equipment that enabled me to write the stories.

A LEISURE BOOK

Published by

Dorchester Publishing Co., Inc.
6 East 39th Street
New York, NY 10016

Copyright © 1987 by Paul Hofrichter

All rights reserved. No part of this book may be reproduced or transmitted in any form or by any electronic or mechanical means, including photocopying, recording, or by any information storage and retrieval system, without the written permission of the Publisher, except where permitted by law.

Printed in the United States of America

1

The blue sky, interrupted here and there by the white fleece clouds, shone through the green ceiling of the thick forest canopy and illuminated a shadowed glade through which a gurgling stream flowed. The stream moved with a cool swiftness that called men and animals to its banks in search of a refreshing drink.

Nick Stack, who stood at the edge of the glade, had already used the stream for washing and shaving, and for water for his coffee and cooking. Now he watched others satisfying themselves on the opposite side of the stream, barely 30 yards from where he stood—close enough for him to use the Savage 99F rifle hanging over his shoulder, almost guaranteeing him a hit. But Stack made no move toward the rifle and continued to watch without flexing a muscle. He stood as immobile as the surrounding tree trunks, blending in with them, his camouflage hunter's uniform aiding his disguise. His eyes narrowed to slits as he watched, fascinated by the deer and her fawn along the edge of the stream. The fawn had lowered its elegant neck to drink from the water. The deer did not drink. The long lashes of her alert eyes fluttered rapidly, indicating nervousness, as she watched the surrounding forest. Gazing left, right, then back again, she craned her head slightly upward and her nostrils flared as she sniffed the wind for any trace of dangerous intruders. So far she had not smelled, or noticed, the human watching her. After a few more sniffs she relaxed her vigilance and decided there was no danger. There wasn't. But only because the watcher had decided not to attack. Satisfied with the temporary security of the forested glade, the deer lowered her head and drank thirstily.

The man watching smiled. For him the scene was peaceful. The gurgling water, the doe and her fawn, the breeze gently swaying the branches of the pines in the forest, shielding him from the civilization beyond. He sniffed deeply. The smell of green things was so good. How he wished he could remain there forever.

But reality quickly intruded. The deer lifted her head and signaled her fawn that the time for drinking was over. With a quick look around they turned and headed away from him into the tree cover 20 yards beyond the stream.

As soon as they were gone, the man headed toward the stream. He went left along its bank until the stream turned right into the trees. There it came to a great outcrop of granite which rose for hundreds of feet.

Stack began to climb the rock mass, pulling himself up, using whatever footholds there were. Halfway up he stopped to rest briefly, then continued the climb, leaving behind the dark coolness of the forest for the brighter, warmer blue of the world above.

His eyes sparkled with interest. His heart beat with the exertion of the moment and the excitement every explorer feels as he moves along new trails.

A few minutes more and he was standing on a ledge of naked rock, looking down at the world beneath his feet. The trees, an undulating carpet of green and dark blue, extended as far as the human eye could see. Endless waves of green stunned and numbed the senses. Mountains were the only islands in the green sea. Stack tried to count them, but gave up after 50. Beyond the mountains of north central California was civilization. A few hours drive to the west was San Francisco, to the southwest was Fresno.

But Stack didn't want to think about that now. He closed his eyes, inhaled, and felt giddy with the freshness of the air and the scent of the forest. Stack opened his eyes and grinned. He was on a ledge 8500 feet above sea level, but he was nowhere near the edge. If he fell, he probably wouldn't even feel it by the time he hit. And nobody'd know he was dead until they found his body some seasons later. There would be nothing left of him by then but his skeleton. Stack grinned at the stupid meanderings of his mind and forced his thoughts onto another track.

He wasn't going to fall. He would just look around and then head back to camp and make himself a final delicious meal. Then he'd packed everything into his red and black Chevy van and head home to his wife, two sons, and daughter back in New York City. It was time to be getting on, he told himself. Much as he had enjoyed these last four days camping, hiking, fishing, hunting, and gathering wild berries, he had another life. People depended on him, on his radio-dispatched private cab company, which he ran in partnership with his father and brother. He couldn't leave them to carry the burden by themselves. Yet, despite the needs of the present, the pull of the wild was too overpowering. Inside, he knew if he didn't go back down, if he allowed himself to stand there like a great bird perched on an aerie, he would spend one more day, then another in the woods. Unlike most city people, Nick Stack had come from a family that loved to fish, hunt, camp, and hike. They were outdoors people. As good at it as those who lived in the country, with as wide a knowledge of the land, its animals and plant life.

Standing there, buffeted by the winds rising from the deep valleys, warmed by the benevolent yellow of the sun above, perfumed by the green scents of the surrounding woods, he closed his eyes again. It was all so good, so peaceful, so addicting to the soul that he never wanted to leave and return to the rat race again. The hell with all the responsibility, he told himself. Everything seemed so unimportant up there.

Then he opened his eyes and let them roam in a

300-degree sweep across the world beneath his vista, his vision blocked to the sides and rear by the rocks which curtained out a slice of this magnificent panorama. But that didn't matter. There was more than enough for hm to feast on.

He cupped his hands to his mouth and shouted out, "California, you're beautiful!"

Stack would not even have known about this beauty firsthand had he not been the one chosen to go out West and close out the estate of an aunt who'd died and left him and some relatives $180,000 in cash, stocks, and property. After wiring the money East, sending the stocks back by registered mail, and selling the properties, he decided he needed a rest and followed three days of business with four delicious days in this mountain wilderness.

Once more he scanned the forest, the mountains, and the endless blue of the sky, unable to take it all in, unable to control his gaze. It seemed as if all his life he had been starved for something like this. Nick Stack loved the wilderness in a way that few men did, and the joy it gave him was obvious from the glow on his face and the brightness in his eyes.

At that moment he spotted the soaring wings of an eagle as it rode the updrafts from the lower valleys, soaring high above the forest, perhaps using its sharp predator eyes, searching for some unwary rabbit or a fish swimming too close to the surface of a glacial lake.

The eagle, a brown-white streak in the distance, rode across the golden disc of the sun. Stack looked away momentarily, stunned by the brightness, then thought he was seeing an optical illusion: a brighter source of light in the direction he had turned toward. But that couldn't be. The sun was high to his left and this globe of growing light was lower down to his right. Then he looked toward the sun. To its left, also lower down, was another globe of fire. Then two more appeared far to the south along the coast. What was going on?

Stack scanned the sky. He counted three—no, five,

then six suns. Each almost as bright, almost as yellow, as the real sun. But then they began to change shape and color. They turned into dirty pillars of roiling reddish-brown that soon glowed with a rainbow of colors, which began to churn mildly like a candy-striped barber pole. As they churned, the pillars climbed higher. The clouds around the raging pillars were quickly painted orange-red like a dying sunset. The pillars grew till they seemed as high as the mountains, then higher. They became thicker before they began widening along their tops, turning into mushroom clouds.

Stack froze in horror, his heart clawing at his throat, while his chest constricted as his breath came in short, jabbing gasps with the realization that these weren't suns! These weren't optical illusions! They were mushroom clouds—the product of nuclear explosions. America was under attack! And there in the mountains, safe for the moment, he was watching the nightmare which all America had so dreaded and which was coming to pass before his very eyes.

"God, dear God. Tell me it isn't true," he screamed at the mute mountains and the blue sky. Still blue where *he* stood, but not out there. Only the sounds of the birds answered his cry echoing across the valleys below. But slowly even the bird sounds died away as the forest creatures became aware of the horrors occurring in the world beyond.

His eyes told him to believe what his mind refused to accept. The reality was out there. And like all overwhelming realities, it penetrated with brute force and made him accept. In short seconds he became a stunned believer, realizing, as he watched, that other such scenes, perhaps hundreds, were going on all across America. Millions were being incinerated in all the cities. He realized that meant New York too. New York, where his wife Marcie, his sons Adam and Grant, his daughter Michelle, his brother Neil, and his father Wallace lived. People so far away he couldn't get to them. Not unless he could grab a plane going east. And

Nick Stack doubted many airports would be open after such an attack.

He looked away from the growing mushroom clouds and back at the forest. It was as yet untouched. He looked out at nearer sky and saw the eagle still soaring as if nothing had come to pass.

"Am I crazy, or is the world crazy?" he muttered. Out there complete chaos, here almost total peace. Stack glanced again at the horizon. Then it struck him. He hadn't heard any sound yet. Why? Quickly, he realized that sound travels at 1100 feet per second. The nearest blast was 50 miles away. Four or five minutes travel time. And how loud would it be at that distance? His question was quickly answered as the first roar reached him. It was muted, yet sinister, frightening sound like that of a whole tribe of disturbed, hungry lions growling deep down in their throats, promising an untimely end to anyone who crossed their paths. This first blast was followed by a second, then another, and finally the remaining three, which came from farther off, but sounded louder. That seemed strange, but Stack remembered reading someplace that in combat the sounds of artillery fire are loudest for those closest to the fighting and those dozens or hundreds of miles away, the sounds reaching them by some strange process.

The arrival of the blast sounds had an immediate effect on the creatures of the forest. There was total silence. A trembling seemed to fill the shadowed glades. Something was happening. Something so overwhelming, like an earthquake, that every living thing took note and waited for the next shoe to drop.

"Why are you standing here, doing nothing?" a voiced screamed to him from deep inside. "Find out what's going on." With a final look at the incredible, deadly beauty of the horizon, Nick Stack began to retrace the path he had taken dozens of minutes earlier. Tensions, like springs uncoiled, were released inside him. He descended the slope like a spastic, slipping, grabbing hold of rocks, cursing, shocked that he was still able to climb down without falling and injuring himself. Stack urged himself to be more careful, trying to ride herd on his nerves, but unable to. Had the slope been steeper, the rocks more treacherous, he would have slipped, fallen, and died—one more added to the casualty lists already swollen with dead and injured. But he didn't. The luck that watches over children and fools took him safely down into the peaceful glade he had left a short time before.

The stream still raced. The water remained crystal clear, full of life and sparkle. But Nick Stack didn't notice. He had to break camp, pack up, get all his stuff into the van, listen to the radio, and get back to civilization as quickly as possible.

Stack reached the spot where he had watched the deer and plunged into the trees, then along a trail which he had followed to this glade, going over dead logs and across soft, spongy, decaying matter. He held up his arms to catch flying branches trying to smack his face, going too fast at the same time, not taking enough care, slipping, almost falling a few times, the trail ahead turning into a stream of shapes and colors, his brain sensing only half of what he saw, his senses operating in a haze, branches catching at his face and clothing, leaving scratch marks and rips in the fabric. But he kept going.

It's happened, it's happened, he told himself over and over. Like many, he had ignored much of the simmering crisis which had been going on for weeks between Russia and America, and had by now become almost routine. Everyone had assumed it was another Cuban Missle Crisis and that an accord would be reached at the last moment. A coup had overthrown part of the Islamic Goverment in Iran. But the mullahs had held on, and now there was a civil war. Russia backed the mullahs and America backed the reformers with arms and money. Russia then occupied that province of Iran known as Azerbaijan, something she had done after

World War II. At the time President Truman had made her give it back. However, America was no longer the power she had once been, and now the Russians refused to budge. The mullahs, needing Soviet aid, backed the Russian stance.

The turmoil in Iran then spilled over into neighboring Persian Gulf oil states, including Kuwait and Saudi Arabia, as Shiite factions inside these nations rose in revolt. They were aided by cross-water Iranian raids. In response, America sent over the Rapid Deployment Force to quell the insurrections and prevent Iranian attacks. This led to American bombing of radical bases inside Iran. In response to cries for help from the mullahs, Russia sent air patrols over mullah territory. On more than one occasion our aircraft clashed with theirs. Strong diplomatic notes were exchanged.

Russia then exacerbated the crisis by staging a coup in neighboring Iraq and setting up a puppet regime friendly to Iran and hostile to other Arab states and America. Syria then signed an alliance with Iraq and Iran, followed by full mobilization of its reserves. Russia then upped the ante by sending ten divisions into Iran to aid the mullahs, who were losing out to anti-radical reformers trying to firm up their hold on most of the country. Egypt and Jordan called up their reserves, as did Israel. Israeli forces in southern Lebanon and along the Syrian frontier were brought to the highest state of alert. More American Rapid Deployment Forces flooded into Arabia and some moved into Jordan to prop up King Hussein, in danger of being overthrown by radicals backed by Syria.

Then Syria, seeking political advantages, with Iraqi help, made a sneak attack on Israel. The Israelis quickly counterattacked and within a week had turned the tide of battle and forced the Syrians to ask for a truce. The Middle East pulled back from the brink and the crisis moved along at a lower level of tension. But the war, amid all the other tensions, caused American forces to be placed on Defcon 3, the third highest state of alert possible. In conjunction with this, the Sixth Fleet was beefed up in the Mediterranean as Soviet naval units from the Black Sea Fleet filled the same waters. At the same time, Russian naval vessels flooded the Baltic and north Atlantic. Incidents between Soviet and American ships, between Russian and NATO task forces, proliferated as Russia sought to dissuade the West from doing anything while she consolidated her holdings and built up Syria for another try at defeating the Israelis. Many of these incidents were not reported to the general public.

But when Russia called home her ambassador for consulation and we did the same with ours, everyone knew. However, this past week the ambassadors had both returned to their posts. Things seemed to be simmering along, but not boiling over.

And now this. Had someone miscalculated, made a mistake somewhere, triggering World War III? Stack didn't know. But this was the aftermath. And now he, like so many others, would have to live with the reality.

He reached his camp, in a clearing, his van in the middle of everything, his tent next to it, a bedroll sticking out of the tent, a dead campfire nearby, with a circle of stones around the enclosure where he had cooked many a good meal and enjoyed warmth in the night while staring up at the moon and the stars. But those memories were no longer pleasant.

He ran to the van, got inside, put down the rifle, started the engine, then turned on the radio. He selected a channel, turned the sound to high, but heard only static. Stack switched from channel to channel. Nothing. Had all the stations been knocked out? He had once read about something called an electromagnetic pulse. A single nuclear explosion high in the atmosphere would send out an electric pulse for 1800 miles in every direction, destroying electronic communications. But it was only a theory. How much of it was reality? Perhaps he could get better reception in another location. Maybe the mountains were interfering with what was being sent out and received. He shut the radio off, then the engine, and began breaking camp, packing everything into the van in a sloppy, rushed manner, his heart beating too fast, his eyes too wild, sweat standing out on his face. But gradually the exertion since he had come down from the granite outcrop caught up with him. At 36 years of age Nick Stack may have been in good shape, but he wasn't 16 anymore. And all the physical and emotional exertion he had been going through would take its toll on an Arnold Schwarzenegger.

He stopped for a breather. The few minutes of rest also gave him time to reflect on how he had been reacting now that the initial panic had worn off. He couldn't go on pushing himself like this without collapsing. The road ahead would be a hard one. In order to survive he would have to pace himself, hold in his emotions, and deal with things as they came up.

His loved ones were far away. Whatever had happened to them, he could do nothing about it from out here. Stack would have to find out if there was communication between the coasts, then try to discover what had happened to his people through the Red Cross or other authorities—if they were functioning. Only then could he try to get back across the continent. But that was later. First, he had to get down off this mountain and back to civilization. Whatever remained of it.

2

He was down from the mountain, having driven across rutted trails, then dirt roads, till he came to a trail which merged with the main highway. He raced between steep-sided cliffs till he reached a flat area, looking all the while for traffic. But he had spotted only two distant cars. He had honked a number of times, but no one had seemed to notice him. Or maybe they hadn't wanted to acknowledge, having places to go and people of their own to search for.

He turned on the radio a few times and got more static. For a brief stretch he did catch human voices saying something about emergency alert frequencies, and then an excited announcer speaking very emotionally about "... a great beast loosed upon mankind ..." and "... the flaming soul of the galaxy unleashed across the face of the earth." And then it was all gone in a sea of static. He tried a few more channels, then shut the radio off because the static was getting on his nerves.

Stack looked out the window at the sky. It had darkened. It was too early in the day for it to get this dark. He wondered why it was happening, then realized that the debris clouds from the blasted coastal cities were coming inland. Clouds filled with radiation, no doubt. He shivered and rolled up the windows. Then, ten minutes later, it began to rain. A light rain which drummed on the roof and made him use his wipers. It went away almost as soon as it came. But the clouds did not dissipate.

And then he saw the girl. She was standing by the road, her thumb up, a small khaki knapsack on her back. She looked about 14, with bright red hair. The first human being he had seen since coming down from the mountain.

He stopped, leaned over, and threw open the door on the passenger side. "Get in," he said as she ran over. "You shouldn't be out there with all this debris falling down." He pointed up. She gave him a bright, toothy grin and got in.

"Thanks for stopping, mister. I didn't think there was a person alive on this road."

"There may not be. What're you doing out here?"

"Trying to get home."

"Home where?"

"Fresno."

"That's about 40 miles from here."

"Are you headed there?"

He shrugged, starting the van again. "I don't know where I'm headed. I came down from the mountains after the bombs went off. I saw them blowing up."

"I didn't. But I saw the rising clouds and heard the alert on the radio. Everyone ran for their cellars. Did you hear the alert?"

"Nope. I was in the mountains the last four days, living the natural life, and sort of lost touch with civilization."

"Welcome back," she said with a quick grin. Stack liked this girl and was glad he had picked her up. No telling what could happen to a young girl on the road, especially at a time like this.

"It's good to see you have a sense of humor after all this. What's your name?"

"Rayisa Gilchrist. And yours?"

"Nick Stack. You can call me Nick."

"I like the name."

"Glad you do. But what're you doing in the

mountains all alone?"

"I'm not really here by myself. I was staying with a widowed aunt in the town of Makepiece—that's about fifty miles from here—when the bombs went off. I knew neither Mom or Dad would be able to come for me. And my aunt's too old and feeble to drive me to Fresno, so I hitchhiked. And now I'll go as far as you're going. Then, if you don't head toward Fresno, I'll just get out and let some other kind stranger give me a lift."

"I'll take you there," he said, the tight grin on his face giving little indication of the tension still dancing inside of him. "I don't think there are going to be many kind strangers on the road today."

He had been studying her while she talked. He found Rayisa to be an interesting and captivating girl. She was tall, with long, slim legs, wearing jeans and a green blouse. She had shoulder-length red hair, freckles, an upturned nose, a mouth that was a bit too wide and slightly crooked teeth—with wise blue eyes which complimented all these features perfectly.

Rayisa had also been studying him while they were talking. And she liked what she saw. Stack was tanned, with black hair and dark brown eyes that had wrinkles around them which made him look kindly when he smiled. His physique, she noticed, was muscular and looked powerful.

He had done the questioning so far, now it was her turn. "Where are you from?" she wanted to know.

"New York City. I came here on business, mixed with a little pleasure. I have a long way to go to get home."

"I'll say you do," she said with a laugh and a toss of her hair. Then she asked, "How long before we get to Fresno?"

"Maybe an hour."

"I hope Mom and Dad are okay."

He frowned. "We'll see."

"You don't think they were hurt?" she asked, worry filling her face.

"We can't tell from here. We'll have to find out."

He fell silent as he scanned the land. He looked down into a valley with a road running through it and spotted some trucks along the road. Stack honked to get their attention, but no one answered.

"It's hot in here," she said. "Can you open a window, or maybe put on the air-conditioning?"

"No," he said too suddenly and startled her. Then he explained. "There's radiation out there. We have to wait till it passes. Then we can open a window. The air-conditioning would just suck the radiation into the van."

"Oh."

They came around a bend and spotted a gas station just down the road. Stack looked and saw that the gas-gauge needle was at the two-thirds-full mark. Grab some gas while it lasts, he told himself. He didn't think there'd be gas left in other places. So he pulled off the road, went across the hose laid out across the concrete apron, and heard a friendly ping as he stopped at the gas pumps. But no one came out to serve them.

Stack hit the horn and said, "Maybe the place is deserted. Stay in the van while I go have a look." As he stepped out, Stack noticed that the gas-station office was open. He walked around to the front of the van as a man stepped into the open doorway. He was bald, in his middle 50s, and wore stained overalls. Behind him stood a teenaged boy holding a wrench.

"Afternoon," Stack said. "I was driving along and saw your station. I was up in the mountains when the bombs struck. Can't tell you how surprised I was," he added, trying to put some friendliness into his voice. But the two in the doorway had a vacant, faintly unfriendly look. "What happened?" Stack asked, lifting his arms out, then letting them drop down.

"Can't tell you more'n you know, mister. I wasn't paying no attention to the radio. Orville here," the man nodded at the boy behind him, half in shadow, "was listening to the radio. The music he likes to hear was interrupted a number of times. He told me something big was about to happen and now it's come. Darned fools couldn't leave well enough alone. Had to put their fingers on those buttons and blow half the world apart."

"Who started it?"

"Don't know and it don't matter, does it, mister? It's all over."

"I wouldn't say it's over yet. There could be millions alive. Enough to pull things together and start over."

'If'n they do, it'll be long after I'm in the ground. And don't think those blasts are the finish. There's radiation, you know."

"Yeah." Stack rubbed his jaw. "Mind if I use your men's room?"

"Nope. Go ahead. Always been free for anyone who comes off the road with nature calling. You'll find it to your left around back."

Stack did. The toilet flushed. He smiled. That showed a few things still worked. Then he looked into the mirror. He was still the same, except that the worry lines on his face had deepened and the tension showed in his eyes. There was a brittle, vacant hardness in them.

He went back around to the front, where Rayisa waited patiently in the van. The man and boy still stood as he had left them, almost like robots. They had a lifeless quality, as if they were going through motions they didn't really mean, motions not connected to how they felt inside.

Stack nodded toward the pay phone against one wall and asked, "Can I use it?"

"If it works." A faint smile appeared on the man's face. Stack went over, picked up the receiver, and listened for a dial tone. Nothing. He tried the operator, then dialed the police and fire emergency numbers. Nothing. He put the receiver back.

"What about the phone in your office?" Stack asked, pointing to the phone on the counter inside. "I'll pay you if I can use it. I want to call New York collect."

"You ain't callin' anywhere. That phone's dead too.

All phone service is out. Phone lines go over or under the ground. When the damn bombs landed they made holes in everything, blew things down, and burned them up."

"How about some gas then? Do your pumps work?" He pointed to them.

"I ain't sellin' any. No new gas is goin' to be produced now. And they probably ain't got no pipe to ship what they do pump from the ground, and no refineries worth speakin' of to refine the oil. Gas is going to be a commodity more valuable than gold."

"Then sell me just a little." Stack took out money. "You'll need cash to buy things. Sell me some of your gas for some of my money."

"If you want my gas bad enough you'll pay my price. I want ten dollars a gallon. That's a fair price for a time like this. Ain't it, Orville?" he asked the boy with a sly smile.

"Ten dollars a gallon! Are you nuts?" Stack exclaimed, almost spitting out the words as he bent forward from the waist. Rayisa sat up in her seat to catch the conversation.

"That's the price, mister," the man said, his face suddenly unfriendly, his voice very cold now. Orville handed him a rifle from inside. The man held it across his chest, his finger on the trigger.

"This is in case you're thinkin' of takin' the gas without payin'. Me bein' an old man and him a boy." He nodded back at Orville. "Now the price is ten dollars. A week from now it'll be twice as much. And when people need what I've got, they'll pay my price. Now how many gallons do you want?"

"None from you." Stack spat, his face livid with anger.

"Then I won't be holdin' you no more, stranger. Be on your way."

Stack didn't answer as he hurried back to his van, started the motor, and drove off. "Mountain people are sure unfriendly," he muttered.

"No, they're not, Nick. You have to get to know them."

"Maybe. But those two back there are real bastards. And I'm afraid they're not the only ones we'll meet. The bombs falling down were only the first broken illusion. I have a feeling a lot more illusions will be smashed along the way. People turn into such bastards when the going gets tough, trying to screw each other and squeeze out every ounce of advantage they can get. I wonder, when we get down to the bottom line, if there's really so much difference between us and the beasts of the field. At least they don't lie, cheat, and steal."

"But they hurt each other all the time," Rayisa countered, "and kill the weak and the young. At least among humans not every fight ends in bloodshed."

His hot, hard anger passed as he smiled at her. "Wisdom out of the mouths of babes," he said. "Let's hope you're right."

They passed a side road leading to a town deeper in the mountains, but continued along the main road, then came to an area with wide, grassy fields, the woods far back from the road and the mountains behind them. When he turned the next bend, instead of more of the same he saw woods close to the road and a flare on the highway about half a mile ahead.

"Maybe someone's vehicle broke down," he said as his eyes became wary and he studied the lay of the land. Just beyond the flare he spotted a house among trees. It was constructed of unpainted wood and blended in with the forest, not being noticeable till he came closer. Then he saw more houses, people, cars. They'd come to a town. The van pulled to a stop near the flare as people came out into the road, one of them a thick man in a sheriff's uniform.

Stack got out and Rayisa came with him. The sheriff walked over. He was a short, broad-chested man with a wide, ham-sized and ham-shaped face. He wore a Smokey-the-Bear hat, a gun on his hip, and a mustache over his upper lip. He didn't seem much of a lawman.

But up here in the mountains they weren't very particular. A man had to be popular more than anything. And he displayed that feature.

"I'm Kurt Willem, the law here," he announced. "You and your daughter?" he asked, nodding toward the girl.

"She's a hitchhiker. I just came down from the mountains where I was camping."

"Heard about the war over the radio?"

"Saw it from a mountaintop. I couldn't believe my eyes."

"None of us could believe it either. We've been waiting for travelers like yourself to give them something to eat and shelter, if need be. If you're hungry . . ." He nodded up the street at a side table where several elderly women were serving sandwiches, lemonade, and soda.

"Have you had many takers?"

"Half a dozen so far, including a trucker carrying a refrigerator full of frozen meat. He ran out of fuel. The truck is parked out behind the town bank. He has nowhere to go and has contributed all his meat for our use."

"Do you have electricity for your freezers and refrigerators?"

"So far. There's a small electric plant which supplies us and the towns around. Our grid hasn't been affected. The plant is coal fired and has a month's supply."

"What happens when it runs out?"

"We'll cross that bridge when we come to it. You're welcome to stay or go on, as you wish. But while you're here please don't spread any defeatist talk. We're trying to keep people's spirits up."

Stack nodded agreement.

"I'm glad you're cooperating. Some people get touchy when asked to help. What's your name, stranger? We might as well get to know each other."

"I'm Nick Stack. The girl's Rayisa Gilchrist. She's from Fresno."

"I saw a bomb go off in the direction of Fresno. All communication is down, so we have no way of knowing how bad things are down there. You from near Fresno?"

"New York. I came out here on business and pleasure."

"Sorry about your pleasure having gone flat, but a lot of peoples' dreams just went out the window."

Stack nodded his agreement. Just then someone called the sheriff, who started away. He was a big, waddling man who gave the feeling of competence, and just might be lethal if that was called for. As he went off, he looked over his shoulder. "If you need me just ask for Sheriff Willem."

Stack turned to Rayisa. "Let me park the van someplace, then we'll get ourselves fed. I think you were right when you said earlier that not all people are bastards."

He parked the van, then they went to the picnic table, where several motherly women smiled at them. It was almost like a church social, except for the tension in the women's eyes and the forced smiles on their faces. It seemed to Stack like an open-air buffet on the deck of the Titanic while lifeboats were being lowered into the water at the other end. How long before the radiation struck?

Stack and Rayisa didn't think about that now. They bit into fresh tuna-fish and egg-salad sandwiches and washed them down with Coke and lemonade.

3

Stack left Rayisa with some girls her own age and they excitedly discussed what a post-nuclear world would be like with that mixture of fear, awe, and adventure which only children can have. Stack took a quick tour of the town. He had not asked its name at first, but he now learned it was Montieth.

Men and women, worry etched across their faces, stood in knots along streets with big trees sheltering cars parked along peaceful blocks. It wasn't a huge town. Maybe 600 people, he judged, maybe less; a big family.

He gravitated to the only tavern in town. Beers were still being sold for fair prices as long as the beer lasted, the owner said. He wasn't going to be a war profiteer, he announced to everyone there—about a dozen and a half people, only three of them women. Stack bought a beer, but drank it mechanically, listening to bits of conversation. One man had a son in the Rapid Deployment Force. There were tears in his eyes as he wondered aloud if the boy was alive and if he would ever see him again. "Bill's only nineteen," the man said. Another patted him on the back. "Don't grieve yet, Sam. He may be alive. Jumpin' to conclusions will only kill ya." Others echoed his words.

Then the blond-haired, medium-sized man in his late 30s wearing a garage mechanic's work clothes entered the tavern. All eyes turned to him. Someone noticed that Stack was a stranger, pointed out the man who had just entered, and said, "That's Bill Grenaugh. He's a ham radio operator."

"What's new, Bill?" one man asked.

"That's what I came here to tell ya. I've been in contact with a number of people despite the static, which severely limits the distances I can communicate over. A good deal of the conversations are garbled, so I have to ask the parties to repeat themselves a number of times. Despite that, every surviving ham operator is just tearing up the air waves. There are so many stories out there. So many tragedies and cries for help." He stopped to brush away a tear.

"In spite of the difficulties, what is happening is that one short-range ham operator talks to another and the messages pass like that, from link to link, over long distances. News has it that one man, who owns a long-range radio and is able to pick up news from all over the world, got part of a Radio Moscow English-language broadcast claiming that this war is all America's fault. That we struck first."

"Bullshit," someone yelled.

"Those Commies will say anything," a woman piped in.

"We sure didn't start the trouble in Iran," a man added.

"Our mistake," the woman said, "was to go into the Middle East, just like we went into Vietnam." There were many voices of agreement. Stack said nothing. He didn't know enough to speak out and hadn't made up his mind about anything yet.

The talk was futile and depressing, like discussing a ball game that's been lost. Nothing will change the score—ever. Stack finished his beer, then stopped at a cigarette-dispensing machine and used all his change to buy three packs of Camels. He had a smoking habit that he constantly broke, but which always came back. And in times like these he was sure to do plenty of smoking. So he bought all the available butts he had change for. No telling where his next smokes would come from and what they'd cost.

Stack headed out of the tavern and back to the refreshment table. When he got there he saw Rayisa leaning against a nearby car, talking with the girls she'd met earlier. When he approached, she waved and introduced her two new friends, Nancy and Belle.

"Nancy's dad works at the power station," she announced. "She's invited me home for supper with them."

"You'll have to give her a rain check. We have someplace to go. Don't you remember?"

She hung her head. "Sorry. This town is so nice that I felt at home."

"I understand. But this is no vacation, Rayisa. There's been a war. It's time we got to Fresno and saw how your folks are. Don't you think?"

Rayisa nodded, then turned and said her good-byes to the girls. They all promised to meet another time. Then Stack and the girl headed toward the van.

"Did you try calling your family?" she asked.

Stack halted, thumped himself on the side of the head, and said, "I forgot in all this turmoil. But I don't think any phones are working. Still, let me try. Wait in the van while I go find the sheriff. Perhaps he can help me."

He found Willem up the block drinking a can of Sprite. The sheriff took the can from his mouth as Stack walked over. He then asked about the phone service.

"We have nuthin'. I don't think the people here know how really bad things are." He dropped his voice. "My brother, Wyatt Willem, is sheriff of a town about forty miles from here. Vista Royale. I can't even get him on the phone. Later, I'll drive out there and see how he's doin'. But right now I've got my hands full here. We don't have much crime in the mountains, so I'm alone. No deputy, or anything."

"You ought to deputize a few people."

"I probably will in the next few days. But to get back to your problem, there's no phone service here. Though there may be in other places and some lines may be up in the next few weeks. But right now I see zilch happening down the road. People are going to have to communicate like they did in the old days. On foot, by horse, or car. Do me a favor, will ya? When you get down to Fresno, scout around. See what's what. Try and contact the law down there. Then, if possible, come back here. Let us know what's happening. We're so isolated."

"Will do. Though I might not be back so soon. Who knows what side roads I may have to go down. But I will keep you in mind." Stack looked back at the refreshment table. "I didn't expect such hospitality after what happened today."

"Yeah. It's every dog for himself," Willem replied. "People get selfish when the chips are down. But not up here. These are good people. They care. You saw the evidence of it yourself."

Stack pursed his lips a second and asked, "How long will they care when the going gets tough? They missed the bombs, but there's radiation, disease, and refugees. The best is yet to come."

Willem shook his head in agreement, setting his chins to wobbling. "I've been thinking about that myself. I don't think these folks realize what will happen. Not too many people are knowledgeable about nuclear war. I used to be in the National Guard."

"So was I."

"So you know what they taught us about it. And what they taught I don't like. But do come back and tell me what's happening down there."

"All this travel takes gas. And while I'm not low yet, I will be having problems. Is there any chance of me buying gas here? I tried to out on the highway and the guy who owns the gas station ten miles down the road told me I could have gas for ten dollars a gallon. Then he showed me a rifle in case I was thinking of taking some, which I wasn't."

"That's Deke Barnes. He said that? Well, he was a bastard even before this war. I guess the dropping of all those bombs didn't make his disposition any better. I've known Deke for quite a few years now. And let me tell you, that guy was aleady a bastard in his mother's womb. Maybe it had something to do with bad sperm. That sonofabitch just didn't turn out right. It goes to show that not all mountain people are nice. We get our share of mean cusses."

"I'll try not to lose any sleep over it," Stack said. "Now what about the gas?"

Willem called over a graying, grizzle-headed man in his 50s. "Virgil, you still got that full fuel can in your garage?"

"Sure."

"This man here," Willem nodded at Stack, "will be doing some scouting for me and needs some gas."

"Come on," the man said and Stack followed him. "I'll sell you that five gallons for five bucks."

"You're much too generous. I'll give you ten. Use it to buy yourself some beers at the tavern."

"Don't need beer. I have a cooler in the cellar full of Coors and Olympic. You can have one on me."

"Thanks, but I already had a beer at the tavern, and I'll be driving. Also, I'm not much of a drinker. A little makes me tipsy."

"Okay, you can have one when you get back." By this time they had gone down a side street, then up a slope lined by comfortable-looking, clean homes on wide lots with great grassy lawns and high shade trees. Swings and walks and white lawn furniture were out front, and picket fences were around some of the properties. Winding driveways up to garages, or around behind the houses completed the scene. A nice place to grow up in. But none of it was far from the claws of war.

They went up one of the walks to a garage, inside of which Virgil gave Stack the five-gallon gas can. It felt kind of heavy and Stack remembered that gas weighed around six pounds to the gallon. He was carrying 30 pounds plus the weight of the container.

They returned to the van, where they made small talk as Stack filled the tank via a funnel. Then he fished into his pocket and came out with a ten-spot, which he gave to Virgil along with the empty can.

Just then a man walked up and stuck out his hand and said, "My name's Stuart Caudell." Stack shook the hand, which was strong, calloused, and hard. He quickly eyeballed the man, who was gray-haired, in his 50s, with a wide, hard mouth, cold blue eyes, and deep lines across his face. Before Stack could do any more analyzing, the man began talking.

"Conversation has it you're going to Fresno."

"What's it to you?"

"Don't get your dander up, mister. I mean you no harm."

"I'm just being careful. What do you want?"

"I stopped here, just like you did, and partook of this town's hospitality. And like yourself I'm heading toward Fresno. I thought it would be better if we went together."

"Why?"

"In case one of us breaks down, or there's an accident, or there are bandits on the road. Who knows what's going on out there?" He extended an arm as if he could encompass the entire world.

Stack scratched his chin. "Sounds like a good idea. Are you alone?"

"Nossir. I've got my wife and son with me."

"What kind of car do you drive?"

"A gray '82 Oldsmobile."

"How're you fixed for gas?"

"I've got more than half a tank."

"Looks like you'll make it. If not, I can give you some of my gas. But not too much. I'll need most of it. A man's got to look out for himself."

"I understand, and I'm glad you're being so decent about the whole thing." Caudell's manner seemed to have changed to one of great relief and friendliness.

"We'll need some tubing, so you can suck gas from

my tank into yours. Do you have any tubing?"

"I have what you need," Virgil said. "Let me go get it." He was back within minutes with a yard of yellowed clear-plastic tubing about a third of an inch thick.

Virgil explained to Caudell, "You use this like a big straw. One end in the tank, one end in your mouth. Suck in, like you're drinking milk till the gas comes two-thirds of the way up, then stop and hold your breath. Pull the tube out, put it into the other gas tank and take your mouth away. The fuel will trickle down. Don't go beyond the two-thirds point. You may get more fuel each time, but you can also swallow some by accident. And that stuff's poison. Getting poisoned is the last thing you need. I doubt there are many medical facilities to take care of you, and poisoning is a painful, lingering sort of death."

Stack knew most of this, but let Virgil talk, seeing the satisfaction on his face that he could give such advice and have it accepted. One never knew when he might need the help of this man or his friends. It was best not to step on any toes, best to be all things to all men. Stack felt a bit phony. But extraordinary times called for extraordinary actions. Stack thanked Virgil for his advice and the other man nodded, then walked off. Caudell called to his family, who came over from the refreshment table, his wife munching on a sandwich. She was a woman around Caudell's age with dyed brown hair. With her was a skinny 15-year-old boy with a long, narrow face like his mother's and straggly brown hair. Caudell introduced his wife, Sally, and his son, Bart. Rayisa smiled at Bart and he gave her a shy grin in return.

"This your only son?" Stack asked.

"No. I've got two more. One's a trucker in Tennessee. The other's in the Navy." His voice almost broke, but Caudell went on. "He's with the Sixth Fleet in the Mediterranean." Stack cast a quick glance at Mrs. Caudell. Her eyes had misted over. Bart was emotionless. Too young to feel the full effect yet.

HELL RIDE

"This your daughter, Mr. Stack?"

"No, a hitchhiker I picked up. My family's back East."

"Well, we'd better get moving," her husband announced. "Have you got a road map?" he asked Stack, who lifted one off his dashboard and showed it to him. Everyone then got into their vehicles and, with a last look at Montieth, Stack led the procession out of town.

Once on the highway, they moved quickly, the altitude gradually dropping. But the road remained empty. This did not last long. Five minutes later they spotted a car heading toward the mountains they were leaving. They honked, the car honked back. Then another car, full of stunned-looking people, went past without acknowledging anything. A third car, with a man and woman in the front seat, honked, then slowed down. Stack and the Caudells did likewise.

They quickly saw the man's and woman's clothes were ripped, their faces were smudged, and the paint on their car was covered with great dried bubbles and peeling in places.

The man leaned out his window and said, "Don't go any further. It's bad down there. Almost complete devastation. Plenty of dead and wounded. I'm from a small town two miles east of Fresno. My house was totalled by the bomb blast, then by the firestorm which followed it. Fires are raging all over. Grabbed what I could and got the hell out. The mountains may not be a picnic, but they're surely better than down there. At least I can hunt. Got my rifle and plenty of ammunition in the trunk." He then asked about the mountains.

"They're still okay, but I don't know for how long," Stack said.

"Did a lot of people make it out of Fresno?" Caudell asked.

"I can't say," the man replied, shifting his gaze. "I didn't stay long enough to see. But it's bad. My kids were in school when the bombs came down. I drove by the place and it was totalled. So I checked with the hospital, which was also badly damaged. But they can't make heads or tails out of the situation and were no help at all. Many bodies are so badly burned they can't be identified. Some teacher from that school said no one in his class survived. Seeing that, I didn't stay around on the off chance that one of my kids might be alive. I left quickly. I'm looking out for number one. My wife wanted to stay," he nodded toward her, "but I convinced her we'd be better off in the mountains. Later, when things settle down, we'll come back to look, though I doubt there's anything left of my family. Well, good-bye. I'll be getting on my way."

As they drove off, Rayisa looked at Stack in shock. "The man didn't seem human. He should have been more concerned for his kids. And his wife didn't even say a word."

"Probably shock, or self-defense. People under stress look out for themselves. They'll kill their emotions, desert loved ones, do a lot of weird things. You're going to learn a lot about people. So, I'm afraid, will I." With that, he took his foot off the brake pedal and drove on.

The road went downhill through a narrow wooded valley. When they came out of the valley they noticed the first signs of intensive devastation. Dark clouds across the nearer horizon and the licking red-yellow of tongues of flame eating into dwellings, woods, and fields. In between were blackened, burned-over areas. Across the faraway horizon the mushroom-cloud monoliths, which had sprouted across the land, had almost completely come apart. The dismal gray of the sky was flushed with red and streaked with black. The sun, slowly heading toward the great Pacific basin beyond, was painting the land and the sky a dull orange.

There was a car off the road about a thousand feet ahead. As they passed it, slowly, they saw a woman sprawled on the ground next to the car. Slumped over the hood was a dead boy. Inside, lying in a jumbled mass, were three people, one over the wheel. All dead.

"What is it?" Rayisa asked in a halting voice.

"Probably the effects of radiation. They took too many roentgens."

As he speeded up, she asked, "What're roentgens?"

"A measure of radiation," he said and fell silent.

They passed a line of roadside stores and houses, all of them badly burned. The trees, bushes, and grass around them were blackened. A number of vehicles, too close to the fire, had also been incinerated.

A quarter of a mile on they passed a grove of trees which were still burning, the flames having stopped at a creek about 50 yards back from the road. Beyond the creek was a farm with cattle in a field. They seemed to be wandering aimlessly, still fenced in. Stack looked around for a farmer or farm hands and didn't see any.

Then Rayisa sat forward and pointed down the road. "Look," she said as he gazed at a woman staggering along. She looked hurt. Her clothes were torn and burned. Stack was wondering if she were walking away from the fire they had passed.

He honked and slowed down, then stopped as he reached her. The woman stopped and gazed at the van and car. There was a wild look in her eyes, as wild as her unkempt iron-gray hair.

"Do you need help?" Stack called out.

"You're too late," she said. "I'm from that burned-up place you just passed. The flash from the bomb started so many fires we couldn't fight them all. The men were away at work and there was no phone service to call the fire department. Some people died trying to go back into the flames to get valuables or save trapped family members. For those of us who survived there was no reason to stay, so we each went our way. Some to the homes of friends or relatives. All on foot. The fires started so fast that what few vehicles there were were burned up. Now I'm trying to get to where my husband works so we can search for shelter together. He's an insurance man in the town of Tustin, five miles down the road."

"We're going in that direction. Can we give you a lift?"

"Yes, thank you."

Rayisa bent forward so the woman could push the back of the seat forward and get into the rear seat. Behind that was the cargo space which contained Stack's gear.

Nobody spoke as they passed woods and fields which gave way to what looked to be a town of 10,000 people. "Tustin," the woman announced. It hadn't been hit by the bomb, but was close enough to get a pretty good dose of the winds and the heat wave. Fires had been started in many places and a number were still burning. The sounds of fire engines could be heard in the near distance. Cars were parked along streets. Some of the cars had been burned, as had some of the houses. There were people on roofs, hosing them down. More people were in the streets. Traffic was light. The woman with them pointed to a corner and said, "Let me out over there."

He did and she thanked him, then was gone into the crowd. Stack reflected a moment and realized she hadn't even told them her name. But then, it didn't really matter. He drove on, noticing that the traffic lights were out. But just ahead, a deputy sheriff, his head swathed in bandages, was directing traffic.

As they drove up, Stack came to a stop, stuck his head out the window, and asked, "How're things here? Is it safe to go on to Fresno?"

"Things here aren't as bad as they might've been. Lots of fires. Small ones. Most people are alive. The hospitals are functioning, most electricity is out. The same for phone service. But Fresno is terrible. Not as bad as some hours ago, but still a bitch. The blast did a lot of killing. It could have done more, but the bomb landed a bit off center. At least that's what some National Guardsman who passed this way an hour ago told me. There's a lot of chaos. Plenty of fires. And the radiation is strong, though not as powerful as right after the blast. Most of it is spreading." He made motions with his hands, then directed some more traffic.

"You folks from Fresno?"

"Not me. The girl. We're trying to find her folks."

"Good luck."

Stack nodded, then drove through town, past some open fields. There were cars alongside the road, some burned out. A few accidents partly blocked the road, but most had been shoved out of the way. Minutes later he saw what had done it: a bulldozer moving along the highway, a tough-looking military man driving it, a cigar clamped in his mouth as he moved steadily along, lord of his domain. He nodded at them as they went past.

More traffic came their way from the direction of Fresno. Badly beaten-up vehicles of every model and make and condition. Also some military trucks. Stack was glad part of the military was functioning. That meant things weren't completely hopeless; someone had his fingers on the pulse of things.

There were more houses now. Villages, single homes with fields, towns, the populated places close to Fresno. And each bore signs of the bomb. Fires, injured people, light traffic, cars and trucks damaged or destroyed along the way, flames still licking the horizon, and constant smoke. Stack was glad he didn't have a Geiger counter. He didn't want to think about all the radiation they were passing through. But the worst had by now lifted. Then it began to rain. A light, dismal rain. The kind that had fallen after the Hiroshima and Nagasaki bombings. Bringing and also washing away radiation.

Stack drove off the road to an abandoned car by the wayside and the Caudells followed. The front tires of the car had been blown out and no one was inside.

Everyone got out. Stuart Caudell came over to Stack and asked, "What's up?"

"I think we may have ourselves a fuel source."

"What if the owner's nearby?" Rayisa asked.

"If it's been abandoned, and it looks that way,

someone will come along soon and start stripping this thing. As long as that's going to happen and we need fuel, we'll take it. It's the law of the jungle, Rayisa. We're in one now and must fend for ourselves."

He told Caudell to get the tubing Virgil had given him. "Bring your car over so it'll be next to this one. After you fill up, I'll go."

It took Caudell half an hour. He was out of breath a number of times. That's when his wife and son took turns. Meanwhile, Stack kept watch, looking for an irate owner, who might return anytime. But no one did.

Once Caudell had taken what he thought was a fair amount, Stack began siphoning. But the tank ran dry before more than three gallons had been removed. Still, he wasn't disappointed. There would be more abandoned cars, more fuel for the taking.

They continued their trip, the devastation increasing in intensity. Blocks with every other house burned down flew past their windows. Burned cars stood in the middle of the rubble-filled streets. In places, the asphalt had melted and cracked. They were now on the outskirts of Fresno, where the fires had burned everything. Not a block had been left untouched. Bodies lay in the gutters to such an extent that the van had to slow down and crawl around them. Lone, stunned stragglers moved along wreckage-filled sidewalks or picked through the ruins of what had once been homes.

"It looks like London in the Blitz," Stack muttered. He looked sideways. Rayisa sat wide-eyed, her mouth open, then she began to cry. Stack wanted to comfort her, but couldn't tear his eyes from the scenes of destruction and utter devastation. He moved more slowly now. There were few street signs left standing. And there were fires, hundreds of them, like the campfires of an army resting from the march, sending up dark pillars of smoke that merged into an angry dark cloud over the ruins, almost blocking out the sun, now an orange orb sinking fast in the west, leaving long shadows across everything.

HELL RIDE

The closer to the heart of the explosion they came, the greater the destruction. At first there were burned blocks with the first stories of the buildings still standing. Then the first floors no longer existed. Just pillars of rubble-filling cellars, some of them still smoking. And soon there were just low hills of rubble looking like cinder dunes on the surface of some alien planet. Only the streets, forming intersecting patterns, remained. And in places even they did not exist. The twisted skeletons of concrete buildings and girders of steel stood like silent sentinels in the devastated desert of nothingness.

"Where did you live?" Stack asked Rayisa as he stopped the van.

She looked around as if he'd pulled her from some hypnotic trance. "I lived on Lake Street."

"Lake and where, in which direction?"

"I don't know in which direction. There are no familiar places I can point to, saying go here, go there. Are you sure we're in Fresno?" She looked at him with vacant eyes.

"Sure as I'll ever be." He got out of the van and walked back to Caudell's Oldsmobile. Caudell was shivering. His wife was crying. His son was cursing quietly under his breath.

"Do you know where your relatives live? We'll look for them first."

"Using what street signs?" Caudell asked. "All I see is rubble. I don't think they're alive. I don't think anyone's alive where they are."

"There must be survivors. We saw some on the streets."

"And how long do you think they'll live?"

"That's not for us to say. They might survive longer than we do."

"I can't believe this," Caudell said, his eyes sweeping the scene. "It's like those pictures of Hiroshima. Only it never occurred to me it would look like this for real. I remember Fresno as a bustling burg you couldn't cover in one day. Full of life and buildings. Now it looks so small. A lot of rubble in a limited space."

"Anytime you knock down buildings or trees the space they used to occupy looks smaller. Ground cover gives an illusion of size."

"I only wish this death and destruction were an illusion."

"Unfortunately, it's real. What do you want to do?"

"I wanna lie down someplace, cover myself over, and die," he said, a look of total disgust and defeat on his face. "But I guess I must go on. I have a wife and children to look out for. They'll need me more now then ever."

"Why don't we see if there's some sort of casualty-evacuation center run by the Red Cross or someone? We might be able to find your people and Rayisa's there."

"Where?" Caudell put out his hands, palms up.

"I've got binoculars from my hunting trip. I'll climb up on the van to give me elevation, then look over the lay of the land to see what movement there is. Where there's a crowd, so to speak, there ought to be some sort of casualty station."

"Sounds good. Go try it."

Stack got the binoculars, then climbed onto the van. He felt the roof sag a bit under his weight, but paid it no attention, as he scanned the terrain in a 360-degree sweep. He saw two likely points of activity and picked the larger, using a prominent rubble landmark to orient himself. Then they all headed in that direction.

They quickly reached what had been a park and was now a half-empty, burned-out field flanked by rubble dunes. A building in the park, with one wall partly blown down and most of the roof gone, held wounded, stunned, shocked survivors who lay in rows on the ground, many of them already dying. More casualties were walking in, or being delivered by comandeered vehicles, some of them military. There were a handful of doctors and nurses in attendance, some officers of the law, and a small number of military people. A few of them looked like they needed help more than their charges, but they continued to work.

Stack and Caudell pulled to a stop where the sidewalk came to an end. Everyone got out and waited while Stack walked over to where an officer was giving instructions to some troops. The officer turned around as Stack approached. He wore dirty khakis and no rank insignia, and was in his 40s. A hard-faced, crewcut, beer-gut, once-tough Marine, the type one meets occasionally. Only he was National Guard, mobilized just two weeks before, he told Stack.

"I'm looking for the relatives of the people who came with me," Stack explained.

"Give me the names. I'll be glad to check them against the casualty list I have. The list is incomplete, so even if they are alive, they might not be on it. Or they could be in the casualty camp across town. I'll check their list too. There's also a chance they're among wounded we haven't identified yet, or who still haven't come in."

"What about those who are in hospitals right now?"

The officer gave a short, barking laugh. "This is the hospital. What used to be the hospital is now tons of rubble. You're looking at the remaining medical personnel in Fresno. Surgeons without operating theaters. No medicine or blood plasma. Whenever there has been severe blood loss, we get some Type-O soldier to lie down and transfer blood directly from him to the casualty. A needle in his arm, a needle in the casualty's arm, and a tube between them. That's what it's down to."

"What about those who need operations?"

"We try and stem the bleeding as best we can, then wait for a helicopter. We're trying to get one. There are still military communications over short distances. Not too good. Lots of static. But it's something. There are still hospitals intact. Bases intact. Small ones. If we can get people there we can operate on them."

"It doesn't sound too hopeful," Stack said.

The officer dropped his voice. "No. I'd hate to be

one of those poor bastards. Most'll be dead before morning."

"How's the radiation in these parts?" The officer moved his palm from side-to-side. "Maybe we shouldn't have come down from the mountains."

"They'll get theirs soon enough. Radiation travels with the prevailing winds and rains. Just don't touch too many objects and dust yourself off a lot. That way you won't pick up much. It's the best you can do."

"I noticed a lot of almost-unconscious people lying about with no signs of bleeding or external injuries. Radiation sickness?"

"You're on the mark there. Those poor suckers are halfway to the grave. Many didn't even make it this far. Young, old, grandmothers, babies. What a disgusting thing war is," he said suddenly, his gruff exterior cracking under the strain. But then he pulled together.

"No use my standing here, chewing the fat with you, mister. I've got a job to tackle and not enough time to do it in. Get me the names of those you're looking for and I'll check them against my lists. Some of the poor bastards here have come in unconscious, or delirious, and couldn't give us their names and didn't have any IDs. Those unidentified have been placed on the left. Have your people look at their faces. They may recognize someone."

Stack called Rayisa and the Caudells over. They gave the officer the names of their loved ones, which he couldn't find on his lists. Then they looked at the faces of the unidentified. None of them were blood relations either, but Rayisa and Mrs. Caudell were crying by the time they were back outside again.

"What do you think happened to my sister and her husband?" Mrs. Caudell sobbed to her husband as she tried to regain control.

"Do I have to draw you pictures, Sally?"

Stack listened to this as he kept an arm around Rayisa, comforting her. Just then the officer he had spoken to came over.

HELL RIDE

"We've got reports of casualties from the center of town and need transport fast to get them over here. I'm requisitioning your van, mister."

"What'll I use?" Stack asked as if coming out of a trance.

"I just need the van for a few hours."

"If you're taking it, you're taking me with it."

"Fine. But we'd better get going."

"This'll use up valuable fuel I'll need to get back to the mountains."

"I can get you a few gallons. Our stocks are limited, but we can spare some fuel. Satisfied?"

"What about the people who came with me?"

"Let 'em stay here till you're finished. We'll feed 'em military rations." Stack told the others to wait for him, then got into the van with the officer.

They drove off quickly, with the officer giving instructions on where they were to go. The officer had a mobile field radio and was talking with somebody not in visible range.

After he had signed off, the men silently eyed the devastation. A sudden wind came up and began driving dust through the open windows. Both men quickly rolled them up.

"That dust's full of radiation," the officer said. "So's everything. We're breathing it, stepping into it, and probably drinking it too."

"You're pretty jolly for someone who's got to stay here. I'm going to be here only a short while, yet I'm nervous as hell."

"I read what you're saying. But this is my duty. Serve and die. The great patriotic bit. No doubt some of us will die of radiation. But many won't. I'll wait and see if any of those tickets out there has my number on it. Right now I'm living this thing one day at a time, and today is just the first day of the war."

"If I had a medal, I'd give it to you," Stack said.

"By the way, what's your name? We've been talking for a while and are going to pick up casualties together, and I don't even know your name."

"Nick Stack. And you?"

"Major Bill Bathhurst from Castro Valley. That's across the Bay from San Francisco." His face hardened. "I haven't been home yet. I heard that the Bay Area cities have been devastated. The Golden Gate Bridge has been knocked into the water, barring passage to ships trying to get in or out of the harbor, except for small craft, which can go through gaps."

"Do you know how your family is?"

Bathhurst shrugged. "I have to wait to find out and take care of these problems first." He gestured out the window with his right hand. "If it wasn't for this assignment, I'd be looking for them now. Or maybe not. I worked for a company in downtown Frisco before I was mobilized. If not for this job I'd have been in Frisco when the bombs came down."

"So, in a way, you're lucky."

Bathhurst's face hardened. He looked sideways at Stack. "Mister, the only really lucky ones are the poor bastards who died when the bombs hit. They evaporated in a fraction of a second and didn't even know they were dead before it was over. They're with God or part of the dust scooting through the atmosphere. But we're the ones who have to scrape and scuffle for life. No one's ever seen a war like this. No telling what kind of world it'll turn out to be."

"Let's hope for the best."

"Those hopes usually don't come true," Bathhurst said grimly. But then there was no more time for talk. They'd arrived at their destination. Four badly wounded civilians were on stretchers on the ground with three military men around them, one with a radio.

Stack pulled to a stop, then he and Bathhurst got out and went over to help load the casualties. Above them the sky darkened another notch as the sun sank a bit further in the western sky.

4

The lone B-52G took on altitude as it left the blue Pacific and came over land. Soon it would have to go higher to avoid the Sierras. The six-man crew was grim-faced. This was probably the only B-52 from their base that had had to abort its flight and could not go on to attack the USSR. The immense power their bomber carried—eight Boeing AGM-69 short-ranged attack missiles, plus nuclear free-fall bombs carried in the thousand-cubic-foot bomb bay, and 12 AGM-86B cruise missiles, six per wing station—would not be used on any enemy, but would remain impotent as the crew looked for a place to land.

Giles Garudet, the youngish-looking chief pilot, glanced at his co-pilot, Brad Osseville, seated higher than his commander. The other man grinned down, then let his eyes quickly skim the cockpit dials and controls, studying height, speed, fuel consumption, and radar position. The plane was kept on track by a Honeywell AN ASN-131 gimballed electrostatic inertial-navigation system called GEANS. Height was given by a Honeywell radar altimeter. Brad Osseville was sometimes stunned by the sheer array of electronic gadgetry jammed into the bomber. The real wonder was inside the plane. Not the impressive exterior and huge size most people commented about: the nearly five-story height of the plane as it stood on the tarmac, or the 185-foot wingspan, or the 488,000-pound maximum takeoff weight. But all of it had been made unimportant by a simple engine failure they could not remedy in the air. And so, unable to complete the mission that would be the culmination of their training and pay the Russians back for what they had done, they were here over California.

Garudet thought back to the previous hours and days. Everyone knew something was up when America went into a Defcon 3 alert, two down from Defcon 1, which was war. All B-52s were ordered back to CONUS—the Continental US. In the case of Garudet's squadron, that meant coming back from Guam to the 93rd Bomber Wing Headquarters at March Airfield in Southern California. There, they remained on a high state of alert, their planes loaded up with a full compliment of bombs.

Then, without warning, it came. What no one had expected in all the endless war games. Hearts racing, they rushed for their planes, thinking, hoping, that perhaps this was only one more readiness alert. And that things would simmer down as a settlement was reached—the way it had been reached in past crises. But this time it hadn't happened. And while the planes were taking off, shields had come down over their 12-window cockpit canopies, and they were steered by internal TV as pilots watched the screens from behind 21-layer lead-lanthanum zirconate-titanate ceramic goggles which turned opaque under bright light to prevent flash blindness. The enemy warheads detonated as the planes were taking off, one after the other, climbing for height, eight powerful engines, each rated at 13,750 pounds of thrust, a total of 110,000 pounds of forward momentum, pushing the bombers as fast as their heavy weight and the force of gravity would allow.

Some of the crew had to fight back tears as they realized the base they had just left no longer existed, and that many of the friends and loyal ground crews they had served with were now just atoms and ashes being sucked up into an endlessly rising cloud of nuclear debris. The force of the blast, like some gigantic backwash, grabbed and shook the plane in a huge, hard fist. But gradually, the power of those eight jets pulled the B-52 free and lifted it higher and higher like some great eagle pregnant with lethal eggs and nuclear death. Eggs it planned to carry across the far Pacific, then over the Pole, or by another route, into Siberia to make their opposite numbers pay for the decisions made by men inside Kremlin walls. Men who by now were safe, whisked away into some deep underground shelter.

Once they were high enough and far away enough from the blasts, the cockpit windshields came down and the crew looked out over a California strange, alien, and frightening as never before. Peppered now with mushroom clouds. Inland, rising mushrooms were over the major military bases, but the mushrooms were thickest along the coast where most of the large cities were. From San Diego, almost on the Mexican border, to Los Angeles and her satellite cities, to San Francisco and her surrounding cities in the north. Far to the east Las Vegas lay under a pinkish, twisting cloud, as did Hoover Dam. Garudet had a sister in Las Vegas. As for Hoover Dam, once it turned into rubble, the billions of tons of water that it held back would charge forward in a 700-foot wall of raging hell, racing down on survivors, killing victims dozens of miles away as the unannounced foaming river plunged down on their heads, snuffing out their lives. The sights the crew witnessed gave added impetus to their determination to make it to Siberia, run the gauntlet of defending Soviet fighters and missiles, and rip the hell out of those who had done all this damage.

Garudet was determined to make it and confident of success. His plane could fly 7500 miles without refueling. Enough range to reach Siberia and almost enough to get home. However, KC-135 tankers were now making their way north and would be there for the survivors to refuel before they headed back to CONUS, or some base in Canada—which would probably be attacked as well, though not as badly. And if no base were available, Garudet planned to ditch the B-52 over some secluded spot before he and his crew bailed out. A waste of a good plane. But it would have served its purpose. First, though, they had to reach Siberia.

His engines had roared with muted power as the B-52 climbed to 30,000 feet. Only when approaching enemy airspace would the bomber drop down and skim the surface, sophisticated radars guiding it. Garudet had looked to his right and left at the six other bombers flying on his flanks. They would keep in formation till they were a hundred miles out over the Pacific, then separate, each plane taking a different path to Russia. That way, if one B-52 were picked up by hunting packs of fighters, only that plane would fall victim. There wouldn't be a whole squadron to feast on. The Russians would have to search for the hundreds of B-52s one at a time. And while they did, electronic ghost decoys would send enemy fighters hunting here and there, with only a few fish falling into their nets as time, measured in minutes, was lost and the real B-52s drew ever closer to the target zones.

Garudet checked his fuel. The capacious internal tanks held 46,000 gallons. Two underwing tanks each held 700 gallons more. Enough fuel to provide six gallons for each mile flown at 509 miles per hour at high altitude. Over 3000 gallons per hour.

Often, during training, the men talked, but not this time. The tension was too great. The realization that this was for real and that their loved ones might no longer exist gave a harsh, surreal feeling to the very atmosphere they inhabited, their minds electronically locked to one another and this great machine which carried them relentlessly toward the homeland of the enemy: a place none of them had ever been to. Giles Garudet, pilot; Brad Osseville, co-pilot; Bob Carbindell, navigator; Todd Stahl, radar navigator; Lance Briggs, ECM man; and Ralph Raditsch, gunner. Men who had come to know each other as brothers. Men who might well die in this flying coffin if the Red Air Force caught up with them, or some ground crew drew the right bead at the right time.

Garudet felt sharp sparkles of electricity rush up his spine, but forced these sensations down, then tried to imagine what was happening in Europe right now, and in half a dozen other flashpoints from the Korean DMZ to the Middle East. The image of it all stunned him as the size and complexity of what was happening filled his mind. Across the screen of his imagination tanks raced through great choking clouds of dust as they converged on frontiers from either side. Armored troop carriers mixed in with the tanks, troops firing in wild abandon, weapons dancing in tightly clenched fists, eyes now wild pinpricks of excitement, rivers of sweat rushing down glistening, greasy bodies as red, pink, and blue tracers flew from reddened barrels, great jerking clouds of smoke erupting from the twisting guns, rounds striking home. Men falling, others grabbing for legs or parts of limbs no longer attached to their bodies. Great masses of men and equipment being turned into blackened, burning rubble as units fought, advanced, and retreated. Tanks exploding with direct hits, or taking the blast, thick armor holding back the killing shell, then advancing, trying to catch the other tank in the death-dealing grip they had avoided, as hundreds of helicopters raced across the terrain, flying low, catching the tanks in the open and blasting them into scrap with rapid missiles tipped with explosive death. Scenes of great red, orange, and yellow rolling balls of flame turning into pillars, then mushrooms of death going rapidly black and dying as ugly puffs of smoke on a hundred battlefields raced across his fevered imagination and made his eyes bright with suppressed excitement as he tried to do his job.

But the images kept returning. He was unable to get any real information, and his imagination supplied him with what it thought was happening. The scenes of war, vivid, violent, bloody, costly, and merciless. And like someone watching an execution he doesn't want to see, but unable to control his fascinated revulsion, Garudet watched while his imagination played out every battle scene he had ever read, seen on TV or in the movies, or heard about from buddies.

It would have continued that way if his co-pilot hadn't pointed to their left and right as the other planes peeled away. Below, the wide, endless circle of blue that was the Pacific flowed serenely. For short seconds it allowed his mind to deny what he needed to deny: that there was a war and that this was not another in an endless series of exercises. But Garudet couldn't force himself to accept lies. Not even with his vivid imagination.

Just then the first tremors shook the plane. The pilots eyeballed their cockpit dials, checking all the indicators and controls, finding no problems. Eyes gazed out cockpit windows and along wings. The plane flew on, seemingly without trouble. But a few minutes later the tremors returned.

Brad Osseville eyed various control dials and told Garudet, "Trouble in right wing engines one and four. Don't know what kind yet," Osseville added, the slightest trace of emotion in his words. "But there's been a pressure drop and power is falling."

"Fuel leak? Compressor blade problems? Something wrong with the air-fuel mixture intake?"

"Can't tell, Giles. Could be this, that, or the other. Let's hope it's temporary and works itself out. Only a ground mechanic can tell us the trouble once he's gone over the plane."

"Where the hell do we get a mechanic now?" Garudet laughed.

The problem soon went away and the men breathed more easily. But then it came back. Crewmen throughout the plane contacted them about it. Garudet used his communications hookup to tell them what he knew and to promise to inform them of any new developments.

Things did not get any better. They deteriorated in a

HELL RIDE

slow, progressive, downward slide. Something somewhere in the big, complex flying machine had gone wrong. Something had broken, or come loose because it wasn't screwed in tightly enough, or developed a hairline fracture under the stresses and strains of constant use. And now, under the pressures of performing tens of thousands of feet in the air, buffeted by high winds, numerous temperature changes, and the stresses of ramming through the air at over 500 miles an hour, the weak link in the chain had come undone. It happened all the time with mechanical things, and especially with highly complex, sensitive military aircraft. But how serious was it?

Garudet and Osseville checked dials and kept glancing out at the wing carrying the offending engines. The strain on their concerned faces and the look in their alert eyes told the story as they flew north.

The fact that two out of eight engines were not putting out enough power meant an uneven push was being developed, adding stress to the other engines and setting up varying air currents along different sections of the wings so that it began to creak with the strain of moving through the air. Indicated air speed began to drop.

"Perhaps we ought to increase the power to get our speed over five hundred miles an hour," Osseville suggested.

"No. Whatever is failing out there will fail faster under greater pressure. Let's see what develops."

"Should we abort the mission?"

"Not at this point. America is going to need every bomber we can get over Russia. And I don't want to miss paying them back for what they've done. Maybe we'll be the ones to get the guys who fired the missiles that totalled our base, or perhaps a few silos won't have the chance to fire missiles they haven't shot at us yet."

"Yeah," Osseville replied. But one could sense the disbelief behind the single spoken word. The B-52 was having trouble and Siberia was perhaps a dozen hours distant. Deep Siberia, that is. And they would first have to penetrate Soviet fighter defenses. And a partly crippled bird was not the desired way to do so.

"Shouldn't we contact someone to get their advice about what we can do?" Osseville asked.

"I'll try. But I don't think communications will be too good right now."

Garudet contacted Bob Carbindell, the navigator, who, with the bombardier, was seated further aft on a different level. Garudet ordered Carbindell to try and contact their airfield. He did and quickly got back to the pilot. "I can't raise the field."

"I didn't think you'd be able to. Try Fifteenth Air Force Command. Tell them our problem, ask their advice. Say we'd like to go on and hit our targets despite the problem we're experiencing."

Carbindell signed off and attempted to make contact while Garudet and Osseville continued to pilot the bomber, paying attention to the various dials, worrying about the future of their mission.

The wing continued to creak. It was not of the latest mechanically flexible type with fiber-glass leading and trailing edges to aero-dynamically take the stresses being placed upon it.

Garudet listened as Carbindell got nothing but static. Finally, he picked up two distant B-52s, one of them from their air base. The commanders of the other planes asked questions, with plenty of static to knock out key words, then offered advice. But there was nothing they could do. They had missions to fulfill and in time of war their orders were to go ahead with what had to be done and leave the others to fix their own problems. Besides, this wasn't some battlefield where they could pull behind some rocks and work on the problem together. In the air you were truly alone. It was every crew, if not every man, for itself.

Garudet got on the radio, thanked the commanders of the bombers for answering, and said he would make

HELL RIDE

the final decision to abort if need be. Once they had signed off, Garudet made one more try at raising Fifteenth Air Force Headquarters, using the AFSATCOM global communications satellite network. But it obviously wasn't working. It looked like the dear old Russkis had used lasars to destroy the network. Something America hadn't developed to the same degree because the anti-SDI darlings had run a tattoo on our defenses. Next, he tried every military airfield in California, followed by Nellis Air Force Base in Nevada, then Eighth Air Force Headquarters—though it wasn't his command, followed by the 42nd Strategic wing of the 3rd Air Division of SAC—his old unit. He got a negative on all attempts.

Garudet stopped trying, then told the rest of the crew, "We're on our own."

"What're we going to do?" Osseville asked. The internal communications net was on so that the entire crew, even those in the farthest parts of the cavernous B-52, could hear what was being said.

"We'll see what the next hours bring. And while we're at it, let's have a look at what our targets are supposed to be."

Garudet took out the sealed envelope provided to each bomber crew. They had been so busy with various details Garudet hadn't even thought of the envelope till then. Now he ripped it open and announced their targets.

"Well boys, you'll be glad to learn that we're going to release our Tomahawks at a dozen Soviet army bases in southern Siberia just north of the People's Democratic Republic of Outer Mongolia. The six short-range AGMs will hit half a dozen airfields in the Lake Baikal region near Irkutsk. Our free-fall bombs will then be delivered in a pattern over Irkutsk itself."

"Irkutsk," Lance Briggs said, "is the largest city in Siberia, and Lake Baikal is the biggest freshwater lake in the world. When we hit it, sir, we'll be poisoning all that water and a goodly chunk of Siberia."

"I guess we will, Lance. But then, a lot of things are being poisoned this day. The men in high places who started this, whichever of them did, should have thought of all that before they acted. But as long as the destruction's begun, a bit more won't matter. Anyway, our's not to question why. Our's but to do and die," he said, quoting a line from a poem. He tried to remember if he'd read it somewhere or heard it in a movie. Just then the wings began to vibrate harder.

Power was really beginning to fail. Garudet looked at the dials. Engine pressure was down even more in the two troublesome engines, and indicated air speed had fallen to 460 miles per hour.

"I'm going to try something," Garudet told Osseville, contradicting his earlier statements. "Perhaps the fuel lines are jammed, or maybe a good pressure jolt is needed to get those parts moving faster in synchronization. I'm going to let the power out full throttle and see what develops. Hold on."

As the power began to flow, they watched the dials begin to quiver, then climb. The plane reacted as if struck by a giant hammer as it arched up and started to climb. Even the offending engines began to reverse their troublesome performance. It looked as if they were over the hump. Within a minute the bomber had climbed to over 40,000 feet, heading toward the B-52's 55,000-foot ceiling. Indicated air speed reached 500 knots, almost 580 miles per hour, close to the peak speed of 595 miles per hour that the bomber was capable of. They had just passed the 44,000-foot mark when something happened which wiped the smiles off the crewmen's faces. The two offending engines began to shudder and spit smoke—whitish smoke at first, with sparks to it, then black smoke, a thin stream which finally thickened. The entire plane shuddered. The trouble wasn't going away. It was multiplying. Despite full power, the bomber's performance began to waver. It was unable to continue the steep climb with the same force as before. Like an old boxer attempting to make one more comeback in the ring, then faltering after a hot start full of punches as the younger, more agile opponent got his balance and responded with a flurry of counter punches, the jet began to slow down.

Rather than push the bomber to the limit, Garudet leveled off at 46,000 feet and looked at the cockpit gauges. Some indicated rising temperatures inside engines one and four. Their peak speed, after leveling off, had been just over 580 miles an hour, and had now dropped to 560 miles per hour. The strain of even that effort was making the whole plane vibrate, just as it did when they made a low-level penetration at an altitude of 200 feet. But they were at 46,000 feet. This should not be happening.

Indicated altitude was beginning to fall. Then Garudet realized he was feeding the engines at full speed. He had not, in his shock, reduced the amount of fuel going to the engines. Garudet immediately cut the fuel flow by 20 percent. Within seconds the plane began calming down. The smoke from the offending engines subsided to a gentle brownish-black stream, which soon frosted over into a fluffy white contrail as water vapor adhered to improperly burned hydrocarbons in the minus-40-degree atmosphere.

Garudet looked over the dials one more time, frowned, then made a quick decision. One he dreaded making and now was forced to.

"Men," he announced, "due to mechanical problems I am going to abort this mission and return to California."

He did not hear any frustrated oaths, just a deadening silence. Were they as disappointed as he was, or glad they did not have to fly across hostile territory, face death from the ground and in the air, and at the end of it all, blast hundreds of thousands, if not millions of people into the endless Valhalla waiting for them?

Finally, Briggs spoke up. "I guess Irkutsk will live after all. Nor will Lake Baikal and a goodly chunk of Siberia be contaminated for centuries to come."

"It won't matter, Lance," Osseville replied in a dead-even voice. "There'll be plenty of radiation from other sources to fuck them up."

No one said anything more as Garudet turned the B-52 around and headed toward California, wondering all the while how he would land now that their base no longer existed. He'd worry about it when he got there. Right now he had enough fuel, if needed, to fly across America looking for a field to land at.

5

They had stopped on the highway, perhaps 50 of them. Hard, muscled, bearded, tattooed men and five women, sitting astride their motorcycles. Men with tough faces and cold, slitted eyes. Eyes that had seen too much. Faces that had been molded by a life wild and endlessly cruel as they rode across the underside of society and lived a life experienced by their kind alone, away from other men, outside the eyes of normal society—most of the time. Fists which had done violence, taken, beaten, stolen, struck, clenched, clawed, grasped, and sometimes killed now held onto the handlebars of bikes as they looked in stunned realization at the march of mushroom clouds across the horizon at the same time that Nick Stack had watched them from his mountain aerie. They understood in the same dumb, silent way that the animals of the field understand the power of forces greater and deadlier than any around them. It was an overwhelming, ruthless evil vaster than anything they had touched or could envision. And in touching this world it had brushed against them, though the distance kept them safe at least for the moment, from this horror visited on the land by men much like them. Only those men wore suits and rode in limousines, not bikes, and at least had the surface respect of society. But none of that mattered now. Society had been brought down to the level of the gutter. And in some dumb way these outcasts understood that the fires that had burned inside them for so long were now burning across the land, bringing to others the hells they had known all their lives.

At the head of the line of bikers who had been taking a jaunt in the country, after a summer of thieving and good living in the cities of the coast, sat their leader. He was 43, though he didn't look it, with a black, gray-speckled beard down to his belly, and hard, wild brown eyes which could burn hypnotically through men and women. He had a short, flattened nose that looked as if it were beaten in, bulbed at the tip, which sat over thin, frowning lips almost hidden in the tattered, dirty, matted jungle of his unkempt beard. He wore a World War II German helmet with a great black swastika painted across the top inside a blood-red circle. The eyes of onlookers were drawn first to the beard and face, then to the helmet, and finally to the great, gleaming, chromed chain he wore around his neck. It hung down onto his belly as his personal jewelry. It was also good for using as a flail during gang fights—or, bunched up, for beating his latest woman when she wasn't treating him right, or acting up, or giving him lip in front of the gang, making him look bad, bringing down his status.

The chain almost always rested on a black body shirt which matched the black of his leather riding pants and big, black, scuffed boots and black-linen riding gloves and black-leather, chrome-studded wrist bands.

Lyle Rokmer, also known as San Quentin Sal for the time he had done in that prison, was as hard and evil and cunning a piece of work as had ever been produced by the bike gangs of California or any other locale. Rokmer was able to hold his own in a fight with almost anyone barehanded, or with a knife, machete, gun, rifle, tire iron, chain, or broken bottle. In his time on the earth he had employed almost all these methods—more than once.

Farther back in the line was his main lieutenant, with the nickname of Samurai Sam, but better known to the police as Lance Zoyas. He was a year older than

Rokmer, his hair almost totally black except for a thick white streak through it. Like Rokmer, his idol and leader, he sported a great beard, a Nazi helmet, and many of the same clothes, except for his buckskin shirt and brown-leather pants. He wore a long machete in a sheath tied to his back and had on goggles against the wind. The girl on his bike was Debbie. She was a willowy, washed-out blonde with a small chest and a big rear. Zoyas liked them big in back, and this made her the girl of his dreams. He'd met her in a police station when he'd been picked up for a local burglary, a charge they could not prove in the end. She'd been pulled in for drunk driving. They'd gotten to know one another while having their vital statistics taken at the booking desk.

And when the police let him go, Zoyas looked her up. One thing led to another. She became his woman, quit her job, sold her car, gave up her apartment, and rode through southern California with him. She found Zoyas a strange, brooding man whose mood could vary from bright—the life of the party, to mild-mannered, generous, crude, rude, lewd, and violent. A drinker who threw fits and beat his woman on the spur of the moment, and then, the next day, told her how much he loved her and showered her with cheap jewelry.

Bit by bit, from Zoyas, his friends, and even Rokmer, she dissected the life of the man she loved, feared, was puzzled and amazed by. It was a life as hard and sharp as his dark face. A face like the prow of a ship. The nose long and bent, the eyes burning brown, hooded, watching, cunning, and scheming. He had big hands as if he had been born to grasp great chunks of this earth and the things on it.

Lance Zoyas, she learned, was the product of a broken home. A not uncommon thing in the circles he hung out in. His father was a Mexican wetback, his mother a Greek immigrant.

When he was fifteen he went away to reform school for the first time. Prison made great, ruthless fighters out of a lot of guys. Zoyas was approached sexually for the first time in reform school and had to fight like hell to prevent the other guy from turning him into a girl. The second time he would not have made it if not for a tougher kid who had taken an interest in him. A kid by the name of Lyle Rokmer. Their first meeting. One in a long series of jail meetings.

It was a murder in a Santa Monica bar with a switchblade, in which he'd killed another leather-jacketed rider, that put Rokmer into San Quentin with a five-year rap for manslaughter. A charge he served no more than three and a half years for because the prison was getting crowded and certain classes of criminals were being released early. It was there that he earned his nickname of San Quentin Sal.

Now Zoyas looked at Rokmer, whose face gleamed with strange fires and whose eyes reflected perverted dreams of wild deeds yet to be done. Rokmer looked back at his fellowers strung out along this stretch of highway, their bikes gleaming in the brilliance of the sun and reflecting the twisted clouds of death across the horizon.

He threw back his head and laughed. Those who had still been staring hypnotized at the mushrooms spawning higher and higher turned their heads, questioning smiles on their lips.

"Look," he said, pointing a crooked finger at the horizon. "That's the end of civilization. Do you know what that means, crazy motherfuckers?" His gaze wheeled across their questioning faces, dumb eyes, and gaping mouths.

"It means no more cops. No more army, navy, or air force. What's left of them won't be left for long. It means no more Folsom prisons." There were cheers. Some of them had served time there. "No more San Quentins." More cheers. Zoyas joined them. "No more Chinos." Greater cheers.

"We can do what we want. Take what we want. Rob. Rape. Kill. Enjoy ourselves till hell freezes over. For it'll surely freeze over sooner or later. We have nothing to lose and everything to gain. Are you with me, world?" he asked. They were the only world he had. The only world that mattered. His mother, father, cousins, sisters, brothers, friends from a host of pens were now ashes or on their way to the grave.

"Yeah," they yelled in unison.

"Good," he said, turning as he started the Kawasaki KDX 80. "Let's go," he yelled over the roar and sputter of the engine and vast clouds of bluish-white smoke. "Let's find some town and party!"

A chorus of hoarse roars followed him as engine after engine kicked over and a host of wild men and women raced pell-mell down the deserted highway, heading up from the valley they were in toward the forested uplands.

Overhead, almost silent, white contrails carved the sky as B-52s headed toward the open sea. One of them was piloted by Giles Garudet and Brad Osseville.

6

Giles Garudet and Brad Osseville scanned the landscape, eyeballing familiar points. The coast, as far as the eye could see, was a checkerboard of green, brown, and burned-out swaths. There were vast areas with hundreds of fires across them and torrents of blackish smoke rising until each black swath had a pillar of roiling darkness four miles high over it, some of the offshoots having joined together. Many of the fires in the center of the swath were dying out, while around the edges flames still burned with great vigor, consuming the plentiful fuel underneath them.

Garudet winced at the thought of how many lives had been wiped out and how many more would end before this day was finished. Then his mind flashed across the scene his plane would have created had it penetrated Siberia and dropped its load. Was he any better than those who had done this before? Garudet quickly forced down the thought. He was letting his insides come out again. Through superhuman control he once more became the professional flyer looking for a place to put down his bird. He told the rest of the crew over the communications net that he would fly to their base to see what condition it was in, if perhaps there was a place to land—though he doubted it.

Garudet looked at the fuel gauge. Thousands of gallons had already been used up. But there was still plenty left. The two 700-gallon fuel tanks under each wing were full. Time to pull in the fuel and dump the tanks. That would get rid of the extra weight and underwing resistance which was downgrading performance. He needed to smooth the airflow as much as possible.

The trembling in the wings and airframe was coming back now as they moved into the thicker, lower atmosphere. Even a speed of 350 miles per hour was too much for the plane to sustain.

"Don't you think we'd better shut down those two engines now?" Osseville asked.

"I'd do it. But then I might not be able to start them again and we'll need all our power for landing, wherever that might be."

"How long till we get to the air base?" Osseville asked.

"Maybe forty minutes."

"Thirty-six minutes," Carbindell piped in.

"Thanks, Bob," Garudet said. "Make a list of all airfields, military and civilian, that can take our plane. We'll try them all if landing conditions aren't right at March."

"Yessir."

The scenes of devastation below gave way to forests of endless green. He kept the plane at 20,000 feet and 350 miles an hour. The fuel had by now been sucked out of the auxiliary fuel tanks. He flicked a switch and both tanks fell away, twinkling in the sunlight like silver jewelry as they tumbled end over end into the vast greenness below, becoming too small to be seen.

"I wonder how Jean and the kids are," Osseville asked suddenly. Garudet looked up at his co-pilot. This had been the first time in the mission he had spoken about his wife and three girls, aged four to nine. Garudet wondered about his own family and thought about the other men in the plane. He saw the troubled look and the worry lines on Osseville's face. Garudet also realized that the interplane communications net was open and the others had heard this. He wondered, and not only for privacy's sake, whether he should close the communications net so that the conversation would be between him and Osseville alone. The worry of one man could become the worry of all of them—except for Raditsch, who wasn't married.

Finally, Garudet spoke in that deafening silence. "We'll find out, Brad. If we can't get a message through, we'll go look for them. All of us will look for our families. But first we've got to get this bird down."

"Yeah," Osseville said, sniffling. "Sorry about my outburst."

"It was hardly an outburst. I thought you were quite controlled."

Osseville laughed nervously and returned to his duties. For the next few minutes there was small talk as the men went about checking indicated air speed in miles and knots per hour, altitude, direction, pounds of fuel consumed, and fuel remaining. There were over 40,000 gallons in the tanks, giving them plenty of flight time to find a place to put down, whether in California or Nevada.

"We're approaching our field," Carbindell announced. "Ten miles and closing."

All eyes in front of windows, or near TV consoles, strained for the first outline of the familiar field they had called home for over three years when they weren't on distant duty in their forward Guam base.

Then they saw the ruins. The runways, hangars, administration, supply, and repair buildings. Most of the buildings were down, some were still burning. The wooden structures were totally gone, nothing more than shadow patterns on the ground, like in Hiroshima. Garudet slowed the jet and brought it lower as they swooped over the base. Then out across the desert, where he brought the B-52 around for another pass.

The concrete buildings were shells. The roofs were blown off. Many of the walls were caved in, or half caved in, on the sides facing the blast, the windows empty spaces like gaps between teeth. The hangar and administration areas were almost completely flattened.

Garudet remembered how concrete had survived somewhat in Hiroshima, even when the blast had been very close. Of course, this blast had been larger. At least several hundred kilotons, maybe ten Hiroshimas' worth. The runways were pitted. One had a 200-foot-wide and perhaps 150-foot-deep crater. That must have been the point above which the bomb went off. He made a third and final sweep over the airfield.

"No good, boys," he announced as he climbed for altitude and put on speed. "We can't land. Our wheels will catch in those holes and the landing gear will break off, causing us to scrape along and explode in a flurry of flames. We'll be trapped inside with no one to get us out. Then the bombs'll go off, finishing what the Russkis started."

"Where to now, Bob?"

"We can try Edwards Air Base near Palmdale. Merced Air Base, Fifteenth Airforce HQ. George Air Base near Victorville. Castle Center near Marysville. Norton Air Base east of LA and the China Lakes Naval Air Station. There are also a host of small civilian airfields."

"Forget them. We need a minimum of seven thousand feet of runway. And even that's cutting it pretty thin."

They reached Edwards first. It was as devastated as March had been. As the bomber passed overhead they noticed some people along the edge of one of the ruined runways signaling them using mirrors and waving. Garudet wiggled the B-52's wings in acknowledgment. But there was nothing else he could do. Landing was out of the question. Perhaps they had wounded down there who needed help, or were in need of food and water. He couldn't even radio for help. He tried again and all he got was static. Closing his eyes a moment and shaking his head, he flew across the desert toward Norton Air Base, east of LA. It was just as devastated as Edwards. Only this time he saw no signs of life.

"Want to try LA International Airport?" Carbindell

asked.

"All right, let's do it." As expected, the airport was one more ruin in a vast plain of ruins. It had been hit as badly as any military facility. The men also stared in shock at what had happened to LA beyond the field. Shaking their heads they headed inland again.

"Let's try the China Lakes Naval Air Station," Osseville suggested.

"We're just wasting our time flying over military bases," Carbindell said. "I don't think there's an intact one left. We've got to try some civilian airfield. There's an abandoned one in north central California. They started it some years ago to open the area to tourism in a big way. There were plans for hotels and a retirement community. Then the money ran out and the field was left unfinished. They put in a runway, but no hangars or administration building, and only a half-completed road."

"Give me the location," Garudet said. "We'll fly over it if we can't land at the China Lakes Station."

Carbindell gave him the information he requested and then the men tensely eyed the terrain below, waiting for the China Lakes airfield to appear. The minutes passed and soon they were over it, discovering another depressing military disaster.

"Okay, boys," Garudet told the rest of the crew, "we're going north to check out that airfield Bob told us about."

As they headed in that direction desert brown began to give way to grassy lowlands, then forests as the elevation grew. The B-52 moved higher. Soon they were over endless sheets of woodland. Blue lakes sparkling in the sun like polished warrior shields lying on a battlefield of long ago. The thin silver ribbons of rivers, creeks, and streams gleamed as sunlight reflected off them. What Garudet wouldn't have given to be down there now, walking through the cool of the woods, or standing in some stream with cold water gurgling past his legs as he fished for trout or wide-mouth bass. He wondered if they were indigenous to these waters.

But such thinking was fantasy, he realized. Underneath everything was the great pall of death. He had only to look to his left to see the dirty black haze across the horizon. And around everything was the radiation driven by the prevailing winds to every corner of the troubled land. In the days, weeks, and months to come men and creatures would fall to radiation poisoning. Nuclear bombs, unlike most others, left behind a silent legacy. At least with an explosive bomb, once the shrapnel had stopped flying, the injured, depending on how bad their wounds were, knew if they would die or live another day. In the case of nuclear weapons, even those without a scratch faced the prospect of an agonizing radiation death or cancer defects for their children decades after the war.

But his mind switched itself back from these thoughts to the cockpit controls. What happened was past and gone. Water under the bridge. Something which could not be retrieved. Garudet and others would now have to live with the aftermath and make the best of what was out there.

He wondered again about the survivors at Edwards and how many others there were like them that he hadn't seen and would never get to see. Guilt stabbed at him for having passed by those who needed his help at Edwards. But what could he in all reality have done? The bomber would have cracked up had he tried to land, and then he and all his crew would have burned up and no one would have been saved anyway. And they most likely knew it down there. Perhaps they only signaled so he could radio somebody to come and help. Well, that was not possible. They would just have to make the best of it, like tens of millions of other survivors. He didn't even know if there were that many. He had read somewhere that this would be the population after a nuclear holocaust. He hoped the numbers were wrong and that even more people were alive. But even a small strike would eliminate tens of millions, more than the losses in the first half of World War II. As for the survivors, they were on land, able to move to a safer place. A lot luckier than those who survived ship sinkings in the North Atlantic during World War II.

Stop it! Stop it! he silently screamed at himself. Can't you control your mind? But he couldn't. This damn thing had him by the throat. Thoughts popped in and out at a fever pace. No sooner had one gone than another took its place. Though not wounded physically, he now realized what it meant to be caught in war's aftermath. A winter chill passed through his bones from deep inside to the surface of his skin. Garudet forced it down as his navigator announced, "Another few minutes and we'll be coming to Amrad Airfield."

"That's what they call it? Not much of a name."

"A company by the name of Amrad was building the field. They hadn't decided on a name yet, so they picked Amrad as a preliminary name and the moniker stuck. They were even going to run a contest to pick the best name for the airport, with the winner getting two weeks paid vacation in San Diego or Las Vegas."

"Yeah," he found himself answering absent-mindedly. But with the other half of his mind he was dissecting the conversation in amazement. Here they were, making small talk, and around them half a planet lay in ruins. In one way it was unreal. But he reminded himself that not all conversations had to be grand and eloquent. This wasn't some movie. Life consisted of grand and banal moments, with the banal providing the rest stops, the pauses between the great. For most people, unfortunately, life was one long feast of banality.

Garudet looked away from the cockpit and up at Osseville, who had a shocked look on his face, his mouth open as if he wanted to speak. But nothing was coming out, his eyes crinkling as if he wanted to break into tears. Garudet was about to ask if everything was okay, but that might start the man pouring out his guts,

HELL RIDE

with others listening in. Others who no doubt had their own worries and tensions and might find them exacerbated by any adverse reaction on Osseville's part.

But now there was no more time to worry about it. Carbindell announced that the airfield they were interested in was only ten miles away. The pilots began bringing the speed and altitude of the B-52 down so they could more slowly sweep across the abandoned field to see if it were possible to land there.

The airfield was located inside a mile-wide, five-mile-long valley surrounded by green-flanked, granite-tipped mountains. The walls of the valley were heavily wooded, but the bottom consisted of grassy, rolling fields and the runway: 8500 or 9000 feet of concrete. Garudet also saw that one had to begin descending right after coming over the mountains. And on takeoff one had to climb sharply for height to go over the peaks, which were at least 8000 feet high.

He made one pass over the mountains and the valley, turned, came back, and went over the peaks, then down into the valley, his hand steady on the controls, the plane going less than 200 miles an hour. He dropped the B-52 lower and lower till they were skimming along no more than 1000 feet above the runway. Then he began to climb again, aiming for a point above the highest jagged peaks of the mountain wall straight ahead. The flight in and out looked easier than it was. This was definitely not the place to put an airfield which mostly less-skilled airmen and private pilots would use.

The fact that they were climbing sharply made the plane vibrate with the strain and effort and the troubled engines started spitting smoke and sparks. But he kept pouring on the power. At 300 miles an hour, they cleared the granite crowns with several hundred feet to spare. He winced at the thought of those jagged talons ripping the stomach out of the bomber, then tossing the flaming debris across a swath hundreds of yards long as great crimson-orange clouds tinged by black smoke rose across the mountain, followed perhaps by the ignition of the armed multi-warhead cargo and the obliteration of those jagged rocks within a nuclear inferno along with thousands of acres of woodland. But it didn't happen.

And then they came around again to dip into the valley a second time. This sweep told him the runway was good. It had been mostly finished, except for 200 feet near one end where rusted steel framing showed through the partly poured concrete. The only worry now was that they might run out of runway before they were finished rolling. But not if he cut his air speed dozens of miles an hour below normal just before they touched down and dropped all his flaps so that they formed air brakes.

That decided, he took the bomber up out of the valley and began turning for another approach. He explained to his crew how they'd make the approach from south to north because the unfinished portion of the strip was at the northern end. He'd try to touch down right at the edge of the runway to give himself enough ground to roll along.

"I could look further afield," he explained, "but there may be nothing out there and we'll just exhaust ourselves looking. This is here now, so we're taking it. To tell you the truth, I'm also worried about those engines. You can never tell when they'll start acting up badly again. And there's the possibility a third engine can go. As it is I don't relish trying to land with four engines on one wing and two on the other. I think we should grab the first safe port we can find while the grabbing's good. Do you agree?"

"You're the captain," Carbindell spoke up. "It's your plane."

"No, it's our plane. Yours, mine, the whole crew's."

Osseville grinned, though trouble stood in his worried eyes. "Does that mean that when you sell the plane, we all get a cut of the proceeds?" That led to laughter from the rest of the crew.

Garudet smiled. "My word of honor. Everyone gets

an even share. We'll split it six ways. I'll put up a sign at the edge of the airfield. CHEAP. SLIGHTLY USED B-52, PLUS 40,000 GALLONS OF GAS. SERVED TWO TOURS IN THAILAND AND INDOCHINA. AVAILABLE FOR ANY PATRIOTIC AMERICAN WHO WANTS TO FIX IT AND USE IT TO HIT THE USSR. NEVER BEEN THERE BEFORE."

"Sounds good," Osseville said. "I may buy it myself. I'm a rich guy, you know," he said, pointing a thumb at himself. "The salary the Air Force pays us has made me rich."

"As long as we're on the subject," Raditsch said over the communications net, "when are we going to get paid?"

"To get paid we have to find someone in charge," Garudet said. "Why don't I try to raise someone before we put down? We might connect this time and be ordered to a base which hasn't been hit yet. If they can repair us we can still make that bombing run to Siberia."

"Yeah," Osseville said, adrenalin pumping through his veins at the thought. The levity and now the possibility of going out to bomb the Russkis had brought them around, at least for the moment.

"Alpha Rose Theta 1191," Garudet called out as he used their code identification. "Jackson Wing. Quadrant Four calling all open channels. This is a Mayday. I repeat, a Mayday. Any channel, please answer. This is Alpha Rose Theta 1191. Come in, please, all open channels." They listened a long time, but across the ether came nothing but static. He tried once more as the big bomber circled the valley.

Garudet looked at Osseville, a grim expression across both their faces. "We're going down," he said with an air of finality.

The B-52 came over the peaks edging the valley to the south, then dipped steadily as the two pilots reduced altitude, making sure not to go so fast that they would strike one of the sloping mountain walls—always a danger with a plane so big. Complicating matters was the fact that they were flying partially blind and could not see the rear of the bomber. By the time the tail gunner could warn them about what was happening it would be too late. So they did things by dead reckoning and lots of experience.

They were now 1000 feet above the valley, which was itself at 4500 feet above sea level. The runway was only three-quarters of a mile distant. Indicated air speed was 175 miles per hour. Garudet now dropped the air speed to 160 miles per hour. The B-52 was just 350 feet above the valley floor as it approached the runway 1500 feet ahead. He took the plane down 50 feet at a time, trying not to misjudge so that they came down on concrete, not earth—which could be spongy, causing the wheels to sink in, stopping the plane with a jolt so that it nosed over, plowing into the ground, hard, breaking open, setting off fires, killing part or all of the crew, and setting off the bombs whose blasts would be thrown back toward the source by the shielding valley walls. Again and again.

Garudet's nightmare did not come true. He flew over the edge of the runway at 75 feet and brought the plane down at 140 miles an hour, perhaps too hard, several hundred feet from the edge. At the last second he thought of breaking off the approach, gaining altitude, flying out of the valley, and coming around for another try. But that might not be any better than this one and could be worse. They were here now. So down they went.

They landed with a jolt and he could feel the rubber burns on the runway, which raced past at a terrifying speed. The edge, some 8000 feet away, was not that distant. Quickly, he brought down all the flaps and could feel an instant slowing in forward momentum from 100 miles an hour to 60. Then he began to cut power to the engines.

The runway, which had looked smoother from above, was not so smooth close up. There were bumps and small depressions where concrete had buckled and sagged under nature's not-so-benevolent touch without any human hands to repair the damage and smooth down the rough edges. The going as a result was a bit rougher, which served to cut the speed of the bomber even more. Less than 3000 feet of runway remained. Then it was less than 2000, and finally only 1000, the last 200 feet of which were too rough for the B-52's wheels. But by then the plane was doing only 25 miles an hour.

Garudet added a little power to the whine of the jets and began to use the wheels to turn the plane on the runway till it was facing the direction from which they had come. Then he shut the engines and let the B-52 move till it came to a dead halt. Not only was the plane at a safe rest position, it was also turned in the other direction, having almost an entire runway at its disposal in case they had to take off again.

There were cheers when he had done it. And then all of the crew were out of their seats, tension sweat making the clothes stick to their bodies as they headed for the exits. Garudet was the first down on terra firma.

He quickly moved out from under the sheltering body of the B-52 so he could look at it from the outside. While doing so he eyed the landing wheels. They were somewhat beaten up. Then he glanced at the offending engines. Their outside appearance gave him no indication of what had gone on within and he had no mechanics to look into the problem.

The others, except for Raditsch, who ran to the side of the runway to urinate, walked over to where Garudet stood. While this was happening, Garudet quickly took in the sight of the B-52 from the cockpit to the tail. It was a big, beautiful, complex bird, and he was proud of it despite the fact that he hadn't been able to fly it all the way to Siberia. Garudet then looked away from the bomber and all around the valley before turning to the men who had assembled on his left and asking, "How do you like your new home?"

7

Nick Stack lit a cigarette, the third one in an hour. The sky was gunmetal gray. The host of fires burning in and around Fresno had only abated slightly. He was filthy, covered with dirt, soot, cuts, scratches, exhausted by the rescue efforts he had been involved in, and sickened by the sight of all the carnage. His face had that hard, wrinkled look one sees so often in veterans of hard-fought battles when they return from the front to the rear for R&R.

This last batch he had brought in had affected him the most. Four groups of six victims each. Blind, barely able to talk, walking wounded. They had been close enough to the bomb to be affected by the heat blast, but not killed. Their eyeballs had melted and run down their faces as they were instantly blinded. And their faces had been horribly burned to the point where facial features were no longer recognizable amid the big, welted, reddish lumps oozing colorless liquid. Where their eyes had been there were now empty, reddened sockets. Their mouths were open, gaping holes sucking air into fevered, wheezing lungs. Their faces were so swollen, so oozing, with the skin peeling off, that their noses were barely visible in all that swollen, undulating mass.

Bill Bathhurst had seen the expression on Stack's face as they had helped victims into the van to take them to the casualty center. "The same thing happened in Hiroshima, only not as bad as here," he had explained.

"The bombs that hit us were bigger. Had it not been for the blast and fires there'd be more cases like this. Most of the victims, stunned and blinded, didn't have a chance. It's pretty hard to get away from falling timbers, girders, and advancing firefronts when you can't see them and are trying to make your way forward by feel."

Stack had said nothing. He just continued loading on the victims and drove them back to the casualty center, where they were laid out on the ground. Later, someone found a wrecked, half-destroyed mattress shop and brought in damaged mattresses to lay the more severely wounded down on. Others lay on stretchers, or blankets, rags, and linens spread out on the ground. The number of survivors in the center was now over 200. But there were more wounded too sick to come in without being carried, and many still undiscovered in and around Fresno.

There were plenty of reports of people trapped in ruins. Bathhurst and Stack went to look for some of them. They saved a few. Very few. A mother. A child. An old man. A teenager. Some schoolgirls who had been playing hookey and survived when the theater in which they were watching a movie partially collapsed during the initial blast. Had they been in school, near ground zero, none of them would have survived. In this case hookey had been the right course to follow. Now, orphaned as well, they were taken to the casualty center.

Heading back out on another rescue mission they passed a place in the road where shadow tracings of human beings were sketched across the asphalt like long shadows in the setting sun. He pointed to them. Bathhurst smiled grimly, his face by now a gray mask of soot, grime, and ashes.

"When the bomb exploded," Bathhurst explained, "the first blinding flash burned the surface of the earth close to ground zero. Where people were in the way, they prevented the light from getting through, so the flash etched the shapes of their shadows into the asphalt. It will remain there for as long as the road surface lasts."

"What happened to the people?"

"They evaporated. The human body is mostly water. The solid matter burns, the water evaporates."

"What a bastard thing nuclear weapons are."

"Yes and no. In conventional wars one third of those who die are destroyed with their bodies. At best, bone chips and ashes are left behind. A buddy of mine told me about some guy he was fighting alongside of in Vietnam. The guy was a big, strapping fella with full combat gear and a backpack. In the backpack he had twenty pounds of C4, a plastic explosive three times as powerful as dynamite. They were fired on by the enemy, so they dropped to the grass and gave return fire. The enemy poured in a heavier volley. One of the bullets struck the backpack and the C4 inside it. There was an explosion. When the guy who was telling me about this looked up nothing was left. No soldier. No helmet. No rifle. No backpack. Nuthin'. War's like that, buddy. Only nuclear war's more of a bitch.

"Look," he said as they passed a block of leveled houses. An extensive brick wall bordered the sidewalk. And fused to the wall were what looked like carbonized crosses.

"I don't understand," Stack said as he stopped the van.

"Those were people against the wall."

"People?"

"Look closer."

"Yes, I see now."

"They were probably walking past that spot when the bomb went off and grabbed onto the wall for support and were carbonized. They weren't close enough to evaporate. The blast knocked down the houses, but struck the wall along the edge without toppling it."

Bathhurst saw the look on Stack's face and decided to get him away from there. "Let's drive, fella. We've got places to go and things to do."

As they started forward a host of rats raced from under twisted girders, trying to cross the road to the next block.

"Get em!" Bathhurst said with sudden passion. Stack, the adrenalin pumping in him as he reacted to the rush in Bathhurst's voice, with the horror and hate bubbling up out of his guts, hit the gas and the van flew forward as the air filled with the high, keening screams of frightened rats. The swift, deadly vehicle loomed down on them like some giant monster suddenly emerged from the bushes. Hard, madly spinning, screeching tires caught a handful of rats, squashing them flat into the road as rodent skulls were crushed instantly and a circular wave of blood, guts, and intestines shot outward from suddenly erupted body sacks, spraying across the asphalt. The surviving rats flew rather than ran through the air, fleeing for the safety of the rubble across the road as the van rushed on—rat fur, tails, bits and pieces of brain sticking to the tires and rotating around and around.

"Goddam muthafuckas," Bathhurst cursed as he shoved a cigar in his mouth and lit it with an old World War II Ronson lighter. "They're coming into the city. They smell the dead. Cooked meat. Food. Shit!"

"How come they weren't killed by the blast, heat, flying debris, and radiation?"

"They probably were, in great numbers. But there are so many of them and they're also better able to survive than highly advanced man is. And in instances like this rats and lice flood into the cities. The same happened in Japan after we dropped our nuclear bombs there."

"I can't wait. And thanks for the education," Stack said sarcastically. "You told me things I wouldn't have learned about otherwise."

"I'm always glad to help a guy find out what it's all about."

By then they had reached their destination. Another nameless mountain of rubble with men, military and civilian, pulling away debris and looking for survivors underneath.

As the two men left the van, Stack pointed to a rubble hill some 15 yards away where rats were nibbling on a burned hand sticking up from the debris.

Bathhurst picked up a baseball-sized chunk of concrete and tossed it at them. It landed and sent up a puff of ashes as the rats scattered.

"Run, you bastards. Lunch is over," he yelled. Then he turned to Stack. "Come. Let's help dig up those survivors—if there are any."

8

It was twilight. The fires which still burned across the blackened hide of the city were reflected in a dull red glow across the low hanging cloud cover. Stack drove the van into the rutted parking area next to the casualty center. Bathhurst was in the seat next to him, exhausted, disgusted, dissapointed. They had found people. But all of them were dead. A mother and two infants, one in each arm, had affected the men most, though their feelings were fairly numbed by then. Bathhurst ordered the bodies buried though he knew that was a futile action. They could not find all the bodies there were. Bodies which were already rotting and soon would fill the air above what had been Fresno with a stench that was maddening while flies and lice congregated and rats feasted.

"One good thing about rats," Bathhurst said in a tired voice, "they'll tell us where the bodies are if we want to find them. And they'll eat the corpses down to the bone. That ought to eventually take care of the stench of rotten meat. That and the prevailing winds."

Stack didn't answer this, but he did ask about food. "I'm hungry and I'm sure those who came with me are hungry too," he said as they stepped from the van.

"To be honest, I barely have enough food for the injured. I can't really feed the healthy. You and the others will have to forage. I'm in the military and I've hardly eaten anything. Sorry," Bathhurst said with a shrug. "But I'll get you the gas I promised."

Stack didn't argue. He just shook his head in agreement, disgust written across his face, weariness in his stance, and shock in his eyes—which burned with the bright fires of the fanatic who has found a new religion. Only he hadn't found anything to believe in anymore. Maybe later, but certainly not now.

Bathhurst was called away by some orderly as Rayisa came running. The Caudells also hurried over. Rayisa hugged Stack, then moved back to look at him. She was surprised by his appearance, but there was no time to ask questions.

Stuart Caudell stepped up and asked, "How is it out there?"

Stack looked at everyone and said, "It's bad. Maybe one in a hundred of those we try to save is still alive, and of those half die while we're digging them out or putting them in the van. But I hear things aren't too good out here either."

Stuart Caudell nodded in agreement and Rayisa began to cry. Stack put his arms around her, doing so automatically, like some robot programmed to act in a certain way when someone acted in a certain manner.

"Don't cry, girl, don't cry," he said in a weary voice.

"It's over, Nick," she sobbed. "No use fooling myself. My parents are gone. I was hoping against hope. But it's useless to go on like that."

"She's right," Sally Caudell added. "We've also been fooling ourselves. No use thinking our people were lucky where so many others lucked out. Entire families are gone. Why're we even in this godawful place? Let's go back to the mountains. It's safer there."

Rayisa stopped crying, looked up at Stack, and nodded agreement.

"If that's your decision, I'm all for it," he told them. "But not tonight. Let's wait until morning. Traveling will be safer by day. No telling what idiots are moving about out there without headlights, or traveling too fast, or are broken down on the highway. We might spot them too late to avoid a crash. Besides, I'm too tired. By morning we'll all feel better."

There was a chorus of agreement. Then Bart Caudell asked, "Did you see about food? I'm hungry. All of us are hungry."

Stack explained to them about the food situation, then added, "However, I'm not entirely without resources."

He looked at the sky. Still flying in the twilight were seagulls, which had moved inland from the ocean, probably disoriented because of the bombings. They rode the air currents over the city where the updrafts gave them power to soar, alighting where there was food, mostly dead fish. Seagulls, he recalled, were scavengers who loved city dumps and edible garbage.

He went to the van, took out his Savage 99F rifle with its five-round clip, then looked at Rayisa and the Caudells before lifting and aiming the rifle. He followed a soaring gull, and when he had held a bead on it long enough, Stack pulled the trigger.

The sound of the shot rang out like angry thunder. Half a hundred heads turned. Bathhurst ran out from inside the half destroyed shelter where the worst wounded were being kept. Stack did not look at them. He watched the gull as it began to turn in a corkscrew manner once the round caught it. The wings failed after a few weak flaps and then it fell from the sky like a lead weight. He watched it come down, looking for some rubble landmark to place it, then aimed for another bird and fired. His aim was good, steadied perhaps by the need for food. As the second gull fell, he turned to Brad Caudell, told him where to go, and headed for the first fallen bird.

He passed Bathhurst, coming toward him. "Just hunting, Major," Stack explained. "I'm sure the earth won't mind the loss of a few fat gulls around this time."

Bathhurst smiled. "I guess not."

"On second thought, I wonder if those birds contain a dangerous level of radiation."

"Not this soon after the blast. But in the end process it doesn't matter. Everything you eat will have some radiation in it as it works itself into the food chain. You'll just have to take your chances. Each animal won't have much. But the damn thing will accumulate. What happens ten years down the road I can't say."

"I'll take my chances," Stack said and headed off to find the downed gull.

By the time he got there a rat was gnawing at white and gray feathers speckled with blood. When it saw Stack, the rat stood on his hind legs, showing teeth, ready to fight for the food. Stack took the rifle by the barrel and swung the butt like a club. But it came down on empty ground as the rat fled.

When Stack got back Brad had already returned. Each held a chicken-sized bird by the neck. Bathhurst walked over and with a laugh asked, "How about shooting me one?"

"I'd love to. And I think your patients would enjoy some fresh meat. But you boys have guns and bullets. And my ammunition supply is limited."

"Okay, we'll do the job." Ten minutes later the area was filled with the sounds of shots as birds fell from the sky. There were more misses than hits and the gulls were soon gone to fly in a safer part of town.

But at least there was enough fresh meat to feed some of the less-serious casualties. However, too many people were deteriorating badly. Their skin was coming off. Great tufts of hair were falling from their heads, which now looked motheaten. Some were so weak they were barely able to walk and just lay there, staring glassy-eyed at the world. Stack and Brad gave their gulls to Mrs. Caudell. "I hope you're good at plucking and cleaning poultry," Stack said.

"Yes, though it's been some time since I've done it. I mostly bought clean poultry parts at the supermarket."

"Something tells me you're going to go back to the old way of doing things. I don't think too many supermarkets are still open."

"Where can I get a knife, some pots and pans, water, and cooking oil?"

"I've got what you need, except for water. When I was in the mountains, I cooked for myself. I'll see Major Bathhurst about our water needs. As for fuel, there's plenty of charred lumber lying about. The fact that it's charred will make it easier to start a fire."

Stack went looking for Bathhurst and found him directing some soldiers removing corpses for burial.

"Can I help you?" he asked when Stack came over.

"We need water for cooking and cleaning."

"Sorry, there's no tap or bottled water, but there is a pond a mile from here. I can tell you how to get there. The water will have to be boiled. Let it sit a while first so the sediment and other gook will settle out."

"I feel like I'm back in the mountains. No running water there either. But at least it was cleaner."

"Out here that pond's the best we can do. Frankly, I'm surprised we're coping this well. I thought it would be worse."

"Don't rejoice yet. The Russians may fire another set of missiles at us."

"To hit what? They've already wiped out almost everything."

"They might want to make sure they didn't miss anything."

"You're a cheery guy to have around."

"I try my best. Now can you give me the instructions on how to reach that pond and tell me where I can get some jerry cans to bring the water back in?"

Bathhurst gave him the instructions, and got him plenty of empty cans and the extra fuel he had promised. Stack made a quick round trip and was soon back with water for washing, cleaning, and cooking. Mrs. Caudell joked that she would now set about to make a dinner fit for a king. Stack also provided her with salt, pepper, and oregano. She didn't have a pot big enough for both birds, so she cooked them one at a time. The aroma of the cooking filled the air. After what Stack had been through, the food smelled good. The roaring fire, the hissing sparks passing into the night, the shimmering air in the cool darkness, the warmth of the flames, the orange light patterns playing across faces, the wisps of smoke passing into the sky all made this seem a cheerier place than it was. Under other conditions, in other places, in earlier, brighter times—now only 24 hours distant, but seeming a million years ago and a billion miles away—this would have been a night for affairs of the heart and soul, for holding hands, for sitting around the campfire, singing songs, and toasting marshmallows. But not now.

Yet there was something about a fire that gladdened the heart and drove away the darkness, enveloping all of them within a cocoon of light, brightness and promise. They sat around the flames, Stack with an arm around Rayisa, who leaned against him for emotional warmth as he smoked a cigarette and vacantly eyed the fire, wondering again about his family, all the while casting glances at the Caudells and Bart—who eyed Rayisa. Was romance blossoming? If so, it was one hell of a time for such things. Better to keep a distance between people, like in combat. If a soldier fell, the loss was his, not anyone else's. No need for emotional baggage. But could men really prevent themselves from loving? he wondered. In time he would find that out too.

There weren't enough pots to go around, so some of them ate first and the rest later. Nor were there enough metal plates and forks. Rayisa had a plate and fork. Mrs. Caudell ripped off a drumstick, then used the knife Stack had given her to cut off a breast, which she ate with her hands. Her son did the same. And while they were eating, the second gull was being cooked. Grease-smudged mouths were wiped clean on shirtsleeves, because there were no napkins, just like in the old days. It was crude, the surroundings were dismal, the future uncertain. And yet, in a way, it was fun.

As they ate, tongues were loosened, and Mr. Caudell

began talking about his younger days and his service in the navy, which was one reason his middle son had joined that service. Then he told about the lumberyard he had established when he was discharged from the navy. "It's probably all burned up, or splinters by now," he added with a bitter laugh.

"Where are you from originally?" Stack asked.

"Yakima, Washington. My wife's a Sacramento girl. That's where I live and have my lumberyard. It's north of here."

"I know where it is, Mr. Caudell."

"Mr. Caudell is too formal. Call me Stu. If we hadn't been vacationing in the mountains we wouldn't even have met. Now tell me about yourself. I've talked too much about me."

"I really don't know what to tell you. Not that many exciting things have happened in my life." He shrugged, thought for a second, then began. "I'm thirty-six, just an ordinary guy who's tried to make the most of what he has. Sometimes I've succeeded and other times I've failed. I started out as a junior high gym teacher in a slum school. I found it to be a hard place full of troubled kids. But I also discovered a lot of young people who tried their best and because of that made it out in spite of the obstacles. The problem for me was never the school or the kids, but the salary I was making. It was never enough, so I had to give up the job, though I cared about the kids. I was forced to open a private radio-dispatched cab service with my brother and father as partners. Dad's the dispatcher. He's widowed and this gives him something to do with his days. We had sixteen cabs and were planning on expanding to thirty before the war. In addition to the three of us, we had a variety of people working for the cab company: out-of-work actors, a medical student, a would-be writer, with myself and my brother also doing the driving as well as office work and vehicle repair to save on labor and garage bills."

"What about your family?" Caudell wanted to

know.

"I have a beautiful blond, blue-eyed wife, Marcie, whom I miss very much. I also have two sons, Adam and Grant, aged nine and six, and a thirteen-year-old daughter, Michelle. Her hair is dark like mine."

Mrs. Caudell looked at Stack, who was around five-eleven, with black hair, brown eyes, a square face, and a good athlete's build.

"When I came out here on business, mixed with a little pleasure, I didn't expect it to end this way."

"Life's full of surprises," Mr. Caudell said.

"Coming out of the forest primeval and watching mushroom clouds blossom across the hide of California is more than the usual surprise. It's an almost indescribable experience."

"You're not the only one who feels that way," Mrs. Caudell answered. Then she looked at the pot and said, "I think your gull's done." Stack took Rayisa's plate to receive his portion.

9

It was pitch black except for some campfires 50 yards away. Low talk came from inside the ruined shelter and from military men going in and out. Stack lifted his head, sleep rapidly fleeing from his numbed mind as he sat up on the blanket he had spread out on the ground. Rayisa and Mrs. Caudell were sleeping in the rear of the van. Brad had taken Stack's sleeping bag and his father was bunked out in the back seat of their car, his legs sticking out the open door. Stack had tried sleeping on the front seat, but found it more comfortable on the ground, in the open, a position he had gotten used to during his camping days.

Rubbing his eyes to clear them, Stack looked around. Brad wasn't in his sleeping bag. Perhaps he had gone to relieve himself among the ruins. But that wasn't the case. Stack suddenly saw Brad off to the side heaving out his guts. Stack rose, looked into the car, and saw Brad's father sleeping on his back, his chest moving slowly up and down, his mouth open.

Stack wondered what was wrong with Brad. Then, as Stack began to walk, he felt a bit woozy and his vision blurred. Stack assumed he hadn't yet fully recovered from his sleep. He shook his head. But that had been the wrong move. Small colored balls of light began flying in front of his eyes. He shook his head again. They did not go away. Maybe he needed a cigarette. Yeah, that would do the trick.

He took out a cigarette, put it between his lips, and lit a match. The flare of sudden light was too bright, making him wince and close his eyes for a few seconds. Strange, he had never been that sensitive to light. He lit the cigarette, then flicked away the match and took a deep puff. But as soon as the smoke touched his lungs Stack felt a wave of nausea. The smoke jetted from his nostrils and mouth almost as if his lungs were spasming it out. Nausea welled up from his stomach into his throat, which was trembling. He began to cough and threw the cigarette away. It fell to the ground, striking it with a shower of sparks, then smouldered there, sending up scrolls of bluish smoke which quickly dissipated in the night air.

Brad was coming back from where he had been vomiting out his guts. Holding his midsection, and in a shivering voice, he told Stack, "I'm sick. I've got nausea, chills, and the sweats. What's wrong? Was it the gull we ate?"

"Could be. I don't know," Stack gasped, not feeling too good himself.

"Look," Bart said, pointing as Rayisa came from the van. She was walking with a stagger.

"I'm sick," she said, fear on her face. She was clutching her middle, and it looked as if she was trying to hold back the vomit rolling about inside her.

"Don't try and keep the poison in. Go to the side and heave it up," he told her.

She followed his advice, but did not even make it to the side before she was barfing up her supper.

"We've been poisoned," Brad groaned. "Those gulls were diseased."

"How the hell was I supposed to know?" Stack asked defensively.

But then he wasn't able to ask anymore as he ran to the side and began bringing up foul-tasting, foul-smelling, acidic, bile-tinged vomit. It just shot from him. When he was finally done, he spit out the last of the vileness, wiped his mouth on his sleeve—wishing he had napkins—and returned to the others, exhausted by the ordeal.

Mrs. Caudell was up now and didn't look too well. The commotion had aroused her husband, who looked all right and asked what was going on.

Something was wrong here, Stack thought. If the gulls had been bad all of them should've been sick. Stack went looking for Bathhurst and found him sitting in a jeep, talking over a field radio with some unseen party.

When he was finished, Stack asked, "Don't you ever sleep?"

"I haven't slept in over twenty-four hours, and I don't think I'll get more than catnaps in the next few days. War's like that if you don't know. How can I be of help?"

"I'm sick, and the others are sick too." Stack quickly related all the details. "Those damn gulls we ate must've been bad."

"A lot of people ate gull tonight. I ate gull. I'm feeling okay."

"You didn't get the ones that were sick or full of radiation. We did."

Bathhurst shook his head. "No. What you and the others are experiencing is radiation sickness."

Sudden fear etched Stack's face. "Does that mean we'll die?"

"I doubt you picked up that much radiation. But this sickness could happen to you and them again and again. Depending on how much exposure you have each time. That's the bitch about this war. Whether you survive and in what condition depends on how much radiation you absorb. Nobody can avoid getting some. Who gets more and who gets less is a matter of luck."

"How come you're not sick? You've sucked up more radiation than us."

"No doubt I will get sick. My time hasn't come yet. Now why don't you get back to your people and see what you can do to help them and let me do my job.

Sorry to be so gruff, but I have work to do and this job has frayed my nerves."

"Sure, I understand." Stack turned and went back to the others. By then Stuart Caudell was heaving out his guts. Stack also became aware in the evening chill of the fever burning inside him. A fever for which there was no medicine. The others were also running fevers.

On Stack's advice they built a large bonfire and sat in front of it, wrapped in blankets, absorbing the heat, their teeth chattering, their bodies uncomfortable with aches and pains from head to foot, their insides one running sore from their stomachs to their throats. Then the diarrhea struck. They ran, one at a time, or in pairs, to different places among the ruins and relieved themselves, then came back to the fire before having to run again and again to seek relief. Rayisa vomited once more and Stuart Caudell had such a bad case of diarrhea that he had to relieve himself half a dozen times throughout the night. Not one of them got any sleep. And when they ran to find relief amid the shadows of the ruins they heard the high, keening sounds of rats in the background. Rats scurrying everywhere. Looking for new flesh to eat. Watching the people around their campfires as if they were future victims and they, the rats, with their red, beedy eyes and sharp white teeth in the darkness, were the alien natives waiting at the jungle perimeter to spring out and attack the intruders.

10

Hours earlier, in the mountains, before the sun went down, while the blue of the mountain sky mingled with the darkened haze of the coastal sky, Lyle Rokmer and his Santa Monica Bloodsuckers—a name he had picked himself and which was emblazoned across the backs of their leather jackets in lurid, angled red—raced down the same road Nick Stack and Rayisa had driven down hours before on their way to Deke Barnes' gas station.

They moved quickly, the sun glinting on their goggles and sun shades and on their Kawasakis, Hondas, and Harley-Davidsons, which moved in tight precision along the almost deserted highway, passing only a few vehicles, the road theirs alone. It was an exhilirating feeling for them—thick with the power which they now held and the hell they wanted to raise in a final Viking orgy as they blazed a path of decadent, flaming glory across the earth unlike any they had blazed before. And this time there would be no one to stop them, no higher authority to answer to. A fiendish joy burned in their hearts. Now every place was the jungle and they were the hunters. And out there was the prey. Anything they came across would be theirs. Every man, woman, and child would have to bow to their will or be destroyed. A surge of malevolent power unlike any they had known before surged through their veins, reinforced by the brute energy of their bikes and the hypnotic flow of the road in front of them. This was better than any fantasy, greater than any drug high.

Rokmer looked down at his fuel gauge. It stood at the halfway mark. All of them would need fuel and they'd get it at the next gas station they came to—and not for money either. Rokmer smiled an evil smile, his teeth glinting in the bright mountain light.

The long line of cycles, with Rokmer leading the procession, took a curve in the road, then another curve. Down a long stretch in the road, before the next curve, he spotted a gas station and lifted his left hand, three fingers in the air. His signal that they would be making a stop just ahead. All eyes were on him as riders began to slow down, the beating of the harsh wind against naked faces and fluttering beards gradually abating. And then they roared, one at a time and in pairs, onto the gas station grounds and congregated around the pumps.

Deke Barnes came out of the office as multiple pings signaled the arrival of many drivers. The bland look on Barnes's face died and a shiver of chills ran up his spine. These were bikers. And they almost always spelled trouble.

"Get the rifle, Orville, and stay behind the counter," he said. "I'll call you when I need you." The boy nodded and went to do as asked.

Rokmer pulled up in front of the office and stopped. "Good day to you, mister," he said, his smile too wide, his tone too friendly.

"Good day," Barnes replied, keeping his voice even, mimicking the falsity of the biker, who looked like Lucifer in human form. It wasn't just his sinister, garish getup. It was the eyes and the face, molded by a hundred back-alley confrontations.

"Passing through?" Barnes asked.

"Right, passing through." So far none of them had mentioned the war. Barnes decided to push this along. No use toying around. The longer it took, the worse things would get. He figured they'd rob him. Let them. They could have the $86.73 in the register. All he'd ask is that they wouldn't hurt him, or the boy. But especially not him.

"If you want to use the rest rooms, they're around back to your left." He nodded toward what was his right as he faced outward.

"Thanks, but we don't need rest rooms." Dozens of eyes were on them. A sea of bikes and bikers clustered around their leader and the pumps, bikes roaring as motors were gunned in nervous anticipation. Barnes wondered why he hadn't just locked up when the war began and gone home to take care of other things. Instead, something deep inside would not let him break routine. As if he wanted to finish the day to keep a vestige of a past that was now gone.

Barnes said nothing now, sensing the atmosphere of danger which suddenly existed. He'd just let the other man do the talking.

"We need gas," Rokmer said, then smiled back at Zoyas.

"Sure. How many gallons?" Barnes asked, a tiny shiver in his voice.

"We want our tanks filled. All our tanks." He waved a hand at the motorcycles all around them. "How much is gas?"

Barnes wanted to say five dollars a gallon, but hesitated. "Two dollars a gallon on account of the war. Deliveries won't be coming regular. You know how it is."

"Yeah," Rokmer answered, his smile wider as he leaned back a bit and crossed his hands over his chest. "But two dollars is a bit steep. Don't you think, mister?"

"We're in a war. Things always go up during wars. But I'll tell you what. Since you people are going to buy so much and you look like such a nice bunch of people, I'll give it to you for a dollar and a half a gallon."

"Still too much," Rokmer said, his smile wider. "We're having a serious cash shortage problem."

"How about a dollar a gallon?" Barnes said,

desperation in his voice. "That's below cost, I cain't go lower."

Rokmer smiled at Zoyas. All the bikers were looking at Barnes with wet-lipped smiles. But Rokmer had had enough fun. It was time to end this.

"I think a dollar a gallon's too much. I think we should get our gas free. Don't you think? Us bein' such nice people, like you said? And this bein' after a nuclear war, and people needin' to help one another?"

Barnes put both hands out in front of him. "Wait a second, boys. I'm just a poor guy. I need to make a living. A dollar a gallon is fair. Much too fair. Be reasonable."

"Fuck you, man!" Rokmer yelled, his face getting vicious, spittle flying onto his beard, the ruthless criminal inside him coming out. "I say it's free, cocksuckin', muthafucka bastard."

Barnes turned his head to signal Orville as he began to edge back into the office, ready to shut and lock the door. Let the bastards take the gas while he menaced them from within. They'd go and leave him and Orville be.

But it was then that he saw the hard biker with the leather jacket, long brown, blond-streaked hair, walrus mustache, and white samurai headband with a big red circle in the center. He had a knife and was almost on Orville.

Barnes opened his mouth to scream a warning that someone had sneaked in the back way when the biker, known to his buddies as Billy Bullshit, leaped forward and grabbed Orville. The youth gasped in shock as the biker cupped the boy's jaw with one hand, pulled back his head, and at the same time brought up the sharp, 17-inch, wickedly curved Gurkha combat knife he was holding and in one swift stroke slashed open Orville's throat and jugular veins. The boy dropped his rifle as a huge, reddish gash appeared and blood sprayed out across the counter and the floor, then ran down the front of his shirt. Orville's hands went to his throat as the biker let go of him. And then the boy sank down behind the counter, gurgling as he drowned in his own blood.

Billy Bullshit—which wasn't his real name, but a handle he had picked up over his years in the gang till they had almost forgotten his real name—looked up from the floor with a smile. Billy's name came from his sense of humor. But it was a humor which could turn vicious, as it had now, when his sadistic bent came to the fore.

He stalked out from behind the counter, his knife dripping with Orville's blood, his hands, outfit, and face spattered with red. Barnes turned to face him like an animal numbed by fear, caught in a trap, facing the hunter who will kill, then skin his prey. For a few seconds he forgot about those behind him. But then Rokmer was on him, pinning Barnes arms to his sides.

"What's this?" he asked in mock surprise, as if he hadn't seen Orville behind the counter. "You tryin' to kill us?" he asked, his voice feigning anger, as he dragged Barnes outside to the cheers of the other bikers and asked, "What should we do with this guy?"

"Hang 'im, shoot 'im, cut 'im up," a chorus of cheery voices cried.

"First, let's gas up," Rokmer said as he handed the gas-station owner over to Billy Bullshit, who kept his arms pinned.

Barnes watched them, his chest heaving up and down in fear, air being sucked down into adrenalin-powered lungs, his heart racing faster than it had in years, his mind jetting along at lightning speed as a host of images from the past replayed themselves—dangerous moments he had faced, then the minutes-old horror of Orville's death and the words Rokmer had just spoken to him. Barnes's heart beat so fast he thought it would come up out of his throat, or at the very least stop working as he had a heart attack and died. But it didn't happen.

The bikers quickly gassed up. Then Rokmer came

back to hold Barnes as Billy Bullshit gassed up last. Some of the bikers had jerry cans and filled them too.

This done, they gunned their motors and formed up around their leader, who was holding onto Barnes. "What're we goin' to do with the old man?" Debbie asked from the back of Zoyas's motorcycle.

Rokmer smiled his devilish smile and pushed Barnes forward. The bikers made way as he pushed the old man to the pumps. Then Rokmer asked one of the bikers for rope. The bikers threw him some twine, the kind used to tie things to the tops of cars and the rear of bikes. Rokmer worked quickly and soon had Barnes secured to one of the three pumps. The old man was frozen in mute fear. He watched as Rokmer grabbed the hose from the side of the pump Barnes was tied to.

Barnes suddenly realized what this biker had in mind and began to pull at the ropes, tugging them this way and that. But he was bound too tightly. Barnes, his face red with fear, the veins bulging blue across his temples, cried out, "No, no. Dear God, no. Let me go. I won't tell anyone. Let me go. In the name of Jesus Christ, let me go. I want to live. Please don't do this."

Rokmer didn't answer. Instead he grinned, then turned on the hose and began to spray Barnes, who twisted left and right, closing his eyes against the spray of gasoline, which ran all over him, into his hair, down his clothes, into every pore. The oily, slimy feel of it was over everything. He gasped, trying to catch his breath and not swallow any as the sharp, acrid smell of the gasoline filled his nostrils. When he tried to plead once more for mercy, despite the flood inundating him, some of the gasoline ran into his open mouth. He spit it out. It tasted horrible and burned his tongue.

Rokmer now sprayed the pump itself, then turned to the bikers. "Go," he yelled. In response, they roared away onto the highway, where they stopped and congregated as they watched Rokmer, who sprayed the ground around Barnes before dropping the hose and going to the other pumps. He took down and opened their hoses, which he also dropped to the concrete. All three hoses continued to pump fuel rhythmically onto the ground, flooding the area around the pumps as Barnes struggled, cried, whimpered, and pleaded hysterically, his voice shrieking to the very heavens.

Rokmer now grabbed his bike by the handlebars and pushed it away from the area. When he was 20 feet from the fuel pumps he mounted the motorcycle, started it, and slowly moved out till he was almost by the road. Then he stopped and looked back.

A number of large streams of gas were running outward to all points of the compass. One of them, like a trail of dirty water, was moving toward him. He sat there and watched it. When the finger of fuel had come close enough, he pulled out a book of matches, lit one, and put it to the other matches. They flared into life, twitching this way and that in the mild wind, then began to burn the cover of the matchbook. At that point he threw the matchbook at the finger of fuel.

It landed just behind the constantly advancing tip. And then, with a whoom and a whoosh, two foot-high orange, blue-tipped flames shot up from the concrete and traveled in a swift line back along the finger of fuel toward the pump island, and from it out along all the other streams of fuel which ran off in different directions. In seconds the island became a bonfire of six, eight, and ten-foot flames clawing at the sky. The fires caught Barnes in their harsh, pinching fingers. He shrieked a blood-curdling curse at the bikers, then cried, "God, God, Gaawwwwd, merceeeeeee," and passed out as the flames covered him from head to foot, eating into his flesh, burning off his hair, chewing at his eyes, licking at his shirt and pants.

Rokmer threw back his head and laughed as he raced down the road before the gas station exploded, the bikers cheering and laughing as they followed him, having, like invading Mongols, put to the torch what they could not take with them and no longer needed.

Barnes stopped breathing about that time as the

flames were sucked deeper into his lungs by his involuntary efforts to breathe, singing the lining of his bronchials, which closed up as they filled with fluid and blood. His chest stopped heaving. Then his skin burst in the powerful heat and fat began oozing up out of him, hissing and sizzling as it burned purplish-yellow. There were barely audible snaps and pops in the louder crackling of the burning fuel as water vapor escaped and Barnes shriveled, turning darker and darker.

The flames went deeper, into the underground lines, then down into the storage tanks below the pump island. And there, in the main fuel supply, it ignited with all the power pent up in the stored gasoline.

The force of the burning turned into an endless explosion, consuming all the fuel in a cataclysmic eruption which, pound for pound, was 18 times more powerful than dynamite. It ripped up from the underground cavern, tore away the cover of earth, concrete, stone, and steel, raged through the pump island, and turned Deke Barnes into a thousand chunks of flaming flesh as it wrenched the pumps from their mountings, sliced them into hundreds of jagged bits of shrapnel, and sent them flying in a circular pattern for 200 yards in every direction.

The bikers heard the blast and looked back as a vast, hundred-foot-wide globe of orange fire erupted into the sky, pregnant with shrapnel and rock and concrete and earth and rubble. The force of the blast smashed the windows of the gas-station house, then broke down the walls, crunching them into hundreds of fist-sized chunks, shredding the counter behind which the now-dead Orville lay, turning his body into chaff which rained down on the woods behind the station, while at the same time twisting and ripping out the lifts, sending tools flying, wrenching off the garage doors and turning them into kindling. The immense power of the explosion shredded Barnes's car, parked alongside the building. Picking it up, sheering off the roof, buckling the doors, sucking out the seats, reducing the fabric to blackened cinders, rupturing the gas tank and exploding it into instant flame, adding to the fire filling and surrounding the car, which was twisted, crumpled, broken in half, and then turned into a hundred smaller pieces. Finally, the blackened, barely recognizable bits rained down across the forest. The engine, the largest remaining solid chunk, spitting pistons, chunks of the radiator, nuts and bolts, almost squashed into a solid mass, plunked into the forest floor and sank two feet into the spongy earth.

The mushroom of fire became a pillar 300 feet high, which quickly turned into a black column of smoke and fell in upon itself. As the black pall was slowly dissipated by the wind, a hole 30 feet wide and 10 feet deep was revealed. The gas-station building had been sheered off almost at the base and was now scattered across ten acres of woodland. Rubble lay on the forest floor or hung from the branches of the trees. A broken toilet seat atop one pine was like an impromptu crown. The concrete apron around the crater had been cracked for 20 feet in all directions.

Small fires had been started in the forest, consuming pine needles and decaying matter first, then the bark of surrounding trees, and finally branches and trunks. The bikers did not see all this. They were laughing too much, enjoying the ride, having almost forgotten Barnes—who had by now disintegrated into ashes and no longer existed, almost as if he had been evaporated in his own small atomic blast.

Rokmer came to a fork in the road. One way was the town of Montieth, the other way the town of Vista Royale. He liked the second name better and, with malice and menace in his heart, led his bikers down that road. They roared after him, framed by trees and dappled by the shadow patterns of the branches as they raced the wind toward hell and destiny.

11

The streets of Vista Royale were almost deserted that late afternoon. For the most part people were home. The TV was dead, so they were trying to catch radio transmission. There were some, but voices were too faint and there was too much static. Whatever came through was garbled.

No children played outside. Swings and monkey bars and sliding ponds and tree houses were bare. On orders of the mayor and the town's single lawman, Wyatt Willem—W.W. to everybody—people were inside. They had been told the prevailing winds would drive radiation-laden dust inland from the coastal cities. By tomorrow the worst of it would be gone. But for now everyone was to remain inside as much as possible. All fruits picked from trees and vegetables harvested from the ground were to be washed to cleanse them from possible radioactive dust. Luckily, water was still running and electricity was being provided by the same grid supplying Montieth.

This logging town of 300 souls was stunned by what had happened. There were about 80 families in town and 90 buildings. There was a small Main Street with a small supermarket; an administration office where Mayor Wayne Strauch and his secretary, Miss Alma Holloway, worked; the sheriff's office; a small jail which occasionally held Eddie Garr, the town drunk; and Emo's Place, the only tavern in town, social hangout of the younger set on weekends and the older set on weekday evenings. On either side of the two blocks which held Main Street were four blocks, two and two, where the majority of the population lived.

No one was on Main Street when the Bloodsuckers roared into town. Some people looked out their second-story apartment windows in shock at the sight on the street below. There were two drinkers in Emo's Place and both ran to the front door to look out. The sheriff was out of town. He had gone to the lumber mill to inform the six men from town who were working the shift about conditions in Vista Royale and to urge them to call it a day and come home, though they were reluctant to break with routine and tried to carry on as if nothing had happened. They were relieved to hear that everything was all right in town. Phone service was down and they hadn't been able to call home. One of them had been detailed to drive back and see how things were. He had left before the sheriff arrived and now was on the road, 20 minutes from town.

Rokmer pulled to a halt in front of the supermarket. So did the others, parking their motorcycles against the curb or in the middle of the street. This was their town. Silently, without a word, they had placed their claim on it and were now ready to enforce their will.

"Are you hungry, people?" Rokmer asked his bikers.

"Yeah," came the answering roar. "Ain't there no McDonald's or Burger King in this burg?" another voice asked.

"We got a supermarket," Rokmer replied, jerking a finger toward it. And then he led the way inside. Only two people were there at the time. The owner, Mr. Pellolosi, a swarthy-skinned, black- and gray-haired man in his 50s, and his assistant, a high school girl by the name of Barbara Sidarsis. They turned from their unpacking as the bikers entered.

Pellolosi began by saying, "Can I help you?" But the words died on his lips.

"Hey, Dad," Rokmer said, "we're hungry. Got

anything good to eat? What's the house special?"

Pellolosi moved forward as if to stop them from coming any further into the store as the girl moved back, her blue eyes blinking back tears of fright.

Rokmer didn't feel playful now. As Pellolosi got in the way, Rokmer dropped his right shoulder, made his right hand into a fist, and drove it in and up, hard, putting all his weight behind it.

Pellolosi folded as his guts exploded in purple fire and his heart felt as if it would burst. He was speechless, gasping, unable to catch his breath. And then Rokmer acted again. A hard fist crashed into the side of Pellolosi's head, driving him in the opposite direction as his skull blazed with sudden yellow fire and great colored balls danced before his eyes. And then, as he tried to recover from these two blows, Rokmer pulled out a knife and plunged it into Pellolosi's back, pulled it out, and rammed it in again. Then he kicked the legs out from under the grocer, who fell onto the sawdust-covered wooden floor and spasmed as he bled to death.

Rokmer looked back at his bikers, their women, and the street beyond the windows. Then he looked at the shocked schoolgirl. He called back over his shoulder, "Who hasn't been laid this week?"

"Not me," one biker yelled out. "I haven't been laid either," another biker screamed. Then a few more, including Billy Bullshit, added their voices. Only a handful of the bikers had steady women. The rest got what they could on the run.

"Well, lads, what're you waiting for?" Rokmer said with a grin as he extended a hand in the girl's direction. She slowly retreated, shaking her head, unable to speak, shivering in fear, her legs beginning to buckle. But then she was caught by the advancing bikers.

"Take her in the back," Rokmer said. The laughing bikers dragged her there before Barbara Sidarsis could find her voice.

As they did so, Rokmer told the others, "What the hell are you waiting for? The shelves are full of food. Get what you want and let's party. This is a feast." Cheers filled the air as bikers rushed down aisles and began opening boxes of cereal, grabbing salamis and luncheon meats from the frozen-food section, ice cream, bread, wine coolers from various shelves, and hitting the freezer section for beers. The girls grabbed cakes and candy from a shelf near the rear of the store and hit the fresh-produce counter.

But while that was happening out front, in the back one girl was learning in a very swift and brutal fashion what it meant to know a man and become a woman. Something which was supposed to be happy and joyful, and usually following marriage or engagement, with someone she loved, would now be taught her by means of rape.

They shoved her deeper into the dark, dingy back, lit only by a single bulb high up on one wall, then rammed her against the wall opposite, laughing, some of them grabbing her substantial breasts, others trying to open the buttons on her sweater. Some of them pressed their faces against hers and kissed Barbara. The beer, whiskey, and tobacco on their breaths, the unwashed man smell of them disgusted her as brutal lips came down on her mouth. She tried to fight them off, but two held her arms pinned against the wall, straight out from her body.

"Come on, let's see what this bitch is made of," Billy Bullshit said as he pulled open her sweater, ripping the buttons, which clicked as they fell onto the bare wooden floor. Then he pulled the sweater open wide and her breasts, unrestrained by any bra, jiggled naked before their gaze.

"Oh, yeah," Billy said as obvious pleasure showed on his face. Then he and some of the others fondled her, working the spongy meat with their hard, greasy fingers, hurting her so that she gasped, making her chest heave and pushing her breasts forward.

Two of the bikers began suckling on the berries of her nipples, their rough, unshaven faces hurting the sensitive flesh. One of them bit her left nipple and forced an "Ooooh" from her lips as pain filled Barbara's face.

"I think she likes it," said the biker who had bitten her, while he held one nipple between his teeth and mumbled the words.

The dim light played across the white of her flesh and their shining, sweating faces, making her look sickly and them look like the demons they were.

Then, before she knew it, one of them began working the buttons and the zipper on her jeans. Next they were dragging down her jeans, exposing her panties as they tore at them.

"Stop, please stop, no," she gasped. But they wouldn't. Her jeans and panties were finally bunched up around her ankles. And then the bikers were grabbing at her crotch, tugging at her pubic thatch, digging fingers into her, pulling at her labia as tears streamed from her eyes.

"No. No more," she began screaming over and over in a hysterical voice. Finally this got to Billy Bullshit, who'd had more than enough. He pushed the others away and shoved his face into her hysterical, tear-stained face.

"You gonna shut up, cunt bitch? You gonna stop that babblin'?"

"Please leave me alone. Please! Show mercy. In God's name, show mercy."

"Ain't no God, bitch. I'm God." He slapped his chest, laughed, and looked at the others. Then he asked, "Are you gonna cooperate? Are you gonna be nice to us?"

"Please let me go. Don't torture me like this. I never did you any harm."

Billy Bullshit was getting mad. She wasn't being cooperative. A hard, fiendish light filled his eyes. An ugly sneer curved his mouth as his hands went to the wide, thick, brown cowhide-leather, brass-buckled belt he wore. He quickly took it off. Then he doubled it over, holding it by the buckle.

She gasped on seeing this. "I think you need some teaching, bitch," he said. "I'm going to learn you some manners so you never, ever again try and get uppity when someone asks you to be nice to him and his pals."

With that, he brought the strap forward in a slashing flight that hit her right breast and upper belly in a hard upper-to-lower cut. The girl shrieked as the belt fell away and left a two-inch-wide, foot-long red streak across her sensitive flesh. Some of the bikers in the room licked their lips and grabbed sudden bulges in their jeans.

Without warning Billy swung the strap again, bringing it down across her belly. Barbara folded in pain, then rose and put her arms out to catch the next stroke. But the pain was such, when it landed, that she pulled her hands back and the next swing of the belt caught open flesh. Frantically, the girl turned around, exposing her back and the jiggling globes of her behind. Billy liked this even more, bringing the belt down on the small of her back. The girl screamed and arched in response, her left hand going back to grab the spot where she had been wounded. But Billy then swung the belt across her hand and fingers, making Barbara pull them back in front of her. As she did so, he began to work a steady tattoo across her behind, leaving thick, red welts which quickly swelled into crooked bumps, on some of which the skin had been whipped off so that blood now showed through. Her buttocks wiggled as she danced against the wall, frozen by fear into that position, her mind now a frantic field of crisscrossing thoughts and fears, none of which she was fully aware of as tears welled in her eyes and rolled down her cheeks while sob after sob was torn from her heaving chest.

And then Billy stopped as suddenly as he had begun, looking at the welts across her behind, upper thighs, and lower back. So many of them that not a square inch of untouched skin could be seen. Barbara Sidarsis was in great pain. Her bottom and the area above and below it was now one mass of heated, aching flesh.

"Turn around," Billy growled. This time she did as he asked, his words ringing in her ears; the fear of him dancing in her belly, the vision of his flying belt imprinted before her eyes.

"Take off your sweater," he ordered. She did that and tossed it aside. The back room was now a womb of silence aside from the sounds of the revelers out front. Then she saw Billy pulling down his zipper and unlimbering his cock, swollen stiff with sadistic lust and anticipatory sensations.

"On your knees, cunt," he growled. She went to her knees, bare flesh touching rough wood, which made her wince some more.

He stepped over to her. "Blow me," he commanded. She looked up at him, the whites of her eyes showing all around. But Barbara knew the consequences of saying no. There was no escaping this fate. She opened her mouth and took in the vile, swollen, repulsive, threatening club, with all the lack of expertise of a virgin who had only read or heard of such things or seen them in porno videos in someone's house during a party.

But her fear, her need to please, the power of the moment as this biker mastered her made the event so very good for him. The sounds of sucking filled the room as others watched her lips flying over the superheated meat, her head bobbing back and forth over his crotch like some golden butterfly while her tresses shook with the effort. Billy was in heaven—his head back, his mouth open, his eyes closed as he gasped and hissed. And then, too soon for him, it was all over as he came and ejaculated inside her.

Inexperienced virgin that she was, Barbara had trouble handling the flow and gagged, then coughed a few times, but was afraid to stop, and kept up the pistoning of her mouth as she arched and the semen shot into her, then flowed out between her half-open lips and down her chin, dripping onto her jiggling breasts and the floor.

Billy slowly opened his eyes and looked down, then pulled himself from her mouth, going over to where her sweater lay and using it to wipe himself off with. Barbara meanwhile spit out what was in her mouth and continued to cough and choke. But then the next biker stepped up to her and showed her his swollen instrument. Her mouth came open and soon the room was once more filled with the sounds of her submission.

She was a bit more expert this time. Not choking as much when the second biker came. He also used her sweater to wipe himself off when he was done. And then number three used her.

Billy watched this and said, "Go, boy, go. Give the bitch the juice. She just loves it. Look how she's suckin' that lob a' yours. Do it to her, man. Give her that cream."

The biker looked at him and between clenched teeth said, "But she chokes on it when someone comes and then it dribbles out over her chin before she spits it out."

"No problem," Billy said. "Swallow it when he comes, bitch." She stopped for a second, looked at him sideways out of one eye, and nodded without taking the biker out of her mouth as she continued her silent lip service. And then, when he came, she swallowed, but still gagged and choked and spit out.

"Swallow it, girl. No cheating. Swallow," Billy threatened, his hands going down to his belt, which he had put back on. So she swallowed it all when the fourth biker came. But that was all she could stomach. Her very innards revolted as she heaved up and began to vomit on the floor all around her.

"What's this fuckin' shit?" Billy asked.

"Screw this," the next biker to be blown exclaimed. "This broad pukes all over the place. Gross. I just lost my appetite for that blow job she's supposed to give me."

He walked back into the front of the store, but the others stayed and watched her. When she was finished, the girl spit out what was in her mouth and looked at Billy.

"Please, no more."

"Okay, since you did such a nice job for us, I'll give you a rest for now. But you've got to finish the other guys, later. It wouldn't be fair to them if they didn't get blown, would it?" he said with a greasy smile. She did not answer that. Nor did she answer when he rubbed his crotch and said, "I think I'll need a little more mouth work later on. You're good, baby. And I just know you'll get better with practice. Me an' the boys will make sure you get plenty of practice. Now put your sweater on," he said, pointing to the garment they had used as a rag. "You're coming with us."

12

People began contacting each other as news of the bikers spread. Then some began to converge in front of the supermarket, where all the invaders were feasting. Where was Sheriff Willem, they wondered, now that they needed him? None of the dozen people who were around the supermarket dared go inside. Most just peeked in and walked away, afraid even to be seen by the invaders because bikers spelled trouble. It wasn't till the third or fourth peek for some of them that they saw Pellolosi on the floor, blood all around him. They realized some of the gravity of the situation without knowing that it went beyond their worst dreams. At that point they began to scatter. It was then that the man from the lumber mill arrived to see how his family and the families of his friends were doing. He saw the bikes blocking Main Street and asked one of those now fleeing what was going on.

"We've been invaded by bikers. They're feasting in Pellolosi's Supermarket. I think they hurt Jim badly. He's on the floor in a pool of blood and not moving." With that, the frightened senior citizen scooted up the stairs to the second-floor apartment where he hoped to find safety behind lock and key.

But Vance Doorne decided to do something. First, though, he would go see if his family were all right. Then he would send his two 11-year-old daughters running to tell the families of his co-workers that they were okay. After that, because there was no time to go get the sheriff, he would organize a posse to get rid of these bandits who had invaded this fine town.

Doorne's red-headed, freckled face blazed with anger as he drove through a dirt lot to the next street, went halfway down the block, righted onto a sidestreet, and drove up his driveway. As he got out of the car, Doorne's wife came running from the house. She had been waiting for him, watching out the window. They embraced as she broke into tears.

"Oh, Vance, look what's happened to this world."

"It's not over. How're the girls?"

"Fine, Vance. They're inside. Sheriff Willem told everyone to stay indoors because of the radiation from the coast."

"I want to talk with Sarah and Janie." They went inside, where he hugged the girls and told them everything would be all right. Then he gave them their mission and told them whom to contact. After they left he told his wife about the bikers.

"Take my car and go get the sheriff. I'll get my shotgun and form up a posse. If we don't confront them they'll come for us. Those kind don't retreat unless they're stopped. Now go do what I've asked." Without another word he headed for the den.

He heard the car pulling out of the driveway by the time he had filled up with shotgun shells and had his gun in hand. As he left the house, Doorne looked up at the trees. It was so peaceful, like a late Sunday afternoon when everyone was preparing for supper. But this was an illusion.

Two houses down he rang a bell. The door came open. He told the man who stood there what the problem was and that he was needed. Then his neighbor's wife appeared at the door and wouldn't let her husband go. Doorne saw the fear in the man's eyes and didn't even bother to argue, but went to the next house on the block. He shook his head, never having figured that neighbor for a coward.

The next man he contacted, square-jawed, bull-necked, barrel-chested John Kritzler, in his late 40s, was a plumber by profession. And he was more than willing to join the posse. He got his .22-caliber squirrel gun and all the bullets he had in the house, and together with Doorne made the rounds, gathering more volunteers. They soon had Vic Lunenberg at their side. Lunenberg, a blond-haired, skinny man with bulging blue eyes, was Doorne's best friend, and there had never been any doubt about his joining them. The next one to join up was Ed Kudner, a fiftyish, horse-faced insurance salesman with a balding head of graying mousey-brown hair. Besides these men, Doorne was able to get four more with which to confront the bikers.

Ann Doorne drove onto the highway, heading away from town. But some of the bikers, coming from the supermarket, saw her and figured she was going for help. They jumped onto their bikes and gave chase, buzzing her car as they racing alongside and ahead, hitting the hood with their hands. She panicked and almost lost control of the wheel a few times as the car began to skid off the road. But at the last moment she managed to pull back from the edge.

They called out to her to stop. But she wouldn't. One of the bikers signaled the others to fall back. They did, letting him pull even with her. And then he took out the pistol in his belt, pointed it at her, and smiled before he pulled the trigger.

Ann Doorne, her mouth open in shock, unable even to scream, saw the gun, with a barrel that looked like a cannon to her frightened eyes. And then her assassin pulled the trigger two times. Twin lashes of flame jumped from the long, black barrel. The sounds of thunder were torn away by the wind flying past the racing motorcycle. And in even less time than that, the two bullets, fired so close they couldn't miss, opened two holes in Ann Doorne's head. One over the left eye. One through her right cheek. She fell forward over the wheel and the car instantly went off the road at 75 miles an hour, plowed into a grove of pines, and was stopped dead as its front telescoped and the engine block caved in while the hood shot up and a lone pine shattered at the base, sending out fresh white splinters. The front tires were twisted like black rubberbands. The front windshield shattered. Anne Doorne, who hadn't been wearing a seatbelt, was thrown from the car by the force of the crash and smashed into the trees just ahead, falling like a twisted rag doll into dead pine needles. It didn't matter. She had been dead even before the car hit the trees.

Within seconds leaking gasoline touched hot metal and ignited. The car burst into flame, pouring white and black smoke through the pines while flames consumed the insides and started eating the trunks of the surrounding trees.

The bikers did not watch all this. They were heading back to town. So was Sheriff Willem. Ann Doorne didn't have to go fetch him after all.

Vance Doorne led his small band toward Main Street. They approached along a side street on the right flank of town. Doorne held up a hand and the others halted while he went ahead to look around the corner. What he saw would have wilted the bravery of most men. Dozens of tough, garish-looking, dangerous bikers were coming from Pellolosi's Supermarket, bringing Barbara Sidarsis with them. Since her sweater had no buttons and couldn't close, Billy gave her an old army jacket he had and a safety helmet for her head as he put her on his bike. Other bikers were also getting on their motorcycles or milling around smoking and talking. They had looted the supermarket of all its cigarettes. Many of them had whole cartons.

Doorne moved back from the corner and signaled his men to advance. They were armed with a variety of weapons. Shotguns, pistols, .22-caliber rifles. Not a great armory. But they weren't lawmen or soldiers, just people with recreational needs, among the few in town who had weapons.

"We'll walk out onto Main Street and block it, then call out to these hooligans to get the hell out of town or pay the consequences. Agreed?"

"Don't you think that's a bit bold, Vance?" one of the men asked.

"What do you want me to do? Mail them a Hallmark card asking them very politely to vacate the premises? We've got to throw the fear of God into them to get these bastards out of town and make sure they won't come back. Are you people with me?" He looked each of them in the eye.

Ed Kudner was the first to say yes. The others quickly fell in line. That decided, Doorne led them onto Main Street. Some of the bikers spotted the eight armed men coming into the middle of the street about 30 feet from where the motorcycles were parked.

Zoyas called out to Rokmer and pointed. About half the bikers had guns. Snub-nosed .38s, Colt .45s, Magnum .357s, .25-caliber Berettas, .22- and .38-caliber Saturday Night Specials, and sawed-off shotguns. The rest had knuckle-dusters, knives, machetes, stillettos, and shivs—including the women.

Rokmer moved forward, wending his way through a mass of leather-clad bodies and haphazardly parked bikes. The eight men stood across the width of Main Street like Wyatt Earp and his deputies. No one had said anything yet.

Farther up the street the mayor and his secretary came running. The mayor had been away from town seeing about the electric supply at the power plant. When he came back one of the patrons from "Emo's Place" had confronted him with the news of what had happened. Now he and Alma Holloway hurried into his office and peeked out, keeping the door open a crack.

Doorne started the confrontation as Rokmer stepped

out in front of his bikers. "We're all here to tell you characters that this is a good, peace-loving town. We're not looking for any trouble and want you out of town fast. There isn't room for you and us here. You've already done damage," he said, nodding toward the supermarket without knowing the full extent of what had happened there.

"Go, and we'll forget what you did. But go quick. Reinforcements are on the way. Our sheriff has gone to surrounding communities for help."

Rokmer thought that over, looked at Zoyas, and called him over. In a low voice, he said, "The guy's probably bluffing, but we can't be sure. Even if the sheriff gets other lawmen to come back with him, most of these places are one or two cop towns. I doubt he's got an army. Look at what this town's been able to cough up. Eight lousy people to fight us. I think the smart thing is to make them believe we're retreating. We get the hell out of town, then come back later and screw the hell out of these bastards. If we pull back and wait, they'll disperse. Then we can take them on one or two at a time, instead of in one group." He hesitated a second. "We can take them now. But why suffer losses we don't have to?"

"Good idea, Lyle."

"I always have good ideas," Rokmer added with a wink.

Rokmer next looked at his gang, winked at them, then turned around and called out, "Okay, we're leaving. We were just hungry and needed a place to eat."

"The next time you're hungry, buy your food. Or haven't you heard of money?"

"Sorry, we didn't have any," Rokmer said, holding his hands out from his body for a second, then dropping them.

"Well, just get the hell out of town and take your gang with you."

"Sure thing, boss," Rokmer answered with a wide,

toothy smile, then went to his bike. The others followed his lead, though they did not understand all that was happening. But they figured their wily leader had an ace or two up his sleeve.

Doorne smiled. This was easier than he thought it would be. Just confront your enemies with force and they fold like wet cardboard. He smiled left and right to the men with him. Doorne was the hero who had saved the town. But there was no time yet to savor the victory.

He watched as the gang started their motorcycles and in great blue-white clouds of pungent smoke roared out of Vista Royale the way they had come. Barbara Sidarsis, dressed as she was and hidden in the mass of humanity, was barely recognizable. Nor did she dare call out for help as Billy, who sat behind her, kept a knife to her belly. In that fashion, she and Billy roared after the other bikers, and still more motorcycles followed them.

Doorne now led his men toward the supermarket. As they walked, people began to emerge. The mayor and his secretary left their office and hurried up Main Street. By now the news that the bikers were gone traveled through Vista Royale like wildfire. Neighbors informed one another by calling out windows as in the old days before phone service.

Only when they entered the supermarket did Doorne and the others discover what had been done. Someone ran to tell Pellolosi's wife and to get women to stay with and comfort the new widow.

Doorne wavered between trying to keep the crowd back, telling them not to touch evidence Sheriff Willem would need, and going after the bikers. In the midst of all this he asked someone to get a sheet to cover the body. It was somehow obscene to leave him exposed for everyone to gawk at. It destroyed what was left of his dignity, Doorne felt. Even a dead man deserved a certain amount of respect.

Out on the road, the gang raced against the wind, Rokmer at their head. He wanted to ride till he found a grassy field where they could assemble, talk this out, then make their plan of attack. Vista Royale was a nice town, just right for them to take over. And no dumb hick posse was going to take from Rokmer what by right of might was his.

In the near distance he spotted smoke, which diverted his attention and thoughts. This was probably from the car some of his boys had forced off the road.

As they drew closer, Rokmer saw the flames had almost burned themselves out and there was a wide, blackened swath around the wreck. He also spotted a parked sheriff's car near it and a man in uniform poking about the wreck. Why, this had to be the sheriff of Vista Royale. Gone for help, but come back without it. Actually, he hadn't gone for help. But that was Doorne's story, which Rokmer believed.

Rokmer smiled as he roared off the highway and rode his Kawasaki almost to the wreck, then stopped. His bikers followed suit and soon were parked in a rough half-circle around Wyatt Willem, who, unlike his brother, was a lean, hard-eyed, mustachioed man.

The shock of so many bikers around him wilted, but did not destroy, his courage. His hand went to the butt of his pistol, but he did not draw it. Rokmer got off his bike and came forward to confront Willem.

"What's happenin', Chief?" Rokmer asked with a much-too-friendly smile.

Willem did not warm up. His face remained grim. "Do you people know anything about this?" He extended a hand toward the wreck and then the body beyond it. "That's Ann Doorne. She lives in the town I'm sheriff of and there are two bullet holes in her head."

"Why ask me about this Ann person, Chief? I'm just a biker. I don't even know her." The other bikers had now gotten off their bikes and come closer. Billy Bullshit held onto Barbara and kept the knife at her belly so she wouldn't cry out for help.

HELL RIDE

"Then why did you stop here?" Willem asked, still grim-faced.

"Curiousity. Wouldn't you stop?"

"Stopping at disasters is my job, not yours."

"Well, I'm curious. All of us are." He pointed to the others.

Still grim, Willem asked, "Where were you people within the hour?"

"In Vista Royale. It's a nice town, sheriff."

Willem lost some color. "What were you doing there?"

"Stopping to have a bite. The food's good." Some of the bikers laughed.

"If I find you've made trouble," Willem said, lifting a finger. But Rokmer interrupted.

"You'll do what? We're law-abiding citizens. You have no reason to go accusing us. We even stopped to ask if you needed help."

"I don't need the help of the likes of you. When something happens it's normal police procedure to question every suspicious person in the area. And you people don't exactly look like the local chapter of the Elks. And while we're on the subject, there's been an explosion at a gas station some twenty miles down the road and there's a fire in the woods nearby which is still raging. Would you people know anything about it?"

Rokmer didn't answer this, but started a tirade of his own while he built to an inner rage which had nothing to do with the accusations, but which was connected to the ends for which he had the means.

"Why is it, Chief, that every time people see bikers they think we're all bad? Aren't there any good bikers?"

Willem smirked. "Are you telling me that you're all churchgoers and that you used to attend Sunday school?"

"Hey," Rokmer said, getting mad, bending forward from the waist, "I believe in God."

"So did Al Capone."

"You can't talk to me that way, fella."

"Watch my lips," Willem said, pointing to his mouth. "I want you to come with me into Vista Royale so I can question you and your people."

Rokmer looked at him in surprise. This guy had balls. That he respected. But he had nothing to back it up with. A single man against 50. He was just bluffing, probably slowly cracking inside. Trying to stare the bikers down. Other lawmen had tried that stuff, and it sometimes worked. But not this time. There was no real law anymore to back Willem up if he got hurt.

"He wants us to come with him. You hear that, people?" Rokmer said with a laugh as he looked back at them. Then he turned to Willem. "You gonna make me?"

Willem hesitated only a second, playing his lawman role to the hilt. "Yeah, I'm going to make you come with me."

"You got balls," Rokmer said in all honesty. "Balls, but no brains." And then he heaved back and punched the sheriff in the face before Willem could react and dodge the blow.

He staggered back till he thumped into his car. Then he tried to stand up and hit Rokmer back. But a second fist, then a third, smashed into him. And then all the bikers rushed forward. Hands were on Willem.

"Let go of me," he yelled. "Let go, I say."

But the hands were lifting him now. Then they began to throw him like a beach ball. From one group of hands to another. This became a game, and the wild, gay voices of ball players filled the air.

Willem was getting redder in the face with each passing second. "You'll all be under arrest for this," he managed to gasp. But talking was now strictly an act of struggle. He was being thrown faster and harder and farther as the play got wilder. The whole world spun around him. His head filled with blood and thumped with the rapid action of his heart muscle.

"Enough," Rokmer shouted, already tired of this

sport. "Drop 'im." And they did. Willem hit the ground with a thump which knocked the air out of him, bruised his back, pulled some muscles, and left him so stunned he was speechless.

But he didn't get the opportunity to recover his senses. The bikers roughly pulled him to his feet while the world still danced before his eyes and he tried to focus on the grinning, mocking faces before him.

With a cold sneer, Rokmer then said, "Snuff 'im." About 20 knives from in front and back appeared at his command. Willem was just barely aware of what was going on when the first two knives went in. One in the back and one in the chest. He shuddered as the cold steel stabbed deep, his eyes suddenly focusing. But only for a few seconds. A third, fourth, then half a dozen blades, followed by still more, stabbed him. Front, back, upper chest, abdomen, lungs, neck, and arms. He began spilling blood like a rusty radiator leaking water, the scene before his eyes turning a furious red before his mouth opened and darkness engulfed him. His legs wobbled and Willem fell. It was over. The knifers pulled their blades out, then used his uniform to wipe them off.

"Drive the car into the woods so it can't be seen from the road," Rokmer told one biker. "But check it for any items of value first. Oh, yeah," he said as an afterthought, "put the sheriff and that dead woman in the back seat. We don't want them lying out here where someone can find them."

"Maybe we should just put them in the woods and take the cruiser," the biker suggested.

"Fool. That would make us noticeable. Besides, we got wheels. We don't need no fuckin' police car. Where were you when God was givin' out brains? In the toilet?" The others laughed as the chastened biker went to load the two bodies into the back seat of the cruiser. Some of the gang members helped him. First, though, they stripped off the dead lawman's gun, holster, and bullet belt. They brought this to Rokmer.

"Who wants a gun and bullets?" he asked. Two dozen hands went up. He gave it to the biker known as The Black Donut, a thick-boned, swarthy con who had turned his nickname into a symbol emblazoned on the back of his leather jacket: a black donut on a white background. Once he had the gun he used paper to wipe off those places were blood was on the gun, holster, bullets, and belt. The ground where Willem had lain was wet with several square feet of dark, sticky red blood.

Rokmer called Zoyas over. "I want you to scout out all the approaches to Vista Royale. Take back roads and trails through the woods. Then come back and tell me where they are and where they lead, the condition they're in, and so on. We're going back to take that town from every angle. Anyone who opposes us we kill."

"Right," Zoyas said, then told Debbie she'd have to wait till he got back. She gave him a good-luck kiss as he got on the motorcycle and roared off down the road.

The biker who was supposed to drive Willem into the woods came over to Rokmer. "Lookee what I found in the trunk." He held up a shotgun and a tear-gas rifle with shells for one and canisters for the other.

"Gimme that tear-gas gun and those canisters," Rokmer said.

He examined them closely as someone else took the shotgun and shells. Then he held up the weapon. "Look, people, I got myself a tear-gas gun, just like a real lawman." He struck a pose with the butt of the gun on one hip, which he arched, while resting his other foot on a boulder. Then he told the bikers, "Rest up, people. Soon we're goin' to be doin' some serious ass-bustin'."

13

Emo's Place was filled. Men and women sat or stood along the bar or around tables. Faces were grim. When Vance Doorne's wife didn't come back, Doorne went looking for her and took along his friend Vic Lunenberg. They found her burned car along the road, but not her body. When Sheriff Willem didn't return, foul play was suspected. No one had to ask who had killed Doorne's wife, or waylaid the sheriff. They all knew. Now they were meeting to discuss what they would do if the bikers returned. Doorne wasn't at the meeting. He was at home, devastated. But Lunenberg was there to talk for him and make sure no one caved in to weakness. The horror of what had happened to them made the greater horror of what had happened to the world fade for a time.

"Perhaps that means they've gone away," one woman suggested.

"Don't bet on it," a man near her answered. "Those kind always return. They pick on easy meat. We're a target of opportunity."

"But we chased them out of town," Ed Kudner said.

"For how long?" Alma Holloway wanted to know.

"She's right," Mayor Strauch said. He had to take the lead. Others had done that so far and it wasn't good for him. Tragedy or not, he had to keep his job. It was the reason for his existence.

"We should get help," Kudner's wife, May, said.

"We can't beat them alone because we don't have the numbers or the weapons."

"Good idea," Kudner seconded her.

"Suppose they're waiting for us on the roads like they waited for Vance's wife," Mayor Strauch said. That caused a low murmuring in the tavern.

"We've still got to try," she said. "We can't just let them butcher us."

"All right," Strauch agreed. "But it's getting dark. It'll be dangerous on the roads. Who knows what kind of ambush they're preparing."

"We haven't any choice," Kudner's wife protested. "The phones are down so someone has to inform others about what's happening and get help."

"It can't be just one person," Mayor Strauch said. He was a man with combed-back, balding black hair speckled with gray, a big belly, a wrinkled face, and an out-thrusting chin which always seemed to be pointing at people as if he wanted to call something to their attention.

"If we sent one person, he might not get through. We've got to send several, each to a different town. One or more will make it. I'm not going to call for volunteers since this is too dangerous. Instead, I'm going to ask everyone here to put their names on a slip of paper. They'll go into a hat or jar. Three slips will be picked and those people will go."

People shouted their agreement as Strauch turned to the tavern owner. "Get some sheets of plain paper. Tear it into one-inch-wide, three-inch-long strips. It doesn't have to be exact. Those who have pens will lend them to others." He took out two of his own pens and passed them around. Alma Holloway loaned out her pen. She was a gentle, sensitive, delicate-skinned older woman who had never married. She always wore her iron-gray hair pinned up and used too much red lipstick.

As the slips were being prepared, one man rose and asked Strauch, "Do you think anyone will come and help us? They're got their own problems. Why should they help us, especially when death could be involved?"

Strauch heard comments of agreement passing through the crowd and worried looks on doubt-filled faces. This was defeatism and had to be fought down before it took hold.

He held up his hands. "Listen to me, all of you. It isn't true we can't get anyone to help us. People always help other people. Sure, there are selfish individuals and cowards and those who lose heart. But that's always been true. Despite it, there are people who have fought and not surrendered to adversity. And it's people like those who'll help us. After all, we can't just give up. We have families, young ones to think about, a town that will need all our efforts to survive in the terrible times to come."

"That's beautiful, Mr. Mayor," Alma Holloway said as she stood up, applauding hard, hoping her mood would infect the others. Many did applaud, including Vic Lunenberg, who called out his support. But there was still a lone voice of doubt.

The man who had objected before continued his attack, his bristling straw-yellow hair and reddish sun-wrinkled face expressing doubt. "The same attack made on our town might be made on other towns. And because these people will think it might happen to them, they will be reluctant to send us help and weaken themselves."

"All the more reason for them to send help and for us to ask for it," Strauch replied, feeling more confident now. This was turing into a political debate and he was a politician. "If they're in danger, we should tell them that. And if they send help we're all stronger in fighting off terror. With help we can defeat these bikers and they won't be able to go on and attack other towns."

"Right on, Mayor Strauch," Alma yelled. Others concurred.

"To quote Benjamin Franklin," he added, "when the patriots were facing attack from the British he told them, 'Gentlemen, if we do not hang together, we shall all hang separately.'"

That won the day. There were cheers, whistles, foot-stomping. The people of Vista Royale were ready to go to war and only needed the tough, vigorous leadership to do it. By then the strips of paper were ready and being handed out. Mayor Strauch put out his hand for a slip. The woman who held them looked surprised.

"I said everyone in the room gets a slip," Strauch said with a serene smile.

When she handed it to him, he grinned at Miss Alma and signed his name. Soon everyone was ready. The tavern owner brought out a vase which was filled with slips. Then he held a length of cardboard over the top, shook the vase to mix everything, and asked for a volunteer to pull out three slips.

Ed Kudner's wife volunteered, closed her eyes, turned her head, and chose the slips one at a time, with Strauch taking them from her. He looked at each slip as he took it, but said nothing. When he had three slips, he told everyone to sit down.

Then, without flourish or ceremony, in a flat, even voice, he called out the three names. "Ed Kudner." His wife almost fainted. "Alan Pinochar." The red-faced man with the hay-colored hair, who had questioned the Mayor's plans, smiled wryly. "Wallis Kreitar." A tall, thin, brown-haired man in his late 40s, with deep creases down the sides of his long, lean face, stood up, nodded to a few people here and there, then sat down with a frown.

"Now that we have our messengers we have to plan how they will leave here, which paths they will take, and where they will go. We also have to prepare a defense in case these animals come back. They took the life of two people that we know about, kidnapped Barbara Sidarsis—whose mother is home in shock, and probably waylaid the sheriff—who is still missing. I've mentioned these things to show you what can happen if we don't stick together."

The debate now got down to specifics about which of them had weapons, how much ammunition there was, and who would stand watch. The weapons situation was not very promising. Too few people had too few guns, and there was certainly not enough ammunition for a war, which was what they were being called on to fight. The sheriff had had the largest arsenal of all, and he had carried it with him. But no one knew where the sheriff was.

Night fell across Vista Royale as the debate continued in Emo's Place, now a beacon of yellow in the greater darkness of the forested night.

Across the forested miles, in the valley of the abandoned airstrip, in a clear place along the runway, a great bonfire had been built against the darkness and the cold. Around the fire sat the crew of the B-52, Lance Briggs eating some of the rations he had brought along for the trip to Siberia. The others had food too, but not for more than one day. They would have to either rely on hunting and berry-gathering or find a civilized place where they could get food. After a group discussion, they had decided that, come morning, one of them would be sent out to find a civilized place while the others stood perimeter watch around the bomber with their sidearms. Meanwhile, they sat around the fire discussing their pasts, what was probably going on right then in America and Russia, and the possible conditions of their families. Once the fire was out, they would return to the plane and sleep inside till morning.

Hours earlier the bikers had waited for Zoyas to return from his reconnaisance mission. When he did get back, he reported everything he had seen and learned. Rokmer then led his gang away, looking for an opening into the woods. He found an old logging road and took it deep into the forest, where there were many connected fields and clearings. There, they camped for the night, parking their bikes, sitting on the grass or the stumps of once-logged trees. Night was coming and Rokmer assigned certain of his people to gather kindling wood, which they made into several bonfires. That far into the woods they were not worried about being seen.

As night fell and owls hooted and pairs of shining eyes watched, Rokmer and Zoyas stood off to one side. Zoyas watched the flames from the fires play across the satanic face of the man who was his friend and leader. He wondered about Rokmer, who had no steady woman, but whored about with this or that pickup, staying mostly by himself. A loner in the crowd. A man who kept his own company most of the time and ruled with an iron hand.

Zoyas took out a pack of Pall Malls and Rokmer asked for a cigarette. Zoyas gave it to him, then lit his own butt and Rokmer's. For a second they looked at the other bikers, frolicking, lighting up smokes, some of them puffing pot, others eating and enjoying the forest. It was almost like a large summer camp. But these two knew death was around the corner for some of the bikers and more of the townsmen.

"Ready to kick ass?" Rokmer asked with a faint smile.

"I'm always ready, Lyle. How long've you known me?"

"Long enough. Maybe too long. Don't you ever get tired of this?"

"Tired, Chief?" Zoyas thought a second. "Not yet. Why? You tired?"

"Not really. But sometimes I wonder how long I can keep going this way."

"When I hit fifty, I'll retire," Zoyas said. "Maybe I'll have enough to buy a house, and maybe I'll marry Debbie."

Rokmer threw back his head and laughed, then took a deep puff of his Pall Mall, still chuckling. Zoyas looked at him questioningly, wondering what was so funny.

"The nuclear war that broke out today might change your plans some. Mine too. Everyone's plans, in fact. All of us might be dead six months from now. Even sooner. That ever occur to you?"

"I don't think that way, Lyle. I always let tomorrow take care of itself. If I take care of today, I'll be around tomorrow."

Rokmer took another puff as smoke jetted from his nose and mouth. "Everybody's got his own view of life. Yours suits you. Mine suits me. In the end we wind up dead or alive no matter what we think."

"It don't matter. That's what you're sayin'?"

"Yeah. You slap life. It slaps back. If your slap is bigger and harder, you win."

"Tonight we'll see how big our slap is," Zoyas answered with a grin. "Do you think those hicks expect us back?"

"They'd be dumb if they didn't." The two stopped talking as the screams of Barbara Sidarsis vibrated through the woods. Some of the bikers were pulling her into the trees across the clearing. They wanted sex and she was going to provide it.

"That's the bitch Billy Bullshit took along out of the supermarket," Zoyas explained.

"She's going to be suckin' more cock than a prison fairy," Rokmer said. "Those boys really know how to put dick to a girl when they get goin'. Especially Billy Bullshit."

"Want some, Boss?" Zoyas asked, nodding in the direction in which the girl had been taken. More bikers were heading into the woods to join the original bunch.

"Naw. Let them have their fun. It'll relax them for the big blast we're pullin' tonight."

"When are we goin' in?"

"Three-four in the mornin', when those hicks are fast asleep. We'll sneak in like Indians invading the stockade and snuff the armed guards, then drive everyone into one or two central locations where we can watch them. The older women we'll turn into fetchers. Get us this, that, and the other. The younger meat will do the same as that bitch is doin' in the woods now. There'll be a nice selection of virgins for you, me, and the boys. There should also be plenty of experienced ones too.

Them we won't have to train much as to how we want things done."

"Fine. Now how do we carry out the attack? Who does what?"

Rokmer didn't answer right away, but inside credited Zoyas with a brain. Most bikers would just talk about the plunder they'd take and the women they'd rape. This biker wanted to know how the attack would go down. The mechanics of making the thing work. One day Zoyas would be a gang leader like himself. In fact, had he not been so loyal to Rokmer, whom he treated like an older brother, he might already have his own gang. Rokmer knew this and was glad that Zoyas had stayed. It was good to have someone loyal who wouldn't stab you in the back. For that reason he never cut Zoyas loose or came down hard when he screwed up. Good people, loyal people, were hard to find.

While laughter, conversations, and flickering firelight passed through the air, Rokmer outlined his attack plan for Zoyas. The attack would enter town from both ends of Main Street so no one could leave via the highway. The rest of the gang would attack Vista Royale from the flanks, parking their bikes in the woods, approaching on foot, not making any noise, sneaking into house after house to arouse the inhabitants, taking them prisoner, and in that way grabbing control before anybody knew what was going on. The first approach would come from the flanks. The attack along Main Street would take place half an hour later by forces waiting just outside of town in blocking positions. Rokmer would move up the highway and onto Main Street, while Zoyas would circle around and come in from the opposite side of town. The biker known as the Black Donut would lead in the attack from the western flank and another biker, a big redhead with a red beard down to his belly known as Monster Man, would lead the attackers coming in from the left flank.

"Go get Black Donut and Monster Man. After they've been cued in, I'll talk to all the Bloodsuckers at the same time. Each commander will pick who goes in his group. I pick first, you pick second, then Black Donut, and finally Monster Man. And when you see Billy Bullshit, tell him we can't be bothered draggin' around that bitch he kidnapped. Tell him to snuff her."

"Right, Lyle."

Mayor Strauch had 18 people with a variety of firearms he could count on. If each put in an eight-hour watch, that meant six guns to guard Vista Royale each shift. But that wasn't enough. Sitting in his office, looking down at the pool of light on the empty green blotter of his desk, he felt the shadows of the darkened room closing in and adding to the burden on his shoulders. If anyone had told him yesterday there would be a war today and that Vista Royale would be attacked by bikers, Strauch would have laughed in their faces. But the impossible had come true. The nightmare to end all nightmares. And it wasn't over. Who could predict what the night held?

Strauch forced these things from his mind. He had a job to do. Three people were leaving here soon. Each wanted a gun to protect himself. It was the least they could expect. But that left just 15 guns until they returned. Strauch then decided that instead of each person who owned a gun standing watch, the weapons would become common property. There would be 15 guns for each eight-hour watch. Anyone who knew how to use a gun, man or woman, would serve. That would spread the work around, increase the number of people on guard at any one time, and not wear out anyone. Many who didn't know how to use weapons wanted to volunteer. But there was no time and not enough ammunition to train them. Only experienced hands were wanted. Many housewives, for want of anything better, slept with a kitchen knife next to their beds. They were as ready as any civilian could be when such occasions called.

Strauch made up a list of who would serve on each

watch and who would use what weapon. Vance Doorne, despite what had happened, wanted to serve, and Strauch allowed it. He would be most eager to do well and was picked for the first watch. Strauch looked at the wall clock. It was almost time for the messengers to leave. He would have to meet with them, give each man his assignment, then go back to the office and wait for their return—if they did return.

Sitting in the kitchen section of the two rooms he rented on the first floor of a private house just off Main Street, Alan Pinochar drank his last cup of coffee of the evening and smoked a cigarette. He looked at his wristwatch. It would soon be time to get into his ten-year-old Plymouth Fury and drive over to Mayor Strauch's office.

Pinochar wondered if this was how fighter pilots felt before their missions. The tension. The knot at the pit of his stomach. The cold sweats. The hot fever inside the brain. The feeling that this great mysterious nightmare called life might end. And the knowledge that he did not want it to. There was so much more to be done. And then he felt the regret that so much time had been wasted running after vain pursuits and foolish dreams. Why did so many plans have to end this way? Especially his, now that it was all opening up for him? Pinochar knew that it was all over for him, even if he survived this night and the radiation peril to come.

He looked across the room at the wooden desk in front of the sliding glass doors which made a big picture window framing the garden he had come to love so much in the almost three years he had lived here. Alan Pinochar, man with a dream. Writer trying to make it in that big world out there populated by so many pursuing their dreams. It sometimes seemed to him that artists, writers, and musicians were mere pinpoints of light, like so many stars, trying to cast their glow across the blackness of the heavens.

And now it was finished. Who would read after this

war? Who would publish him? When those bombs went off his profession became obsolete. Reading was the luxury of comfortable, secure societies. Now only necessities would count. All those years, all those efforts down the drain. Might as well be dead, he thought. Then he chided himself. At least he was better off than those poor devils who had been burned to a crisp.

Too many thoughts filled his head. Pinochar didn't know which way to turn. Finally, he surrendered himself to cosmic destiny. He would become a chip of wood on a great, endless sea and let the ocean of life carry him to whichever shore it wished. This was one destiny he would not fight. Alan Pinochar had finally come to a wall he could not climb.

He rose from the table, scraped back his chair, spilled into the sink what remained of the coffee, washed out the cup, put it aside, shut off the light, and left without locking the door. A minute later he was driving out to the mayor's office on Main Street.

The others were there when he arrived. Strauch gave them ashtrays. "You may smoke if you want to," he announced. Pinochar frowned. This sounded like a briefing before a bombing run over Germany during World War II.

Strauch told them what towns they would be trying for and the alternatives to try for if they were unable to get to the primary target. He outlined possible routes they could take, urging them to be careful. One word in five penetrated Pinochar's ears. He was thinking of other things and faraway places. The South Seas he had dreamed of as a youth. The Riviera, where he had once pictured himself writing—not these mountains and not in this post-nuclear nightmare.

Ed Kudner looked excited, as if this were the adventure of his life. Pinochar watched him with faint contempt. Wallis Kreitar sat there with the pallor of death. Or maybe it was just the lighting in the mayor's office. What characters. What a time. The idea for a short story came to Pinochar. He knew of half a dozen markets, having run the gamut of the writing scene. He could go home right now and in a day or two, after some rewriting, have it ready to send out. But reality slapped him back to the present. There was no mail service. No magazines. The hydrogen bombs had also eliminated most of the reading public.

Strauch began talking to Pinochar, who missed the first words, but quickly switched his attention from the inner to the outer self.

"You're to leave in half an hour. We're sending you three out at staggered intervals so, if one car is smashed and we see a flash of fire in the mountain darkness, we'll know enough not to send the others out. No reason to send everyone at the same time and risk losing you all. This is not to say the same thing will happened to you as happened to Doorne's wife."

Pinochar pushed that away. Inside he thought that Strauch was sending him first for bad-mouthing his plans in front of the whole town. Perhaps that was for the best. The enemy might not expect him, so he would get through. Those who followed wouldn't.

"When you get to your objective, the town of Malloy, go to the sheriff there, his name is March Kozniak. He's a good man. Let him know everything that's happened and tell him we need help. Drive carefully. It should take about an hour to get there. Any questions?"

"No. Where's my firearm?" Strauch reached into his desk and brought out a .22-caliber pistol. Pinochar picked it up contemptuously. "This is a bird gun."

"Point it at someone's head and pull the trigger and you'll see birds aren't the only thing it can kill. I'd give you a bigger firearm, but that's the best we can spare with our skimpy arsenal."

"Never mind. I'll take it." Pinochar pocketed the weapon with a look of disgust and started to leave.

"Where are you going?"

"For a beer. I'll be back when I have to leave. You two," he pointed at Kudner and Kreitar, "can decide between yourselves who'll be second and third. Good-bye and good luck." With that, Pinochar stalked out into the night and headed for Emo's Place.

He did not do much talking there and had two Michelobs, not one, then went back to Strauch's office. They were waiting out front. Kudner said he would be the second to leave, followed by Kreitar. Pinochar nodded, not really interested in all this. In the end it didn't really matter.

They wished him luck as he got into his car. He nodded farewell and drove out of town with a last glance at Main Street in his rearview mirror. The road ahead was a blur of shadow-streaked asphalt, the dark sentinels of pines and spruces marching right up to the side of the road. He went past a large burned-out place where Doorne's wife and Sheriff Willem had died.

Pinochar took the .22 from his pocket and placed it on the seat next to him just in case. His eyes were watchful, but he saw no one. Glances in the rearview mirror showed no motorcycles following. Minutes passed and Pinochar relaxed somewhat. If they had a trap prepared they would have sprung it already.

Pinochar had an urge to put on the radio and listen to some music, but remembered there was only static out there. It made him wish he were traveling by day so he could stare out at the sights. Instead, he was moving through a narrow lit corridor being blazed out of the blackness of the night.

Finally, he came to a fork in the road, went right toward Malloy, and looked at his watch. This was taking too long. He could cut down on travel time if he added some speed. Nobody was out there, especially after dark. Pinochar floored it. The Fury hit 70, then 80 miles an hour, and finally 95. This was more like it.

The trees flew by with such rapidity it was almost impossible to discern individual trunks. He had the window down just a bit and a trembling wind entered, bouncing off the top of his head, mussing his hair, tugging at his eyes, making him feel a bit better. The wind was thick with the night scent of the forest. A scent so full of life he doubted for a few seconds that they had gone through a nuclear war. But no matter how often Pinochar and others tried to deny it, this was one reality which could not be forced down.

The road was coming to a curve. Pinochar slowed down, riding the brake as he took the sharp curve at 70, drifting into the opposite lane as he moved around the pines edging the curve, his hands skillful on the wheel. Pinochar smiled at the power of the car and his ability to control it, if not the greater flow of events around him.

And then, as he came around the curve and prepared to straighten out, he spotted the truck coming toward him in the same lane he was using. A truck full of chickens that some driver was taking from his farm near the coast to the safety of his brother's farm in the mountains.

The drivers spotted each other at the same time, headlights blinding each of them as they fought to get their vehicles out of the way, riding brakes, trying to turn wheels. But they were too close and Pinochar was going too fast.

The force, when they met, was jarring. Pinochar was thrown forward through his windshield and out across the hood of his car, which was already being turned into an accordion as it met the mass of the truck. The engine block caved in under a combined contact speed of 130 miles per hour.

Pinochar continued his flight across the hood of his collapsing car till he landed on the grille of the truck, then became part of the collapsing mass of vehicles. The truck driver, who wore a seatbelt, stayed in the crushed cab of the truck.

As the vehicles crunched together they went out of control and began to tumble off the road, tossing scrap all over the place, leaking burning fuel from smashed gas tanks, orange-yellow flames filling the night, eating into dead and maimed chickens, many of the birds now freed as their cages cracked open. But, as they tried to fly in the terrifying, screeching, flaming hell of collision, they were propelled by the momentum of the vehicle they were leaving and smashed into the road and earth at 60 miles per hour. The sounds of numerous splats filled the night, leaving behind crushed, bloodied, feathered streaks.

The vehicles rolled into the trees, being stopped by a line of spruces which were half-uprooted by the force of impact. And there the flaming scraps burned furiously, incinerating their trapped drivers like the sailers on some Viking funeral ship. The conflagration started a small forest fire which, together with the vehicles, burned till half past three in the morning—when a sudden downpour put out the flames in the forest. Then there was darkness again.

14

As the night progressed, the sickness and most of the chills and diarrhea passed. The warming glow of the fire, the crackle of the flames, and the atmosphere of cheer they created dissipated the internal darkness to some degree. When Bathhurst came to see how everyone was, he brought coffee he had just made and they drank it eagerly from metal army cups.

"How does everyone feel?" Bathhurst asked.

"A bit better," Caudell replied.

"But still not good enough," Mrs. Caudell added.

"What do you people intend doing?" Bathhurst asked. "Would you like to join us in searching for more victims, or perhaps go to work in the casualty center instead of returning to the mountains?"

"I don't think so," Stack answered.

"There's nothing for us here," Rayisa added. "If our loved ones were alive we would've found them. But they're dead, like so many others."

"Come morning, we're history," Stack said. "In fact, we're going to start loading up right now. I don't think any of us are going to sleep for what's left of tonight."

"Can't say I blame you. If I didn't have to work here, I'd leave."

"How many people do you figure survived in Fresno?" Caudell asked, abruptly changing the subject.

"I've seen hundreds," Bathhurst answered. "There

might be thousands who've gone to other places. There were two hundred thousand here before the war."

"What a bitch," Caudell exclaimed. Bathhurst nodded to them and started back to his headquarters. Stack walked with him.

"I want to thank you for all the help you've given," he said. "I also want to say I'm glad I met you. This has been a unique and interesting experience. I don't know if I'll see this place again. But I do hope our paths cross. You've been a great guy to know."

Through the tiredness in his face, Bathhurst smiled. "The same goes here. Thanks for all your help. If we survive the next bunch of months to come down the pike, I hope we'll be able to meet and have a drink in some bar when the country's rebuilt and on it's feet."

The two men did not say anything more and stood there for a few seconds, hands clasped in a handshake. Then they walked apart, Bathhurst to continue his work and Stack back to the people who depended on him.

Earlier, in the mountains, two of the three men who had been sent out from Vista Royale reached their objectives and made contact. The town Wallis Kreitar came to was shocked by what he told them. He got the sheriff out of bed first, then the sheriff woke the mayor. But they were unable to send any help. Radiation-laden winds, containing an unusually potent concentration, had already passed through and many people were coming down with radiation poisoning. The only doctor in town had his hands full. The sheriff's deputy was sick and the sheriff himself was not feeling too well. But the mayor promised some help if Kreitar could wait till morning.

Ed Kudner, known to his friends as King Kudner, reached Montieth shortly after Kreitar reached his objective. The streets were deserted. He did not know where the sheriff or mayor lived, but he did know Kurt Willem was Wyatt Willem's brother. Kudner drove around till he found the Willem nameplate on the mailbox in front of one house, then parked and went up the walk to the front door. He leaned on the doorbell till the light came on upstairs and Kurt Willem leaned out an open window, squinted, and said, "Yes, what do you want?"

"I'm from Vista Royale. Your brother's town. I've been sent by Mayor Strauch."

"Wait. I'll be right down," Willem said, an edge of tension in his voice. If someone was waking him up in the wee hours of morning it meant trouble.

The door came open a minute later as Willem, his uniform half on, buttoned his shirt. "Come in. We don't have to talk on the doorstep. The neighbors might hear."

He took Kudner into a modern kitchen, got soda from the refrigerator and two glasses from a sideboard. "Want something to eat, Mr.—?"

"Kudner, Ed Kudner. No thanks."

They sat down at the table while Willem poured for both of them. They both drank, then wiped their mouths as if this were whiskey and not ginger ale. Kudner got to the point.

He told Willem about the biker problem and the help Vista Royale needed. "I'm only one man here. We'll have to talk with Mayor Oppelin and his advisors before I can take any steps. We'll also have to protect ourselves first. Those hoodlums might try to attack Montieth."

"I know that. Mayor Strauch spoke about the needs of the surrounding towns. But each must cooperate in helping. If every town looks out only for itself those bikers will be able to take us out one at a time."

"Did my brother send you?"

Kudner hesitated. Willem wanted to speak, opening his mouth but saying nothing. Kudner then began. "Your brother is missing." He looked into his lap a second, then up at Willem. "Maybe the bikers caught him on the open road."

Willem looked down, his face grim, the family

ressemblance between him and his brother very apparent now. Finally, he said, "Let's go see the mayor."

They woke Cy Oppelin and two of his advisors, the town's leading lawyer and the only resident physician. They met in the mayor's house while his wife, in curlers and bathrobe, made coffee and sliced Sara Lee cake for them.

Willem wanted to go to Vista Royale immediately, find the bikers, and punish them for what he felt was the death of his brother. But the mayor held him back. He had his duty to Montieth. What if the bikers made a surprise attack on the town by night? Who would protect them? So Willem drew up a list of all those who had guns and knowledge of weapons. Some would become part of the town defense force. The rest would go to Vista Royale. Next it was decided who would inform the other towns further afield of the danger in their midst. After the lists were made up, Willem and the mayor's assistants were sent to wake up key people for an emergency meeting about how the defenses would be organized. There were many surprised faces when they realized the extent of the danger now threatening them and how far things had gone in so short a time.

While this was happening the finishing touches were being put on Rokmer's plan. Bikers and their women, all armed with guns and knives, moved into position. Rokmer, Zoyas, and others now called themselves by their nicknames as if these strange, sometimes vicious monickers could transform them into comic-book hereos impervious to the gunfire and knives. Soon they would know how true their myths and beliefs were. Shivers of excitement passed through San Quentin Sal, Samurai Sam, The Black Donut, Billy Bullshit, and Monster Man as they moved out. This was to be a night of conquest, bloodshed, and pillage. Like the Vikings of old they gloried in combat, but they also feared it. Death or maiming might be out there waiting for them.

Still, it would be worth it. This was more exciting than any gang rumble, which was just a fight for small stakes. This was a war for real turf. An entire town, with slaves to serve them, would be theirs if they came out the victors. The excitement was so great they could barely contain themselves. But they kept control and moved to the attack in the pattern outlined by Rokmer.

He approahched Vista Royale with his men, moving up the same road The Bloodsuckers had left town by. They approached slowly, without lights, and spotted the pickup truck pulled across Main Street, blocking it, the armed men behind it, both smoking—which would have given away their position had no lights been on in town. A hundred yards outside of town Rokmer led the dozen riders with him off the road. They hid their bikes inside the tree line, then, on foot, approached to within 50 yards of Main Street, guns drawn, sharp, swift breaths coming between the teeth of opened mouths. Senses were at a peak, eyes were alert, and ears picked up the snap of every twig.

Approaching Main Street from the other side of town, Lance Zoyas and his people were carrying out the same maneuver. On the flanks the hulking giant Monster Man, and The Black Donut, an oily killer with 20 years as a biker behind him, led their people through the woods. With Monster Man was Billy Bullshit. He hadn't killed Barbara Sidarsis as ordered, but instead had let her go. Before doing so, he said, "I hate to kill a good piece of ass. And you've earned your keep. So run into the woods. I'll tell the others I've snuffed you. But make sure no one sees you. 'Cause if they do I'm dog meat and, the next time I see you, I'll surely slit your pretty little throat." He took her into the trees to say this, then gave her a shove. She ran into the deeper darkness, less afraid of the unknown woods at night than of the living animals who had taken her there. And now, as she grappled in the dark, among the undergrowth and the slapping pine-needle branches, the bikers coming in from the flanks did the same, cursing under their breaths, having left their bikes in the woods where they would find them, come morning, if they were victorious.

It was dark in the woods. So damn dark they kept banging into trees and each other. The worst part of it was that they could not curse out loud, but had to keep the tension inside. Finally, they spotted the lights of the village. They were heading in the right direction and soon would be out of this damned hell. Few of them hated the forest as much as Billy Bullshit did. He was thinking to himself that someone ought to come along and chop this place down. What the hell did they need woods for? The hell with the ecologists. More minutes passed till they reached the edge of the tree line. Then they stood just inside the green cover, looking into backyards.

A biker by the name of Ivan, a dark-haired giant with a beard down to his belly and straggly brown hair down his back, known to the others, depending on how the mood struck them, as Ivan the Terrible or Ivan the Not So Terrible, was the first to emerge from the woods on the left flank of town. Black Donut had been trying to restrain him all the way through the forest. Ivan could not be held back. The killing lust was in him, the urge for action. Maybe it was the effect of the plunder earlier, or the position of the moon, or the fact that half a world had gone up in flames. It did not matter. Ivan advanced across the yard he had entered as The Black Donut waved to the others to follow along.

The yard was attached to the house owned by Paul Carnessa, in his late 60s. He was in bed now, thinking about his offer to join the defense force guarding Vista Royale. But he had been turned down as too old. This bothered Carnessa, who had fought in World War II and served in Korea. He had been wounded in both conflicts, twice in World War II.

Neither Carnessa nor his wife heard the rear door being jimmied open and the bikers stealing in, moving through the first-floor rooms, picking up anything of value, then, like thieves in the night, coming up the stairs. They opened Mrs. Carnessa's door first, Ivan leading half the band in, while The Black Donut led the others down the hall to her husband's room, the light from it streaming under the door and casting a long, wide glow across the hall carpet.

When Mrs. Carnessa saw the door open and the invaders come in, she almost fainted and opened her mouth to scream. But nothing came out. The bikers did not wait for Mrs. Carnessa to find her voice. They rushed across the room, Ivan with a big Bowie knife in hand—he didn't have a gun yet—which he plunged into her chest while throwing a big paw over her mouth. The first thrust caused her to spasm violently. He pushed her down, pulled the knife out, and then rammed home twice more. Her eyes closed and she stopped spasming. He left her like that atop the bedcovers, bleeding across the bed, as he wiped his hands and knife on the sheets and began looking for valuables. The Bloodsuckers were a very democratic mob. No arguing over spoils. Whoever put his hands on something first owned it.

As Mrs. Carnessa was being knifed, her husband's door was thrown open. His heart almost stopped as they came into the room quickly, not even allowing him time to think. A fear as great as any he had experienced, greater even than in the Ardennes during the Battle of the Bulge, filled him as six invaders came across the room, their big boots clopping on the floorboards till they lined both sides of the bed. Then four grabbed him. One for each arm and leg. One watched while the sixth pulled Carnessa's pillow from beneath his head and put it over his face. The biker held it there till a struggling Paul Carnessa stopped thrashing about, which wasn't long, then took the pillow away. Carnessa slept the eternal sleep. He looked at peace. How he felt while choking to death none of them could tell and none of them cared. As soon as the pillow was taken away it was thrown aside and the murderous scavengers began going through his things looking for money, valuables, and whatever else could be of use.

They did not spend much time in the house. Their orders had been to move from place to place, herding people together so that control could be established without wasting precious minutes. Time was everything, Rokmer had told them. He had read someplace that every great general taught his troops that. And today San Quentin Sal was a general of sorts.

On the other side of town Monster Man, Billy Bullshit, nine other bikers, and one biker's woman—half armed with guns, the rest with knives—entered the house where Vera Bullock and her two 15-year-old daughters lived. Vera was a widow and the defense force, at her request, had stationed a guard outside her house. He was 60 and had a .22 rifle, but it still made her feel better.

Billy led the team into her house. When he was coming up through the cellar, having broken in that way, he was spotted by one of the girls, who had gone down in the middle of the night to raid the refrigerator. She began to scream in fear, but Billy ran forward and with one mighty punch connected with her jaw and knocked the girl out. Another biker grabbed her as the rest rushed upstairs on the double.

The scream had been heard by her mother, who sat up in bed and called out, "Betty? June? Did any of you girls cry out?" Quickly she put on the light, got out of bed, and reached for her nightrobe. June, her other daughter, had slept through all this. But the scream had been heard by the guard outside the house. He looked around, eyes slitted, face wary, gun ready. He saw the light come on upstairs and started up the path to the front door.

At the same time, the bikers who rushed upstairs ran into hall furniture, banged their legs, stifled curses. Then the door at the end of the hall opened and Vera Bullock stepped out. She ran into The Black Donut and the biker woman with him—a wide-bottomed, red-headed bitch in her 30s with a sagging chest and a crooked, foul mouth. Vera's shocked look was quickly answered as The Black Donut slammed his hardest punch into her face, breaking her nose, and knocking her unconscious. He turned to the biker girl and said, "Watch her." Then he and the others began to go through the remaining rooms, in one of which they found June and dragged her out of bed. The horror of being awakened by these monsters caused her to gag for a few seconds. She was then dragged into the hall, where she began to sob violently at the sight of her unconscious mother on the floor, thinking perhaps that the woman was dead. One of the bikers stepped up to Betty and slapped her twice, hard, saying, "Shut the fuck up, bitch." In fear, she tried to comply.

Billy Bullshit walked over, saw her substantial chest, and took a breast in each hand and began to palpitate them. Then he let go and turned to one of the other bikers and said, "Nob City. We keep this one. I want first go at her."

As this was happening the guard outside knocked on the front door. He knocked three times before The Black Donut whispered to two of the bikers, "Let whoever it is in and then kill him." They rushed downstairs. The door opened and the unthinking guard rushed in. He was grabbed from behind. Another pair of hands wrestled away his .22 at the same time that a hard knife plunged up and in between his ribs, ripping into a lung, which soon filled with blood. Three more times the knife went into him in various places while a smelly paw over his mouth kept him from crying out. And then he was released, groaning and already half-dead as he leaked blood onto the hallway carpet. They left him like that, the door half-open as they raced upstairs.

The bikers worked fast. In a few minutes Vera, holding her broken nose, which was leaking blood, and her frightened daughters, still in nightclothes, were hurried downstairs. The biker girl, using a snub-nosed .38 loaned to her by another of the gang, guarded them, while the other bikers went to the next house in line.

Just outside of town, Lyle Rokmer looked at his watch. There were 20 minutes more before he and Zoyas made their run onto Main Street and began the final assault. He wondered how the penetrations on the flanks were going. It was a pity they had no walkie-talkies to communicate with. Not knowing what was going on was maddening.

What he did not know was that the bikers who had come in on the flanks had broken into four teams, each taking down a house every five minutes. But there were more than six dozen homes. The majority would still be free by the time the half-hour he had given them was up. And at each home the teams had to leave behind someone to guard the prisoners. There simply wouldn't be enough bikers left by the end to carry out the mission he had given them. Rokmer was not the great general he had imagined himself to be.

Any progress the flanking teams did make depended on their not being spotted by the guards. So far one of the guards had died when he entered the Bullock house. Another was killed when he was caught visiting the home of a friend to see if his wife and kids were all right. While there he used the bathroom. When the bikers broke in they quickly overwhelmed the man of the house and grabbed the gun which the guard had left outside while he went in to use the bathroom. As one invader held a gun on the family, another ran forward, his big, booted foot kicking open the door, breaking the flimsy lock inside. There he found the surprised guard on the toilet, his pants down around his ankles. Before he could close his surprised mouth or rise, the biker rushed forward, pressed the small-caliber gun he held to the man's chest, and pulled the trigger. The bullet went through the heart and emerged out the back. The sound was muffled because the gun was pressed against the victim. His mouth opened wider, blood gurgled out and ran down his chin, and he slumped on the toilet, closed his eyes, and let his head fall back. The biker grinned at how ridiculous the man looked, then walked back out into the hall and returned to where the others were.

Monster Man walked in. "Let's start herding everyone into a central location where we can have just two people watch them all." And so it began. Among the prisoners were women who'd had knives on their bedstands but hadn't used them when confronted by so many armed invaders. Their knives became additions to the invader's arsenal.

Vance Doorne, returning to his house to use the bathroom, spotted Monster Man leading three hostages. "Stop, you bastard," he yelled as he raced forward, lifting his gun to fire, hate blazing in his eyes as he realized that the town had been penetrated. His anger gave him courage and a desire for revenge blazed in his heart as fire flew from his gun.

But the bullet went wild. Monster Man then fired and also missed. Doorne tried to hit him again and struck a nearby tree. Wood chips flew as the people Monster Man had been leading into captivity fled. Bikers close enough to the scene ran toward the fighting as Monster Man dropped behind some bushes and began to advance in a crawling fashion. But Doorne stood his ground, the anger inside him blazing like a pure white fire.

Monster Man chose that moment to leave his unsafe position and ran for the shelter of a nearby tree trunk. Doorne aimed carefully, then fired. The shot caught the huge biker square in the forehead, just over the nose, spinning through his sinus cavities into the soft brain tissue behind. Like Goliath felled by David's stone, Monster Man crashed to the ground, the pistol falling from his suddenly limp fingers. Doorne grinned, then wheeled as another biker, this one with a knife, came

HELL RIDE

into view and ran for the gun. Doorne aimed and fired as red flame lashed out into the night.

But the biker dropped down and dodged the bullet. Doorne pegged another shot at the elusive target as the biker made it behind a hedge. Suddenly out of bullets, Doorne rushed behind a car to reload, giving the biker his chance to get the pistol. He ran full speed toward the dropped gun as two more Bloodsuckers came running with the red-haired biker girl behind them.

The fighting was heard out on Main Street. Two guards ran toward the combat and two more joined them on the way. The free-for-all had started. Rokmer heard the fighting too. It was still six minutes to the main event. Should he go in now? No. He'd hold back and let them shift their forces in the direction of the fight. Then he'd strike. It would make things easier for him, but harder for the bikers getting it in the neck. However, that was their bad luck. Rokmer hoped and prayed Zoyas would not panic and lead his attack in now. Hell, why couldn't they have had walkie-talkies? What he wouldn't have given to be able to speak to all his unit commanders right then.

The town was now awake. People were mobilizing. They knew the attackers were there. The bikers on the side of town opposite the fighting hurried along, knowing that time was running short. They figured the attack on Main Street had gone in early. Perhaps Rokmer had been too eager to wait. It did not occur to them that one of the flanking moves had been discovered.

One of Vista Royale's defenders ran to wake Mayor Strauch. Another, taking two armed men with him, hurried to see if anyone had penetrated the quiet flank of town. People called to them out of open windows, asking what the problem was. One of the men answered, "Stay inside. Keep your doors locked."

They reached the end of one block, turned the corner,

and spotted three bikers coming out of a house
diagonally across the way. The town's defenders took
shelter behind some trees lining the street and opened
fire. The bikers quickly scattered and fall down behind
cover.

The defenders tried to end this quickly, but the
invaders now had their weapons out and were prepared
to put up a fight. Shots began to fly left, right, up and
down, back and forth, red lances cutting the night still-
ness. One teenage boy, listening to the exchange inside
his house, thought it sounded like a Fourth of July
celebration and was glad he was not outside.

One of the advancing defenders was hit in the thigh.
He grimaced in pain, stumbled, then fell as he dropped
his pistol and grabbed for his leg. One of the two others
still moving forward turned to help him and caught a
round in the side of the head. Red ran from his ears,
then he spit blood, staggered a few feet, and fell down
dead.

The last of the trio retreated behind a tree and
shivered in fear. The man who was shot in the thigh,
lying now in the open, called out to his friend behind the
tree to pull him away, but the other man did not
respond. Shock had him by the throat. But then the man
on the ground stopped calling for help as more bikers
arrived and began advancing up both sides of the street,
using front yards where they were overgrown, or
peeking out from behind cars lining the curb.

Several shots rang out and the man in the open was
killed. Then one biker popped up, drew a bead on the
defender behind the tree, and pumped two rounds into
him. The man fell down mortally wounded, flailing the
ground with his arms and legs as pints of blood spilled out.

On the other flank of Vista Royale the fighting had
also grown hotter and heavier. The four men who had
rushed to that area were now fighting alongside Vance
Doorne. That left just five defenders out on Main
Street. It was at that point Lance Zoyas, his mind filled
with images of bikers being cut to pieces, rushed in to

the attack. His bikers advanced up both sides of the road, firing pistols, rifles, and shotguns.

The pair guarding that end, behind an '82 Dodge pickup, were caught in a deadly crossfire. The defenders never had a chance. They tried to fight back, but both were hit. One was killed outright. The other, with two bullets in him, fell to the asphalt and fired from beneath the truck, catching one biker in the calf. He screamed as his leg folded under him and went down hard on the road, painting the asphalt red. The other attackers quickly found cover, spotted the defender under the truck, and killed him. Then they rose and advanced.

The three men fighting to hold the other end of Main Street saw what was happening and began to move toward that side of town. At that moment Rokmer, cursing Zoyas for having been panicked into attacking earlier then he should have, gave the attack signal. Firing erupted as his men advanced toward Main Street. They forced the three defenders to hide behind their truck and give return fire. Two bikers were killed almost immediately, dimming some of the enthusiasm with which Rokmer's people moved into action.

"Keep going, keep going, or we'll lose this war," he yelled. "We're almost over the top," he lied, not knowing the size of the enemy force, or if they had reserves coming, or how the battle was going elsewhere.

Vance Doorne's people were doing well as they advanced behind cars and trees. They had killed two bikers and wounded another. None of them had been hit yet, though return fire kept slamming into trees and cars, sending chips and slivers of wood flying, starring glass windows, punching holes in metal flanks, and making cars vibrate.

"Keep up the attack, we're winning," Doorne cried out.

On the other side of the street scared bikers were crawling to avoid incoming fire, looking for guns lying next to dead or wounded Bloodsuckers since few of them had the arms they needed. One biker spotted a gun lying on the grass and ran from behind a tree to grab it. A trio of .38 slugs caught him in the head, arm, and chest. He went down like a felled redwood.

Across town the bikers came into the open and began picking up weapons and ammunition from the dead. Their prisoners, now guarded by one girl with a gun, dared not run. The Black Donut picked five men and led them toward Main Street. Victory had already painted smiles across their faces.

The defenders of Main Street were done for. To their rear Zoyas and his people were moving forward slowly, looking for hidden defenders, and in front of them Rokmer's force was narrowing the distance.

Soon Rokmer was close enough to fire the tear-gas gun he carried. He loaded and fired quickly, letting the defenders have canister after canister. They landed all around the truck. Within seconds clouds of acidic gas filled the air, engulfing the defenders, who began to choke. One of them quickly dropped his gun, then another. They couldn't control themselves as they rose from behind their concealed positions and began to twist about in agony, coughing, spitting, gasping, grabbing at their tearing eyes. Rokmer stopped firing.

The bikers now advanced more quickly. Were it not for the clouds of gas limiting their vision, they would've killed all the defenders. But now the gas was clearing some and they were too close for comfort. The attackers charged the pickup when the men using it as a barrier staggered back. A volley of shots rang out. Bodies convulsed and the trio of citizen fighters fell dead as the bikers overran their position. Those without guns picked up weapons from the dead, searching their still-warm, bleeding corpses for ammunition.

Rokmer grinned now that victory was seemingly in his grasp. However, fighting still continued on the left flank of town, though the gang members did not seem to be bothered by it as they started the pickup. Half a dozen of them got in front or back.

"Head toward the sounds of gunfire," Rokmer told

them. "Our boys seem to be having some trouble there." The driver of the pickup nodded, then roared off, turning left at the first side street. "Go to it, boys. Ride in shooting," Rokmer called after them.

Once they were gone, Rokmer began to worry that Zoyas and his band, approaching up Main Street, might mistake them for defenders and a needless and costly gun battle would then ensue. To prevent this, he walked out into the middle of the street and called out, "Samurai Sam, this is San Quentin Sal. Main Street is clear."

Zoyas heard Rokmer, walked out into the middle of the street, and called back, "This is Samurai Sam. I read you and I understand. But there's still fighting going on near here."

"I know. I've already sent men there to help. Come to me, Lance." Both groups started toward one another. As this was happening, The Black Donut and his men emerged onto Main Street. All three teams and combat leaders met there, embracing amid war whoops, backslaps, and rebel yells.

But things had not been so rosy in the battle zone. A few minutes earlier Billy Bullshit, fighting off three of the town's defenders, killed one of them and almost wounded another. At the same time Vance Doorne took advantage of his diverted attention and raced across the street. Hidden by cars lining the curb, he advanced up the block, popping up to fire at this or that biker. He even drew a bead on and killed the only female in the group when she began firing the pistol she had picked up from a dead biker. She took Doorne's slug high up in the chest, grimaced in pain, then dropped the pistol and fell to the grass. There the girl groaned for help as she slowly bled to death. The bikers, unable to get to her, listened to her agony till she passed away.

The biker guarding the prisoners they had gathered in a nearby house looked out the window at the fighting and some of his captives took the opportunity to go out the back way. Finally, he forgot all about his charges as he left the house and joined in the battling. Taking prisoners was no longer on his mind, just survival.

Vance Doorne moved forward two car lengths. Then, without warning, he suddenly rose and shot Billy Bullshit between the eyes. Billy looked surprised that he'd been hit and fell over dead, realizing perhaps in those milli-seconds before life fled that the fun and games would be no more.

Only five Bloodsuckers and four defenders were left in this particular sector. Just then one of the defenders called out his congratulations to Vance Doorne for the good shooting he had done. But that was the wrong move. The man drew attention to himself. One of the bolder bikers moved forward, aimed, and fired two slugs into the defender's abdomen and chest, killing him instantly.

"Everybody down," Doorne yelled. "Be careful. The object is to kill these bastards, not join them in hell. Just keep up the pressure. We're winning. Listen. The firing has died out everywhere but here. We've won in the rest of town, now let's finish it here."

As he was shouting this, the pickup with the six gunmen roared into the street. Guns blazing, they killed the first two defenders. Vance Doorne than ran for it, firing over his shoulder as he retreated. The pickup took on speed and raced down the street, catching him in its headlights. Four guns blazed away and bullet after bullet slammed into his body. Doorne staggered, then arched as he realized in that final second of life why the firing had stopped and that all his efforts had been in vain. The pistol fell from his fingers as he crashed to the sidewalk. A second later the truck rolled up over the sidewalk and crunched his bones into chips as it ground him into the pavement. Doorne did not feel the pain.

Across Vista Royale the war whoops of Bloodsuckers filled the air. Meanwhile Rokmer gave instructions to have the townspeople herded into the local church, where he would give them their orders. Wounded bikers were brought to a central location as others headed toward Main Street for a big celebration.

One of the bikers broke into the mayor's office and there found the mayor and a frightened Alma Holloway hiding out. Both were brought before Rokmer. In a display of bravery, a gasping Strauch, his belly heaving in fear, his cheeks flaming, his eyes wild, said, "I'm the mayor of this town, and I demand you get out. What you've done is against the law."

"Fuck you." Rokmer spit, leaning forward from the waist. Then he took out his gun and fired four rounds into Strauch, who dropped to the road.

"Now I'm the mayor," Rokmer announced to the cheering bikers. Miss Holloway fell to her knees and sobbed as she cradled the mayor's head in her lap.

15

Stack, Rayisa, and the Caudells headed toward the mountains as dawn broke over the horizon. Major Bathhurst was not even there when they had departed. Several hours earlier he'd had a bout with radiation sickness. Then, partly recovered, he'd driven off with a jeepload of troops to help dig out some trapped survivors in a house somewhere in the ruins of Fresno.

No one even looked up when they drove away from the casualty center. Nor did any of the travelers look back, all of them glad to be out of that place. The trip went quickly this time. The land looked as devastated as ever, but there were more survivors visible now. More vehicles were on the road, vehicles in every state of disrepair that one could imagine. Not many of them, but more than during the trip down from the mountains. There were also people along the roads. A number tried to hitchhike. Stack did not stop for them. He had given enough of himself since yesterday and decided to let someone else play the Good Samaritan for a change.

It was not yet nine in the morning when they reached Montieth. There were people on the streets, their faces looking grimmer than yesterday. Stack, Rayisa, and the Caudells were hungry. They hadn't eaten since last night and had vomited out most of that.

Stack and Caudell found parking spaces. Then everyone got out and stretched their legs. Sheriff Willem spotted them from a block away and hurried over. Stack saw the sheriff and, hands in his pockets, waited for Willem to reach him. The Caudells and Rayisa, not having seen Willem, headed for the refreshment table, which was open again. A few more strange faces were in town. Stragglers no doubt.

Willem's face had a strained, tired look on it. "Morning, Stack's the name, right?"

"Unhuh."

"Back from Fresno so soon?"

"Nothing for us there. We couldn't find anyone. The place looks like Hiroshima after the bomb."

"A lot of dead?"

"Most of the town. Plenty of radiation sickness. We caught some of it. But not that bad compared to what others went through."

"Yeah," Willem answered absentmindedly. "Everyone got screwed in this war. Me too. My brother's missing." He told Stack the story.

"I got the mayor out of bed and his advisors. Then they got a number of leading citizens together. We've had some meetings about what to do. The last one two hours ago. Then we decided to send emissaries to other towns to ask for volunteers so all of us, together, could descend on Vista Royale, ambush those bikers when they launch their attack, and wipe them out in one fell swoop. We've been trying to get things going since way before dawn." He looked at his watch. "It's now nine in the morning and we still haven't achieved a damn thing."

"How many people have you got so far?"

"Twelve-fifteen tops. We don't have tons of people with guns to choose from. And a certain number will have to be left behind to guard each town in case trouble should come down the highway."

"How many people do these bikers have?"

Willem shrugged. "Could be dozens. Nobody's counted. Wanna come?"

"No thanks. I've had a day and night I won't forget

for a long time if I live to be a hundred."

"Then I'll be taking my leave of you. I've got things to do," Willem said.

"Good luck," Stack called after him, but Willem didn't answer as he hurried off. Two men called to the sheriff from another direction and he changed his angle slightly as he walked toward them.

Stack took out a cigarette and lit it. He felt tired and hungry at the same time. A rare state for him. Without thinking more about it, he moved toward the refreshment table. Rayisa was standing there with a half-eaten sandwich in one hand and a can of soda in the other. She was talking to one of the girls she had met yesterday. There seemed to be a warm glow on her face as she temporarily forgot the hells of the moment.

Youth, Stack thought. How resilient. They recover so quickly. For one long moment he wished he was 15 again. But there was no magic well that made wishes come true, so he did the best with what he had.

In Vista Royale, Lyle Rokmer had gone to bed in one of the houses that had been cleared as his headquarters. He hadn't slept in more than 24 hours and now felt exhausted by a long day and night of almost unbelievable activity. Before he went to sleep he gave orders to the only biker he really trusted, Lance Zoyas.

"We've got this town. It's ours. All the people are concentrated into four houses so we can more easily guard them. Fine and good. Some of our guys want to loot. Others want to separate out the young girls and the more appealing women and enjoy themselves in an orgy of rape. Well, not yet. There are more important things."

"Like what?"

"Suppose some people got away while we were rounding up everyone in town. It can happen. We haven't got eyes in the back of our heads."

"So some people got away. You figure they went for help?"

"Could be. They might bring people back with them. We've got to put armed guards all over. In case anyone comes, we'll give them a reception they won't forget and send them back with their tails between their legs."

"Why don't we just get what we want and scoot the hell out of here?"

"If they can stop us here, they can stop us anywhere. I say they can't. We're here and we mean to stay. We leave when we want to. Not when those bastards tell us. It's a new world. A new game. And we're playing hardball."

"Whatever you say, Lyle. You're the boss."

"And you know it. Also, when you set up those guard positions, put a forward patrol on every road going out of town. Use one man in each patrol. Send him about half a mile out of town. Have him go off the road and conceal himself in the woods. Then, as soon as someone moves past, heading toward town, have him move out and race past the vehicle so he can get here first and inform us. And use people who're reliable. I don't want anyone going to sleep on me. Also, what's happening with our casualty situation?"

"Of the five wounded we took, two have died. We got that doctor who lives just outside of town that the people here told us about. He's takin' care of our wounded and theirs too."

"Fine. Now go do what I told you." With that, Rokmer jumped into bed and Zoyas left. He was in command now, and gave orders as if he had been doing it all his life.

One of the bikers he sent out on forward patrol was about to go off the road and conceal himself in the woods when he spotted someone walking along the highway about three-quarters of a mile ahead. He raced out in that direction and stopped in the middle of the road near the stranger, a friendly-looking man in his middle 20s with a big, square head and sincere eyes. He was wearing an Air Force uniform. He said, "Hi." So did the biker, falsehood in his face and voice.

"What're you doing out in this road alone, soldier?" the biker asked, still pretending to be friendly.

"I'm trying to find some civilization. Maybe you can tell me where there's a town or give me a lift there. I'm looking for food and water for my crew."

"Crew?" the biker leaned forward.

Lance Briggs, the bombardier, explained about the B-52 in the valley and how he had been sent out to find a town while the rest stood perimeter patrol around the plane.

The biker's face was poker-player bland, but his voice was a bit sly. "You do need help. I just came from the town of Vista Royale. Maybe you'd like me to take you there. Hop on."

Briggs got on and held on tight as they raced back to Vista Royale to see Lance Zoyas. When they arrived and Briggs looked around at all the bikers, a knot of worry began making its way up from his belly. The biker meantime related to Zoyas all that Briggs had told him. Zoyas grinned at Briggs as if he was a mink about to be skinned and made into a coat for a lady friend.

"Let's take this gentleman to our leader," Zoyas said. Briggs wanted to say something, to ask some questions, perhaps to protest. But then he saw the guns and knives they were carrying and knew he had blundered. Badly.

Zoyas woke Rokmer, who cursed as he opened his eyes. But then he saw the bikers in his room and the strange-looking military man.

"What is it? We been invaded by little green men from Mars?" Rokmer asked, shaking sleep from his head and wiping the blurring from his eyes.

Zoyas quickly explained who the airman was and about the B-52, full of H-bombs, on a deserted airfield not far away. Rokmer sat up, the sleep fleeing from his eyes, a devilish smile crossing his lips.

"See that this gentleman," he said sarcastically, grinning at Briggs, "is taken to a house not occupied at the moment, placed under guard, and given all the hospitality we can extend."

Briggs wanted to protest, but guns were drawn, and he was hustled out. When he was gone and Rokmer and Zoyas were alone, Rokmer said to him, "This is our meal ticket." He jumped out of bed and in his shorts walked back and forth nervously, talking fast, like a madman with gold fever.

"We've got to get that bomber and all those bombs. With them in our hands we'll be kings of the mountains. No one, no one will dare oppose us for fear that we'll nuke them. Any riches we want, any car we desire, any woman we see who pleases us will be ours."

Rokmer stopped pacing back and forth, looked Zoyas in the eyes, and said, "We'll have it made in the shade with Kool-Aid."

John Kritzler and Vic Lunenberg had been walking since well before dawn, going off the road as vehicles came by, then back on it, taking shortcuts through the woods on occasion, resting, drinking from creeks, shaking their heads at the horror which had befallen Vista Royale.

They had awakened in the night when the firing began and found themselves without guns because the men on the first watch had them. By the time they were out of bed, dressed, and had found others who were supposed to be on duty during the next shift, most of the fighting was almost over. And, as they ran to the scenes of the fighting, without weapons, they arrived in time to see the final, horrible stages of defeat. So they fled back to their homes. Rather than be taken prisoner, and unable to drag along their wives, Kritzler and Lunenberg, unlike many others, escaped from Vista Royale to go find help.

Now, after hours of marching, exhausted by the ordeal, their hearts pumping too fast, they staggered into Montieth, where they were given water to drink, then taken to see Sheriff Willem and Mayor Oppelin. They told them everything that had happened, and also informed Willem that while going through the woods they spotted the hidden police cruiser. Inside it were the bloodied bodies of Wyatt Willem and Ann Doorne.

Kurt Willem had been expecting his brother's death. Yet now he barely controlled himself. After a few moments, he asked if Lunenberg and Kritzler wanted to join the group being formed to help liberate Vista Royale. They readily agreed. Willem then sent for Ed Kudner, who quickly arrived. The men embraced like long-lost brothers.

Willem got them guns and introduced those they would be fighting with. After which everyone piled into the four vehicles detailed to take them to Vista Royale. Willem's police cruiser led the procession.

Most of the men, armed with a variety of weapons, weren't too happy with what they had to do. Besides the volunteers from Vista Royale, the cars contained people from Montieth and two other towns. The place Wallis Kreitar had gone to did not send anyone. The radiation sickness there had gotten worse with the passing hours.

As the minutes and miles ticked away, many in the small convoy wondered why they were on this mission into hell. But the time for questioning was now over. In less than five minutes they would be approaching Vista Royale. Sheriff Willem planned to drive to within 500 yards of the town, then park in the woods and envelop the place on foot in a pincers movement from the flanks. But, as they passed the half-mile mark, a motorcycle shot from the woods and raced down the road toward Vista Royale.

"Shoot the rider. Shoot him," Willem's voice boomed. Shots flew outward toward the fast-receeding biker. But the swiftly racing man wasn't even touched.

"Shit," Willem exclaimed as he led the cars off the road and got out. All the men crowded around him.

"What do we do now?" a brown-haired man in his 40s asked.

"We continue with the plan," Willem told Brian Salamuth.

As this quick conference was going on, the sentry rider reached town and spread the alarm. Rokmer came running. Zoyas suggested they take the fight to the enemy and not wait. Get them before they had a chance to mount an attack.

Rokmer agreed and led a charge of 20 picked bikers. The rest stayed and watched all the approaches on Main Street and on the flanks of Vista Royale. Huge rewards would be theirs if only they could hold on a while. Vista Royale was their base of operations and now had to be protected at all costs.

The angry, armed bikers raced into the wind, the roar of their bikes carrying through the air as they approached. Willem and his men, still standing around discussing their attack plan, heard, then saw the enemy coming. They broke formation and ran behind cars or sought shelter behind nearby trees as adrenalin pumped through veins and sweat ran down suddenly heated faces. This was it. Death was coming. Few of these men had served in the military. Only one had been in combat, Willem. The rest were rank amateurs. The only action they had seen was on TV and in the movies. But the bikers out there had been in the military, many of them in wars, and all were veterans of a score of battles in the alleys of half a dozen cities. They were no strangers to death.

Rokmer saw the invaders and signaled to his men, and they drove off the asphalt about 150 yards diagonally up the road from where Willem's force was. They drove into the tree line, got off their bikes, and began to advance through the woods with Rokmer leading the attack.

About 100 yards from the bunched cars they began to fire. The force from Montieth fired back. Quickly the smell of burned powder, the long smoke fingers of dozens of expended rounds, and the whiz of bullets barely missing heads, arms, and chests filled the air.

They mixed with the thunk of slugs going into cars, punching holes in metal, starring windows, and blasting open tires. Some of the men with Willem were so scared they fired off their ammunition wildly without hitting anything and soon had to reload.

The bikers were also scared, but less so, and were more controlled in their fire patterns. They continued to move behind cover till they were parallel to the force on the other side of the road.

The man next to Brian Salamuth, his 64-year-old neighbor, was hit in the head and groaned. Then he grabbed himself and fell down dead. Another man was then killed, and two more were wounded. So far none of the bikers had been hit. Then Willem took aim and hit a bullseye. A big, balding biker caught a round in the chest and went down spitting blood. He wasn't dead, but badly hurt. Willem aimed and fired. He hit another biker, this time in the calf. The man went down hard and grabbed at his leg. Salamuth took aim, pumped two rounds into the hoodlum, and killed him.

But the bikers weren't taking this lying down. They poured enough fire into a '79 Biscayne to star all the windows, ripping out great chunks of glass, and also killed one of the wounded lying on the ground. A slug then penetrated the gas tank and the car went up with a whoosh. It began to burn furiously, sending great clouds of white and black smoke rising as flames jumped up to lick the branches of an overhanging spruce.

Those who had been using the car as a protective barrier now rose and tried to run back toward the next car in line. Two of them, one being Vic Lunenberg, were killed outright. Another caught a bullet in the back and fell down screaming, "Medic, medic." There was no medic. He'd probably seen too many war movies."

The rest began to panic. "Let's get out of here," one of them shouted. That was all they needed. They began to pile into the remaining two civilian cars. And, as Willem screamed out for them to stand their ground, they fled. Only Willem, John Kritzler, and Ed "King" Kudner remained and fought.

Seeing this, the bikers began to advance. The three men pegged a number of rounds their way to get the enemy to keep their heads down. But all three of them knew they were outnumbered and doomed if they stayed. So they made a conscious decision to withdraw and grabbed the wounded man who had cried out for a medic. He now screamed louder because of the pain of being moved as he was rushed into the back seat of the police cruiser. They crawled to the other wounded man to get him but found that he was already dead. They then piled into the police car and fired a flurry of shots from the open windows as Willem got them the hell out of there. Slugs zinged into the trunk of the car and starred the rear window. Willem raced away hunkered down in his seat.

He returned to Montieth five minutes after the others did. The whole town was buzzing with news of the defeat. Willem was confronted by the mayor and a number of citizens. When he asked Kudner and Kritzler to get the wounded man from the back seat, they told Willem the man was dead. There was blood on the back seat and a pool of it on the floor of the car. The jolting 50-minute ride to Montieth hadn't helped any.

There was a lot of flack as Willem began to complain about how most of the people with him had deserted. Had they held, he said, the battle might have been won. The others, except for Kudner and Kritzler, countered that he had led them into a death trap.

Mayor Oppelin decided that under the circumstances there would be no more attacks against Vista Royale until further notice. But even if he had given permission for another attack, Willem had almost no one to help him. And Oppelin would now have trouble just getting people to guard Montieth. Those who had come from other towns now returned to them. The threat of imminent death had sobered a lot of people up. Talk of war is one thing. Going into combat is another.

Stack stood on the sidelines, listening to what was happening. Kurt Willem looked deeply troubled. A lot of people were now against him, as if he had brought them a tragedy that otherwise wouldn't have happened. And Mayor Oppelin pulled him aside twice to whisper things into his ear. Kurt Willem wiped sweat from his forehead as he took his hat off, using a big polka-dot handkerchief to do so. Stack felt sorry for him.

Finally, as things quieted down half an hour later, Willem noticed Stack, who called the sheriff aside and said, "Sorry about what happened. I took a nap in my van, but all the commotion as your people came back into town woke me. What I want to say is that if you need my help in the future, feel free to call on me."

Willem smiled grimly. "Where were you when I needed you?"

"I wasn't thinking when I refused you. I was tired. I'd been through a lot and didn't feel like helping anymore."

"And now, after a short nap, you're ready to help again?" Willem asked, acid dripping from his words.

"I'm sorry. Mea culpa. I'm guilty." Stack touched his chest. "I want to make it up to you. I know you're mad, but I didn't see what was about to occur. I'm no prophet, just human. And I've been shaken by this war as much as you've been shaken by what happened near Vista Royale."

Willem looked down at the ground a moment. "Okay, forget it. I'm sorry I was so hard on you. I've had a tough morning and a not much better afternoon. That's on top of this war and losing my brother."

"Sure, I understand."

Mayor Oppelin now interrupted as he called out to Willem, "Kurt. We've got some cases of nausea and diarrhea being reported."

"Those are the first signs of radiation sickness," Stack yelled back. "We had them down in Fresno during the night."

"How long did it last?" Oppelin wanted to know.

"Five, maybe six hours. I can't guarantee your people will have it as hard—or better. Only time will tell."

"Thanks for the information. Anything they can take for it?"

Stack shrugged. "I'm no doctor. Maybe home remedies. I don't know."

The streets of Vista Royale were festive. The bikers were drinking, drag-racing down Main Street, and enjoying their victory. Rokmer wasn't part of the festivities. He was in the bathroom of the house he had taken over, vomiting and suffering with diarrhea. Fear. Cold, clammy, stomach-wrenching fear had him by the gonads. This was the result of all the radiation that was spreading. How long would it last? Would it be fatal? He didn't know. And he wasn't alone. Some of the bikers, including Zoyas, had come down with the radiation sickness. The people of Vista Royale were also coming down with it. The bathrooms in the houses occupied by the people of the town were filled to capacity. The bikers had to move them into other houses to get more bathroom space.

Rokmer had called for the doctor. But all he could do for Rokmer and the others was prescribe aspirins and antacids. He had nothing with which to fight the plague.

No one knew how far this would go, or how deadly it could be. So everything was put on hold as they wrestled with this new dilemma. The bikers made the doctor treat them first, then he was allowed to treat the people of the town. Whenever anyone asked the doctor how long this would take and what the outcome would be, he shrugged. It might last an hour, or days. It might be mild, or fatal.

Toward evening Rokmer began to slowly recover. He still had chills and was feeling out of sorts. But he pulled himself together, got dressed, and went out to tour the town and give orders. A leader couldn't lie there on his back. Zoyas was one of those he visited. Rokmer thought he looked like one of the living dead.

Zoyas was laid out in the master bedroom of the house he had taken over down the block from Rokmer. There was a pillow under his head, his boots were off, and Debbie was trying to get him to drink some sugary tea. She looked worried. Zoyas was gasping and wheezing, having trouble breathing, shivering from all the chills passing through him, his skin tinted almost green. Rokmer spent only a short time with him, realizing Zoyas was of no use now and might not be of any use at all if this got worse.

Rokmer checked every place. The symptoms of radiation poisoning seemed to be abating somewhat, but were still bad. For every person who got better and was able to get about on somewhat wobbly legs, two more went under with the first symptoms of the sickness. It was a confusing, new, terrible world that he didn't understand.

And those weren't the only things bothering him. Rokmer decided to send out scouting parties to check on what was happening in nearby towns in order to discover if any new offensives were going to be mounted against the Bloodsuckers. Each reconnaisance team consisted of two motorcylists. His orders were that they hide their bikes in the woods outside town, then scout around on the fringes, looking for signs of armed men on patrol or gathered around vehicles ready to go someplace and attack somebody. If necessary, they were to take prisoners to bring back to Vista Royale for questioning about what was going on.

It was after dark when one of these patrols reached Montieth. It consisted of Angel Tortellino, a tall, darkskinned, pimply-faced, black-haired biker in his middle 20s, and Todd Zenthelm, a blonde Viking with a red face and steely blue eyes.

They spied with skill and stealth, moving carefully through the forested night, silently pushing aside branches, moving noiselessly over leaves and pine needles, studying everything there was to be seen in Montieth. The lit streets, the yellow of shaded windows against the greater blackness of night, the cars parked along the curbs, the men with guns who patrolled here and there, the refreshment table that was still open, the park, the meat truck, Sheriff Willem, and the dark-haired, tanned man who walked with him.

Now that they had seen it all, they would grab a hostage who would talk and tell them about how things were in Montieth. Coming along one deserted side street were two teenagers, Rayisa Gilchrist and Nancy Winston—one of the girls she had befriended.

Tortellino pointed to them and the Viking gave him a wicked smile. Young stuff. They could question them, then have their fun. Rokmer did not say who to bring back, just someone. And a young one was as good as an old one. A young one would also scare faster and talk sooner. Yeah. The two bikers emerged from the woods and headed down the dark side street along the block opposite the one the girls were on. They walked till they drew parallel with their intented victims, then crossed over, moving between cars.

The girls, deep in discussion, did not notice them coming till the last second. They stopped walking, questioning looks on their faces, studying the two men who headed toward them. With that primitive warning system the body has, they instinctively realized this was danger on the hoof and began to run. But the men were faster. Tortellino grabbed Rayisa. The Viking grabbed Nancy, but lost his grip. She ran as fast as her legs could move, faster than ever in her life. So fast the landscape became a blur of motion. She did not stop till she reached her house and began ringing the bell and pounding on the front door.

But Rayisa had been captured and heaved over Tortellino's shoulders. He held her by the legs, her face and head over his lower back. "Forget about the other bitch," he gasped at the Viking. "We've got our prisoner. Come on." Rayisa found her voice and cried out. The bikers began running, hoping to reach the woods, their bikes, and the safety of the open road before the alarm spread and the townspeople came down on them, hard.

Rayisa screamed for help with the deep-down fear of someone being carried off to a fate worse than death. She screamed harder than ever in her life. Lights came on, windows went up, heads peeked out. The world for her was an upside-down blur of running feet, trees, cars, and lawns flying past. And then, before she knew it, they were into the woods, branches striking it and scratching her.

She continued to cry out despite the fact that her throat hurt, her lungs were on fire, and her head felt like a ton because of all the blood which had run down into it. "Someone help me, please," she yelled over and over. "I'm being kidnapped. Come get me. I'm in the woods." She repeated it till her mouth hurt. They had reached the motorcycles by then.

Tortellino put her down a second as he got onto his bike. Rayisa wanted to run, but her head was swimming. Before she could recover enough to do anything, he forced her onto the bike, making her sit in front of him, his arms on either side of her on the handlebars. And then they began to move out of there, rolling along a dirt trail which turned to grass. Suddenly they were on the highway, racing off into the endless night.

16

The alarm was sounded throughout Montieth. Mothers pulled children off streets. Armed guards grew more vigilant. A crowd filled the two-block stretch where the girl had been abducted. Sheriff Willem came running. Mrs. Caudell heard what had happened and ran to tell Nick Stack. Together, they hurried to Sheriff Willem's side and found him heading for the woods.

"Wait, I'm going with you," Stack said. Willem nodded agreement and together they plunged into the undergrowth and darkness, the sheriff using his flashlight as they made their way wildly forward, not really knowing where they were going, just moving, listening for the sound of a human voice, or screams above the racket they were making. But nothing came back to them except the noise of the woods at night and the rustle of their own feet flailing through the undergrowth amid the tom-tom beat of their overworked hearts.

After a hundred feet Sheriff Willem stopped, as did Stack. Willem swung the flashlight in a wide arc, then said, "I'm afraid they're long gone. And in these woods," he put his arms out, then dropped them to his sides, "we're sure to find nothing."

"Who do you think it was? The bunch from Vista Royale?"

"None other. First they take over a whole town, and kill my brother and who knows how many others during the process, then they begin kidnapping human beings from other towns."

Willem headed out of the woods. Stack followed. "Will we at least organize a posse to go get her?"

"I'll try."

Hot rage filled Stack. "You'll try," he yelled. "A girl's been taken and you'll try?"

Willem stopped and turned around. Stack stopped too, his face red, his breathing deep and angry so that his chest heaved up and down.

"Look, mister. We attempted to get into that town, and we got screwed but good. I couldn't get many people to come with me in the beginning and those that did punked out when the going got tough. Do you think they'll go back just because one girl got taken? It's her ass, not theirs."

Stack shook his head as if he didn't believe this, not knowing what to say, then asked, "Why do you think they took her?"

"She was available and maybe the guy who kidnapped her liked young girls. Who knows?" Willem turned and continued leaving the forest. Stack followed, his face dark and hard, a mean, smouldering look in his eyes.

He had not realized how much the girl meant to him till then. She reminded him of his daughter back home. And now she was gone. Taken by beasts. Well, he would not let this go by.

As they emerged from the forest, Mayor Oppelin ran up to Willem, the mayor just having been informed of this latest disaster. Before he could say anything, Stack shoved himself between the two men and demanded a posse be raised to go to Vista Royale and rescue the kidnapped girl.

Willem agreed to go along, but the mayor said, "I can't let you go, Kurt. We need you here. You're our only law. The only man we can depend on." Willem wanted to protest, but Mayor Oppelin held up a hand, then turned to Stack.

"I'm sorry. What was done was dastardly. But she's only one person, and I've got to see to the protection of an entire town. You saw what happened—or rather you heard what happened when we tried to free Vista Royale—and you saw the aftermath as the survivors came back. We just can't do anything. She'll have to remain in their hands for now."

"Remain in their hands!" Stack exploded. Willem put a restraining arm on his left shoulder. Stack did not move from his place and talked on. "Do you have any idea of what monsters like that could do to her in the meanwhile?"

"I know. I know. But what can I do?" Mayor Oppelin put his hands out, palms up, and shrugged, then dropped his arms to his sides. Finally he said, "Look, if you can get some volunteers, you're free to try and get her back. But I can't really help. I will, though, put out an appeal for volunteers."

He walked away, leaving Stack deflated. But Stack would not let this get him down. Determined to act, he called out to all those standing there, asking for volunteers. No one was eager to help. The fear in their eyes, the indecision on their faces made him sick to his stomach. He turned to Stuart Caudell.

"Will you come?"

Caudell began to stammer. This was the real thing, and people got killed when they acted for real. "I'm not sure. I'm too old. I don't even know how to use a gun."

His wife chimed in, "Stuart can't come. I'm sorry, but we need him here. What if he were killed? What would Brad and I do?" She put an arm around her son. "This is going to be a frightening world after the bombs. A woman with a young son, without a man, won't survive for long. I need Stuart. I'm sorry." Caudell wanted to speak, but fell silent and hung his head.

Brad then stepped forward. "I'll go. I'm not afraid to fight, Mr. Stack. I like Rayisa. She's my friend."

"No," his mother said and pulled him back. "He's

just a boy," she stammered. "A boy who'd get killed going up against those monsters."

Stack was disgusted. Nor did he know what to say against her reasoning, which sounded as if it made such sense right then. Confused, shocked, stunned, not really knowing what to do, he headed toward Main Street to find Sheriff Willem, who'd walked off during his talk with the Caudells. He didn't see him, but learned that Willem was in Oppelin's office five buildings down the street on the right. Stack walked in without knocking and found them sitting there, the mayor behind his desk, Willem in front of it. Both had pained, troubled looks on their faces.

"Any results?" Stack wanted to know.

"Nothing," Willem said with a shake of his head.

"No one volunteered?"

"You have to understand, Mr. Stack," Oppelin began, "these people aren't bad. They're just scared. They've never faced anything like this before."

"Neither have I," Stack said, pointing to himself. "But I'm ready to act. They should have guts. Where's the old saying? 'When the going gets tough, the tough get going'? Or are these people just all talk?"

"No, they're not all talk. But sometimes they reel a bit after a hard slam across the head."

"Then at least let Sheriff Willem accompany me."

"I can't. I'm sorry." He looked down. Then he looked up. "You talk about the tough getting going when the going gets hard. Why not do this yourself?"

"I intend to if there's no other choice."

"It might be better that way. They wouldn't be expecting one man. Do you know your way around the woods?"

"Yes."

"Have you got weapons?"

"A Savage 99F hunting rifle that holds a five-bullet clip, plus additional ammunition and various knives."

"Have you had commando training?"

"I was in the National Guard, I also took some commando courses."

"Well, they should come in handy now. Good luck."

"The same goes here," Willem said. "I wish I could go along. But in the end I'm a public servant. I must listen to the mayor or be removed."

Stack said nothing as he turned, walked from the office, and headed for his van. On the way there he spotted Stuart Caudell. Caudell wanted to explain himself, but Stack waved it away. He was disgusted with Caudell. He didn't want to listen to anymore reasons why anyone couldn't or didn't want to fight. He just wanted to get away from there, find Rayisa, and bring her back. His course decided on, he got behind the wheel of his van and started the motor. Caudell ran up to the van, but Stack pulled out and headed for the highway leaving the other man behind as he screamed out, "Wait, Nick. Let me explain. I can explain all this."

The lights and sounds of Montieth and the voice of Stuart Caudell died away as the blackness of the forested wilderness enveloped the van and its rider. In the far distance a red rim in the sky showed where the coastal fires burned on. But he looked mainly at the road ahead and formulated his plans of attack. If he went in hot and heavy, he would die. They had the numbers and the guns. He would have to ride herd on his temper, call on all the skills accumulated in a lifetime of mostly civilian and sometimes military pursuits, and employ them against an enemy that had a numerical advantage.

The van chewed up the miles and gradually the glow of Vista Royale, which lit up the low cloud cover, became visible. It was drizzling as he drove the van off the highway and up a dirt road into the woods. When he had driven far enough to hide the van he parked and got out.

He had expected a guard along the road from the

experience Willem and his men had had earlier. So he avoided approaching too close to town. Now he took out his knives, rifle, and ammunition. The rifle he hung by a leather strap over his shoulder. The sheathed knives went onto his waistbelt. Then he filled all his pockets with bullets and loaded clips. Stack also took along a compass with the direction marks painted on the face of the instrument in luminescent paint.

Now that he had everything, he headed off the road into the trees, moving with slow caution, allowing his vision to get used to the night, noticing the pairs of eyes which watched him, listening to the sounds of the nocturnal creatures stalking or being stalked. There was not a lot of underbrush in this section, so he was able to make swifter progress than expected. Some of the falling rain struck his determined, unsmiling face. But most of it coated the roof of the forest and trickled down the gnarled bark of slicked tree trunks. He wondered, as he went along, how much radiation there was in the rain. He couldn't guess, and in the end it didn't matter. There was a mission ahead which he had to fulfill.

He did not look at his watch during the trek through the woods. The worst thing one could do was constantly look at a watch. It made one nervously anticipate the end of the trek and every step would seem a hundred times harder and the trip a dozen times longer as a result.

He ached for a cigarette, but dared not light up for fear of attracting notice. A light in the woods could be seen a long way off. More time passed. And then, before he knew it, he had reached the edge of the forest along the left flank of Vista Royale. Most of the houses were dark. Stack guessed the reason was that most of the inhabitants of the town had been herded into just a few buildings so they could be more easily watched and controlled. That's how he would have done it.

Still inside the forest, he moved along the edge of town studying every street, every house, every guard on every corner within sight. When he had eyeballed the entire left flank, he moved north, through the woods, away from town, till he came to a dark stretch of road. Then he raced across it back into the forest. He approached the other flank of town through the trees and again studied the streets and houses. When he had seen all there was to see he went a bit deeper into the woods and sat down against a broad pine to rest up, running all the details he had witnessed through his mind while he made his plans.

About 15 minutes passed as he rested up and completed his attack plan. Then Stack rose and moved along the fringe of the forest till he came to a backyard that was particularly overgrown with bushes. He emerged from the trees, looking left and right, then moved from bush to bush till he was against the back of the house to which the yard belonged. No one seemed to be inside. But two houses to his right there was light and noise.

He slipped across a number of narrow alleys and backyards till he reached the yard belonging to the house from which all the noise and light came.

The rain was falling fairly heavily now, wetting his hair, running down his cheeks, collecting on his chin, falling off onto the khaki of his hunting clothes, making his hands slippery wet. Just then the back door came open.

A big, bearded, wild-haired biker in his 20s, with a hard face and mean eyes to match, stepped out of the warmth and light of the kitchen and tossed a bag full of garbage into the backyard. Stack stood two feet away jammed against the wall of the house. Then, as the biker turned to go back in, he spotted the intruder. Their eyes locked for one second.

"What the hell are you doin' here?" the biker growled as he stepped forward, moving away from the lit rectangle of the open doorway into the darkness and the rain.

Stack moved away from the wall, swung both hands

up, and, before the biker could respond, clapped them down hard on both sides of the man's head over his ears. As the palms landed, hard, the force of air rammed back in burst the biker's eardrums and sent a gush of purple pain through his head so that he screwed his eyes shut as his hands rose to his head. But they never got there. Stack let his hands fall away and made two fists, which he brought up hard, directly under the biker's chin. The double thud rammed the man up on his toes as his head flew back. He reeled back several feet and went down. Stack raced forward, one of his hunting knives out, and jumped on the biker, jamming a palm over his mouth so he could not cry out as Stack began to ram the knife, again and again, into the big, greasy body under him. Some of stabs were deflected or stopped by the leather jacket he wore. But most of them went through the chest and abdomen and into the neck. Stack stoped himself before the killing frenzy took over completely. He was acting in fear and pent-up tension and realized it as he rose and looked down at the blood shooting in jerking streams from the still-warm and twitching body on the ground. Stack then looked down at himself and saw the blood smears across his chest, legs, and arms. He accepted that as something which could not be avoided, and wiped off the bloodied knife on the clothes of the dead man and returned it to one of the four sheaths he wore around his belt.

Stack quickly walked over to the open doorway and looked in. No one was in the kitchen, but he heard voices from other parts of the house. He stepped into the kitchen and with a quickly beating heart closed the door behind him. Then he went up the hall leading from the kitchen to the living room. There was music in the living room, probably from a cassette player, and laughing voices and sharp orders being barked at people. Stack spotted a closet to his left, opened the door, stepped inside, pressed against clothing on racks, smelled the odor of camphor balls, and shut the door almost all the way—except for a small crack. Through it he watched a harassed, frightened woman being driven from the living room into the kitchen by a tough, redheaded, red-bearded thug who ordered her to make more sandwiches. Stack heard the refrigerator being opened and shut.

Then he heard the biker asking where Ralphie was. "Perhaps," he said to a girl biker who walked into the kitchen, "Ralphie's gone outside for some fresh air."

"In all that rain?"

"I guess not. Maybe he's upstairs," the biker said.

In a few minutes they all left the kitchen with the woman holding a stack of freshly made sandwiches on a tray. "Good," someone cried out as she entered the living room. A young boy's voice asked if he could have something to eat because he was hungry too.

"Later, you slimy fuck," a gang member told him. "First we eat."

Stack decided that staying in the house was too dangerous. He stepped from the closet, closed the door, and headed into the kitchen toward the back door. Once outside, he closed the door and moved toward the body of Ralphie. It would not be good if they found the body just yet. That would alert them that someone they didn't want was in town. Battling all those goons while he was trying to find Rayisa was not what he had in mind for this rainy night.

Stack pulled the dead man into the bushes, then made his way across yards till he came to the next occupied house. He didn't think Rayisa was in the house he had entered. They had taken her for a reason. And because of that, they would probably have her in a separate place and not with a large group of people.

He went around the rear and sides of the house, peeking through unshaded windows to see who was there. Lots of frightened people, but not one was his Rayisa. Stack peeked into the street. A biker was moving past slowly on his motorcycle, looking along both blocks to see if all was well. Then he turned a corner and drove away. Stack hurried out along the driveway, then crossed the sidewalk and street to the opposite block. He rushed across a lawn, then between two houses, and repeated his forays across a number of yards as he spied through the windows of occupied houses. It was time-consuming work that eroded his hopes and filled him with images of frightened people and arrogant, strutting gang members who thought they had the world by the tail. And in a way they did.

He went to the next house he planned to spy on and began peeking into windows all over again, being careful to use no more than one eye so that only a quarter of his head would show. He kept each peek down to three seconds or less to minimize the danger of being spotted.

He looked into the living room, saw no one, and then the kitchen, which was also empty. Then he looked into the downstairs bedroom, aware that if he did not find anything there, he would have to check the upstairs rooms there and with every house he had checked so far. But not till he finished looking at all the likely places in town.

When Stack peered through the fourth window, he spotted a man in Air Force overalls. A biker, holding a rifle, was with him. The airman sat tensely on a chair. The biker was more relaxed, one leg crossed over the other, the rifle crosswise on his lap, his finger on the trigger. He was drinking a beer, a sneer on his lips every time he took the beer from his mouth. For two cents Stack would have wiped the sneer off his face. But that wasn't his task. He had many choices, only one of which he had come here to exercise. The liberation of Rayisa Gilchrist.

Stack went to the next window in line and froze. Rayisa was inside, buck-naked and crying. Two bikers were on either side of her, each holding an arm straight out so that she was held as if crucified, unable to get away. She was facing the window and behind her, swinging a long black-leather strap, stood a laughing biker. There was a sharp crack each time the leather connected with her back or buttocks, causing her to arch forward as a scream was torn from her lips. "No, no," she gasped and shuddered, almost as if this had been going on too long and now she could no longer control her will to resist or cry out.

As the strap cracked down again across her naked flesh and made the girl arch up and cry out, he realized he was glued to the window and pulled away. He was forgetting himself, he realized. If he allowed what was happening to affect him and did not act professionally, exercising self-control, he would blow this and wind up dead, and Rayisa would not escape all the things fate held in store for her.

"Will you cooperate?" someone inside the room asked.

"Yes, anything. Please just don't use the belt anymore. I'm only 14. Nobody's ever beaten me this way before. Why are you hitting me? I never did anything to you."

"Shaddup," the same person as before snarled. This was followed by the crack of a hand connecting with flesh. Rayisa began to sob.

"On your knees, bitch," the voice ordered.

Stack peeked in again. With one hand Rayisa was rubbing her face and with the other hand her behind as she alternately hissed and sobbed. When the girl turned sideways, Stack saw the swollen welts across her backside and the red mark on her face.

"On your knees," a big, dark-haired, heavily bearded hooligan repeated as he put the belt back on his pants. He made a motion as if he might take it off again. She quickly got on her knees.

Stack pulled himself from the window even though what he was seeing had frozen him in his tracks. "Do something," he whispered under his breath, and began moving along the house, looking for a way in, trying to move cautiously. But hate, shock, and a rapidly increasing heartbeat moved him along quickly. He came to a door. Locked, dammit! Then he saw a half-open window. He tugged and the window came all the way up. Stack climbed in, aware that if someone entered the room at that moment he would be at a disadvantage, his head down and half his body hanging out the window.

But no one entered, and he was soon inside, taking the Savage off his shoulder and moving forward cautiously, listening for any movement in the house. He looked into the hallway, and from a room down on the right heard Rayisa begging for mercy one last time, followed by silence, then the sounds of a biker gasping. That meant she was giving him sex. Stack wanted to rush forward in anger. But he held back. Lose your temper and you lose your head, he told himself. With that, he stepped out into the hall and headed toward the room where Rayisa was being held captive.

Stack came to an L, with the base of it going left to the room where the military man was. But straight ahead, through a slightly open door, he could see the girl on her knees, giving the biker oral sex. Stack quickly looked back up the hall to make sure no one was sneaking up from behind while his attention was focused on the scene ahead.

Stack no longer had any choice as to how he would proceed. He would have to move fast and take out everyone in that house. It would mean making a lot of noise and alerting others that an intruder was inside Vista Royale. But that was what separated the men from the boys.

Stack watched her mouth glide along the swollen shaft of the biker whose pants were now down around his knees. The biker's head was back and his eyes were shut tight. The goon was in heaven. His hisses filled the air.

Stack grew very cold now. He aimed the rifle at the base of the thick shaft. Then, as Rayisa pulled back, letting the hoodlum out of her mouth, almost to the tip of the cobra-hood head, Stack fired. The sound of the shot reverberated in the hallway as the goon's shaft disintegrated into strips of bloodied meat and hundreds of flying droplets of blood. Rayisa screamed as she drew back, the stub of his now-destroyed manhood falling from her mouth, while blood jerked from the crotch of the screaming hoodlum, who was quickly going to his knees.

As this was happening the biker from the room down the hall, on the left, moved into action. At the same time, the door just ahead jerked open and two stunned bikers advanced toward Stack. One was going for the gun in his belt. Stack let him have a round in the upper chest. The biker grabbed himself as he went down gushing blood. Stack then swung his rifle and pumped a round into the head of the second man. The bullet plowed through hard bone, then into softer brain tissue underneath. All this happened in under two seconds. And then he wheeled around the corner to confront the biker who had raced from the room into the hall at the end of the L. The biker got off a wild shot, which chewed into the wall three feet above Stack's head. A second later, almost as if in slow motion, Stack pumped round number four into the running hoodlum. As the biker began to fall, a grimace of pain on his lips, Stack heard feet racing down the stairs at the front of the house.

He spun around as two men, one with a rifle, the other with a Saturday Night Special, and a half-clothed girl behind him, flew from the bottom of the stairs into the hall.

Stack fired the last round in his clip and watched plaster fly as he swung around the corner of the L. Then, once behind cover, he ejected the old clip and rammed another into the rifle. When he peered out for a look wild shots came his way. Stack moved back, letting them fire at will. Once they stopped, he knelt down to present a lower target than expected, leaned out, and fired three times, fast, evenly spaced across the width of the hallway. There was some return fire as he swung back behind the protection of his corner. But one of the attackers had taken a round in the abdomen and another had barely missed having his forehead turned into a radiator.

Stack popped into view, then pulled right back again as a volley of shots tried to catch him. Within seconds he heard what he had been waiting for. The hoodlum who had not been hit experienced the clicking which tells every gunman he's out of ammunition and needs to reload. And while the biker frantically tried to get bullets from his pockets, he saw Stack appear and tried to flee. But flying rounds have always been faster than running legs. The biker took two bullets. One in the neck, one in the upper back. He went down gushing blood, strangling as he drowned in his own life fluids. The woman next to him went down on her knees. "Frankie, Frankie," she screamed, trying to get him to breathe, to talk. But he was already halfway gone.

Stack didn't stay to watch. He ran to the room around the corner of the L, from which the gunman had come, and saw the military man emerging, after at first holding back, and going for the dead hooligan's gun.

"Grab it and come with me," Stack said, not having time to explain. Lance Briggs grabbed the rifle from the dead biker as Stack ran into the room where Rayisa was and found her sobbing hysterically in one corner. He looked at the bikers, two of whom were wounded but still alive. He picked up one of their guns, then pumped a round into the head of each man, killing them. Without wasting a second, Stack ran back into the hall to kill the biker who had been wounded near the stairs. The girl, trying to revive her dead friend nearby, looked up in fear. But Stack did not shoot her.

Instead, he grabbed the guns on the floor and any ammunition the dead men had on them and shouted at Briggs to do the same. Then he raced back to Rayisa, found her clothes in a pile on the floor, grabbed them, and hoisted the nude, crying girl over his right shoulder.

"No time to let her dress now," he explained to Briggs. "We've got to get the hell out of here before all hell breaks loose." The airman nodded in agreement as Stack pulled up the window, sat the hysterical, sobbing girl down on the sill, and climbed out, trying to make sure he didn't drop any guns as he did so. Once on the ground, he grabbed Rayisa around the waist and pulled her out. Briggs came next.

Stack, carrying Rayisa, and Briggs raced across the yard into the woods. Out in front of the house, bikers were riding past, trying to ascertain where the shots had come from. Others raced into various houses. Two of them ran into the house Stack had attacked and found carnage as they sprinted from room to room. Then one looked out the rear window into the yard and thought he saw movement in the woods beyond. He climbed out the window and ran across the yard. At the edge of the woods, none to eager to go in and get what the other bastards had gotten, he stood and tried to peer into the darkness, but saw nothing.

A hundred feet in, Stack and Briggs stopped and dressed Rayisa. Stack kissed her on the forehead. "Calm down. Soon you'll be away from this terrible place and things will be made good again."

She was shivering, but cognizant of what he was saying. Stack didn't believe his own words and was only saying them to calm her down and offer hope. In reality, he didn't think she'd ever be the same again, but hoped against all hope that things would be better some days from now.

"Can you walk?" he whispered. "Answer in a low voice. Sounds travel and we don't want the devils back there," he nodded toward where they'd come from, "to know where we are and come after us."

"I can walk," she said, then embraced him in fear.

He patted her on the back. "Don't worry. You're safe now. Come."

They headed off through the woods to where the van was, with Stack using his compass. Briggs didn't talk. He followed Stack and the girl, casting occasional glances at the trail behind them.

Stack moved across the darkness, his eyes watching the terrain ahead and the ground underfoot, while his ears listened to the far-off sounds of motorcycles racing across streets and a town being checked for the whereabouts of the now-vanished intruders. And yet Stack's mind wasn't on all these things. It played back what had happened in the house. Everything had gone down so fast he didn't have time to think about it. Under stress he had almost become another person. He had attacked the bikers out of hate and a need to save the girl. But doing that, he had crossed a bridge he would never be able to cross back. And yet Stack did not regret his deeds. All he felt was a terrible, empty numbness. Had he been asked that morning if he could do such things, Stack would have answered no. But, coming to this place, he had learned something about himself, almost as if he were standing outside his body looking down at this stranger who had been living inside him all these years and now had emerged. And this was a stranger he would have to continue living with from now on.

But the discovery did not trouble him greatly. A state of acceptance filled him. Having realized all these things, he forgot about the recent past and concentrated all his attention on the job ahead.

When they reached the van, he put the guns in back and told Briggs, "Keep one and some ammunition. You might need it. The other guns will come in handy so we can arm more people to oppose those bastards back in Vista Royale."

They got into the van, Rayisa next to him and Briggs next to her. The dirt road the van sat on wasn't wide enough to turn around in, so Stack slowly backed out, the bumpy ride tossing them up and down in their seats. Once on the highway they headed quickly away from there, Stack looking into the rearview mirror to see if any motorcycles were coming in pursuit. But the road behind them remained empty.

Stack looked at Rayisa. "You all right?" She nodded

up and down. "We'll talk more once we get to Montieth." She nodded again without speaking.

Then he said to Briggs, "My name's Nick Stack. What's yours?" Briggs told him. Stack then said, "You look like an airman. What brought you to Vista Royale?"

Briggs quickly related his story about the bombing mission that had gone bad and the B-52 now parked on a deserted airstrip. He explained how he had been captured by The Bloodsuckers after being sent to find help, and the plans Rokmer had for the plane and the bombs it contained. Plans which had been shelved for now because of the outbreak of radiation sickness.

"Shit!" Stack exclaimed, cold sweat breaking out across his forehead. "If those bastards get hold of the bombs on that plane we're all dead. They've got to be stopped immediately. How many people do you have guarding the plane?"

"Five."

"That's nothing. Once those bikers make their move your people will die fast and they'll have the bomber."

"Even worse," Briggs added, "is that they might start a fire during the gunplay, which will set off a fuel explosion and trigger the bombs. They're set to blow. Normally there are seven locking mechanisms which have to be opened, one after the other, before the warheads will detonate. But once they're set to go, like now, all the locking mechanisms are open."

"That's all this place needs, a multi-nuclear-bomb detonation."

"Even if we weren't killed by the blasts," Briggs explained, "we'd die from the downwind radiation, or the huge forest fires set off, which would catch people everywhere. They wouldn't be able to flee fast enough."

The van took on speed as Stack raced through the night. He cast glances at Rayisa, who was barely aware of what was happening. She had her own internal conflageration. One that wouldn't go away with the coming of morning.

Few words were exchanged during the rest of the trip. When they pulled into Montieth, Sheriff Willem was waiting, leaning against his police cruiser, near the refreshment table. Only now the table was empty and most of the town was off the street.

Stack brought the van to a halt, got out, and went over to Willem, who looked questioningly at him, then at the van where Rayisa and Briggs still sat. He wondered who the military man was.

But now his attention turned to Stack. "You did it?" he asked in an incredulous voice. Stack nodded. Willem looked at him with new respect. "You're all right. With a guy like you on our side, maybe our problems aren't so big. Care to be my deputy?"

"Anytime. As for our problems not being so large, I'm afraid they've just begun."

Willem lost the smile on his face. "What do you mean?"

"That guy in the van," Stack nodded back toward Briggs, "is from a B-52 which landed at a deserted airfield several hours drive from here. It's full of primed H-bombs which the bikers want so they can be kings of the mountains."

"Goddam!" Willem's face fell. "We gotta go see the mayor. Things could get real mean damn fast."

"That's what I've been thinking and would've suggested if you hadn't. We've got to see Mayor Oppelin immediately. We'll take Briggs—that's his name—with us. But before we go I need to have a doctor look at the girl."

"What's wrong with her?" Willem asked, looking beyond Stack to the van. Stack quickly told him the whole story.

"Those guys are bastards of the worst sort," Willem said. "It'll be a better world when they've been removed from it."

"First we have to remove them."

"Let's go see the mayor. Take the girl along. We'll get the doctor to look at her."

Willem and Stack went to the van, opened the door on Briggs's side, then asked him and the girl to come with them. Willem started to pat Rayisa on the head. He wanted to ask how she was, but quickly pulled his hand back when he saw her cringe at his touch. He cast a quick glance at Stack, who'd seen the girl's reaction, but said nothing.

They went straight to Oppelin's office in a small building about a block away. Willem had them sit in the waiting room while he knocked, opened the door, and went right in. There was a whole lot of talking, the words unclear through the wooden door. But a few minutes later the door came open and both men stepped out. Oppelin looked grim. He tried to manage a smile for Rayisa's sake, but didn't bring it off very well.

"I'm going to get the doctor," he told Stack. Then he looked at Rayisa and, in a very gentle voice, said, "Our town doctor will take you to his office where you can talk to him. Then he'll give you an examination and a sedative so you can sleep through the night. You'll feel better in the morning."

She nodded without blinking.

"I understand you've made friends with one of the girls in town."

"Yes, her name is Nancy."

"I know Nancy. Let me talk to her mother. I'm sure you could stay at her house for the night. How'd you like that?"

"I'd like it fine," Rayisa said without much enthusiasm, speaking and acting almost like an automaton. The horror of what she'd undergone, the vile thing she'd been made to do, then the maiming and death of the biker she was fellating and the others in the room with him had been almost more than her senses could encompass and her emotions digest.

Oppelin then excused himself and left to get the

doctor. Stack took out his cigarettes and offered butts to Briggs and Willem, who declined. Stack then smoked alone. No one said anything as they stood there and waited for Oppelin to come back with the doctor, who would take Rayisa away. After which they could get down to men's business.

The hunt for the intruder or intruders in Vista Royale had come up dry. And now Lyle Rokmer had called a war council. Lance Briggs was gone. The secret of what they wanted to do was out. They would have to act quickly, he realized, or their ace in the hole would be taken before they knew it.

"Get the men together. We're going out to the airfield to take that plane over now," Rokmer told Zoyas.

"How many men?" Zoyas asked, looking at the confused, sweaty, slightly red face of his leader.

"What do you mean, how many?" Rokmer asked, a bit confused. The first time Zoyas had seen him like that in a long time.

"Ten, twenty? How many? Don't forget, we have to leave people here to guard this place and keep the population in check."

"Right," the other man said, almost as if his mind were too tense for him even to think of that possibility. Then he said, "Pick twenty men. Our best. I'll personally lead the attack. You stay here and run Vista Royale."

"Can't I go?"

"I want you here," Rokmer said, and looked him in the eyes. "I need a competent man to run things."

"Send me and stay here."

"No. This is too important. I have to lead the attack myself. If those bozos hit the plane it'll go up and good-bye bombs. I'm going to have to cue them in on how to fight this. And it's not just the bombs I'm concerned about. That plane contains forty thousand gallons of fuel." His eyes sparkled. "You know how much that is? It can power our bikes for a year. Now go do what I said." Rokmer turned and picked up the pack of cigarettes on the table near his bed. Zoyas nodded and without another word left the room, then the house.

All around the dark shadow of the B-52, camouflaged darkness in the greater darkness of the wilderness night, on and off the runway, at five equidistant points, were bomber crewmen armed with Colt .45 handguns. Each man alone with his thoughts. Some of them merely nervous, others much too tense. Being alone in this great silence was more than they could take. To be alone was to think, and to think was to die a little. Too many things which had remained hidden in all the long, hard hours when they had been together in the air were now coming out like worms wiggling up from the innards of dark, moist soil into the sunlight of day. Brad Osseville was probably the most troubled of all. But each had their concerns, and the biggest one at the moment was the whereabouts of Lance Briggs. He should have been back with help by now. What had happened?

Mayor Oppelin's office was thick with smoke and concerned men. It reminded Stack of the mythical smoke-filled rooms politicians inhabited during conventions. He wanted to smile, but the gravity of the moment never allowed the smile to come to his lips. Oppelin now began to speak.

"I've called certain people to this place without announcing to the whole town what Lieutenant Briggs," he nodded toward the flyer, "told me. I didn't want to create an alarm that would set off a stampede out of here and spread in stages to other towns and villages. Instead I've decided to trust key people. I'm asking all of you to volunteer for this assignment because we no longer have any choice. Time is running out for us as it is for everyone. I know what I'm asking each of you to do is dangerous. But the cost of not doing anything has risen. A number of you made the attack on Vista Royale, which failed. But that doesn't count now. This time you must succeed. And so I'm asking you to volunteer again. Please don't refuse this request."

He eyed each of them, knowing he could count on Briggs, Kudner, Kritzler, Willem, and Stack. But the others, six of them, might waver. And that wouldn't be good.

Oppelin put out the cigarette he was smoking and lit another. He waited for their answers, and they weren't long in coming. Brian Salamuth volunteered first, then his next-door neighbor, then two more men, and finally the rest. Men like Willem and Stack didn't need to volunteer. They already had.

"Good. I'm glad to see we'll have at least eleven men to go and fight for freedom," Oppelin said.

"That's not enough," Brian Salamuth pointed out. "We had more yesterday and lost."

Oppelin nodded. "But we have Mr. Stack now," he pointed him out, "and he did pretty well earlier on. With his help we'll be able to push this thing over the top. And don't forget, you'll have the five-man crew back at the plane to help you."

"What about more volunteers," Salamuth's neighbor, a fat, hard-faced man, asked. "We can go to other towns and get more people—"

"There isn't time," Briggs said, cutting him off. "We have to act now. Do you think those bikers are delaying putting their plans into action?"

"He's right," Stack added.

"Then we'd better get going, gentlemen," Willem announced as he rose.

"I still wish we had more people," Salamuth told him.

"We don't," Stack said. "And when we don't, we make do with what we have. That's what I did. And you know the results." He pointed to Briggs, and added, "There's a little girl who's sleeping now, who would have been through a lot worse than she experienced if I hadn't acted."

HELL RIDE

Still only half-convinced, Salamuth shook his head and announced, "I'm going into this with both eyes open, but I don't think we're in for an easy ride."

"I never said this would be easy," Stack replied.

Doctor Ozeron drove Rayisa to the Winston home. He had been over there half an hour earlier, before he'd examined the girl. Now Nancy and her Mom and Dad waited. Doctor Ozeron had already explained everything to them. They stood there with strained smiles on faces which tried to be gentle. Rayisa understood what they were doing and tried to smile back as she walked toward the house, confused, scared, yawning from the sedative the doctor had given her. In that moment the images of what she had gone through—the kidnapping, the beating, the deaths, the escape, the ride back in the van, the doctor's cold, probing hands, his embarrassing questions, her shame, her feelings of being violated, made so small and vulnerable—came to her in a rush. And the warmth and friendliness which emanated from the house reminded her of how life had been and now no longer was, and how things had been before this horrible war came and put Rayisa in her present state.

And then Doctor Ozeron was saying, "Here she is," as he brought her up to the open doorway, one hand over her shoulders. Before she knew it, Rayisa was being welcomed inside, with Doctor Ozeron coming along into the parlor. Mrs. Winston bent down, the pained smile still on her face as she asked if Rayisa wanted some milk and cookies. But she didn't. She yawned and just wanted to sleep. Dark, wonderful sleep. It would take her away from this nightmare and allow her to forget for a while what had happened. Mrs. Winston, with Nancy tagging along and prattling on about how much fun they would have together, led Rayisa to the room reserved for her and explained it had belonged to Nancy's older sister before she moved away to work in Lake Tahoe. Then Nancy began to prattle on again about all the things they would do now that

Rayisa was under the same roof, but a look from her mother shut the girl up for the time being.

From somewhere in the house, Rayisa heard Doctor Ozeron and Mr. Winston talking in serious tones, though the words were mumbled. She suppossed it was about her, but didn't care. She was so tired and wanted nothing more than to lose herself in the oblivion of sleep as the sedative took a stronger hold on her body. And then she was undressing, telling Nancy and her mother that she was all right as she slipped between cool, clean, smooth, comfortable sheets, and was out like a light as soon as her head touched the pillow.

"Come," Mrs. Winston whispered as she took Nancy's hand. "Let's let the poor girl sleep."

Willem, Stack, Briggs, Oppelin, and the rest walked from the mayor's office as one of the few men left to guard Montieth came running. "Sir, sir," he said as he ran up to the Mayor breathlessly, then looked at Sheriff Willem. "There are bikers in town. They just rode in." He pointed four blocks up the street they were on, which was Montieth's main drag.

"Goddam! Those bastards have more balls than a tribe of bears," Willem exclaimed. "Come on, men. We have to fight to hold Montieth before we can go off and protect that bomber. Mr. Mayor," he said, "I don't know if we can even spare eleven men to go save that bomber if this town's in danger of attack. As it is we're leaving only a skeleton force behind."

"Just take care of this menace," an excited Oppelin said. "Then we can worry about the rest."

The small force trotted up the street, their guns at the ready, as the motorcyclists came into view. An even dozen of them had parked along the sidewalk up ahead and had dismounted and were standing around now in a tight knot. Some of the volunteers prepared to shoot.

"Wait," Willem said. "I don't see this bunch showing guns. Just hold it." They moved closer. The bikers had seen them now and were taking off their

HELL RIDE

helmets. Some of them smiled and waved.

"Be careful," Stack said. "This may be a trick."

As the distance between them closed from 200 feet to less than 10, Willem and Stack saw that these bikers weren't like the hooligans in Vista Royale. No leather jackets. No harsh, bearded faces. They looked like yuppies, middle-aged businessmen, tourists. But none of the defenders let down their guard. They kept their trigger fingers ready as they came closer.

And then Willem saw the emblems, the HOG belt buckles, the Harley-Davidson stickers on their helmets, jackets, and Harley-Davidson bikes. These people weren't part of The Bloodsuckers.

"Howdy," Willem said, as he stopped, as did the gunmen with him.

The motorcyclists also said, "Howdy," but in a somewhat subdued manner. They saw the guns and the looks on the men's faces.

"What're you people doing here?" Willem asked in a bland but cautious voice.

"Passing through," the leader of the group said as he moved forward. Willem quickly catalogued the features of a man in his middle 40s, with faded sandy hair and a wide friendly face ending in a small mouth and spade jaw.

"And what might be your name, stranger?"

"Bay Courtner. And yours?"

"Sheriff Kurt Willem. Where's your group from?"

"Various places. Oakland, LA, Las Vegas, Santa Fe. But what is this? Why the guns?"

"Just being cautious."

"We mean no one any harm. We were touring the desert when the war broke out and came up into the mountains and were camping out till we hit this town. We wondered if there were any lodgings for the night."

"We haven't any hotel, or motel, if that's what you mean."

"I guess we'll just have to camp out again."

"What's the HOG on your belt buckles and emblems

stand for?"

"Harley-Davidson Owners Group. We're part of a fifty-thousand-member company-sponsored motorcycle club. Sort of a big, extended family. We get together for tours, buy various Harley-Davidson gear like shirts, clocks, belt buckles, and watches. We also attend Harley-Davidson receptions and rallies, factory open houses, national motorcycle events, and that sort of thing."

"I see. And that's what you were doing when the war broke out?"

"That's right. We were down in the desert and have been making our way north, keeping together instead of breaking up. We've decided to visit the home of each man to see if anything is left that can be saved, and if there are still survivors. Right now we're headed for San Francisco to see how Tom's family is doing." He nodded toward a dark-haired, short man in his late 40s.

"What did you do for a living before the war?"

"I was an accountant for the firm of Cutler and Brayne in LA. And now, sheriff, could you please level with me and let me know what's going on?"

"I guess you're all right and should know what's been coming down." As briefly as possible Willem told them what had happened in the mountains over the past 24 hours. The quizzical smiles died on their faces to be replaced by grim looks.

"And you thought we were part of that gang?" Courtner asked.

"Yessir. You guys might've ridden into town while we were leaving for the airfield and we would've assumed you were gang members coming to get us, and then we would've blown you to Kingdom Come."

"Goddam," Courtner exclaimed. A murmur of wonder and shock passed through the motorcyclists with him. Courtner looked at all the guns the men around Willem were carrying and said, "You oughtn't to jump to conclusions like that. A lot of innocent men could get killed that way. Most bikers are good people.

Only a small percentage are like The Bloodsuckers, or Hell's Angels."

"We kind of forgot that," Stack said. "But you can see what these people went through and why they would react that way."

"Yeah, I can understand. But I don't like it when me or my friends could've been lying on the ground with our guts spilled out all over the place."

"Then help us end this scourge and make these mountains safe for all decent people. I see rifles on some of the bikes. That means you're hunters too. We need men with guns. After all, if those bombs go off and you're here, you'll die just like the rest of us."

"I can't speak for the others," Courtner said, "but I'm willing to do my part in keeping this country safe. After all, America needs us now more than ever."

It sounded like a campaign slogan to Stack, but he welcomed the man and his sincerity.

Courtner now turned around and looked at the others in his group. "What about it, Ray?" he asked one man. Then he looked at another. "Ready to say yes, Tom?"

"Not all of us have weapons," Tom reminded him. "Can you supply guns?" he asked Willem.

"I've got a few. How many do you people have between you?"

"Three," Courtner announced. "One of them is mine. But I still don't know how many of my people are willing to go."

"Count me in," Tom said. Ray seconded that. Then two more men joined and another after that. That left six who hadn't said yes. But that wasn't of major concern to Willem, who didn't have weapons for them all.

Lyle Rokmer's heartbeat increased as he led his force to the top of the rise and looked down into the valley below. It was a large place, and in the darkness many landmarks were difficult to discern. They were too high up, the night too dark, and the valley too large for them to spot the plane. They would have to go down into the valley itself to find the bomber. They had come this far along roads, then dirt roads, and finally rutted grass trails.

The Black Donut rode up the line and stopped abreast of Rokmer. "Do you see it?" he asked.

"We wouldn't see it from up here," Rokmer answered.

"Maybe that bastard flyer lied to us about where it was so we'd go off chasin' our own tails."

"We'll know when we get down there. And if we can't find it in the dark, daylight's only four-five hours away."

"I still think we've been sent on a wild-goose chase. Something as big as a B-52 would be visible, even in the darkness."

"We'll see. Now why don't you go back in the line and rest your brain. Thinkin's never been your strong point." The Black Donut said nothing and did as requested. He could tell Rokmer was troubled and deep in thought.

He sat on the crest for several minutes, thinking through his options and the possibilities, then yelled back that they were going down. They followed him, a long line of motorcycles, moving like a snake down the overgrown mountainside dirt road. Some of the men around the B-52 spotted the string of lights in the distance and wondered if it signaled some flow of traffic going from one place to another. They watched it for a few minutes, then ascertained the traffic was coming down into the valley. Osseville ran to tell Garudet and he ordered the men to gather around him, calling out to them at the top of his voice, being seconded by Osseville.

"It looks as if Briggs came through at last," he said with a smile.

"Suppose they haven't been sent by Briggs," Raditsch suggested. "They might not even know about us and are heading someplace else in the valley."

"I doubt it," Garudet said. "This place isn't inhabited. They're coming down these mountains because Briggs told them where we are. They're coming to rescue us."

The five of them now fell silent and watched as the line of lights reached the valley floor, then began to move slowly toward the runway. Garudet turned to Carbindell. "Run into the plane and get my flare gun. I'm going to let them know where we are."

"Aye, aye, captain," Carbindell said jokingly and ran to do as asked.

He was soon back with the flare gun. Garudet loaded and fired it. In the far distance, Rokmer looked up in shock as a starburst of sparkling colored fire etched a pattern across the heavens. Rokmer quickly stopped his bike and the long line following him did the same as he wondered what all this was about. Then, as a second star burst in the sky, he realized they were signaling him.

"They think we've come to rescue them," he called back to his men with a laugh. After all, they had no way of knowing Briggs hadn't fallen into the hands of friends.

"Let's go save those sons of bitches," he yelled as the motorcycles raced onto the runway and toward the bomber.

Nick Stack sat in the front seat of the police cruiser, between Sheriff Willem, behind the wheel, and Lance Briggs. In the back seat were Bay Courtner and two of his friends who had volunteered for this mission, Tom Grushin and Joe Angelicus.

"How long before we get to the valley?" Stack asked Willem.

"Two hours, maybe less."

"Can't we do it any faster?"

"Only if we had a helicopter, and we don't. Are you afraid those bikers have beaten us to the punch?" Willem looked sideways for a moment.

"That had occurred to me."

"Nothing I can do about it. We went as fast as possible. Organizing a posse isn't as easy as one man deciding to go someplace on his own. You'll just have to hold your impatience in and we'll see what's gone down when we get there."

Stack nodded and clutched his rifle tighter, half his mind on the mission and half of it on Rayisa. He had gone to the Winston house, before he left Montieth, for one last look at her. Mrs. Winston opened the door to her room and Stack saw her there, her red hair spread across the snowy white of the pillowcase. She looked so serene. How unlike the turmoil she had undergone. She was only now at peace because she had been drugged. What would she be thinking tomorrow? And would he be there when the sun rose, to give her comfort? Stack didn't know the answers, and that bothered him. There were so many things he didn't know the answers to. So many uncertainties clouding his future and the futures of a good many people. How hard and cruel life could be, he realized. Not the first time he had realized that, but the first time it had come home to him with such force and enormity. At that moment life seemed like a great black mountain of naked rock. Yet Stack gritted his teeth, his jaw full of determination. This was one adversary he was not going to allow any victories. Too many people depended on him. Here in the mountains and back in New York City.

The Bloodsuckers raced across the airfield, their motorcycles bouncing as they went across uneven places in the concrete. A cold forest wind played across their faces, ran hard fingers through their beards and hair, and filled their nostrils with its scent. But there was one more thing they smelled, and it wasn't on the wind. Victory!

Then, suddenly, the giant bomber loomed up out of the darkness. And then, off to one side, they saw the five crewmen. The bikers let out war whoops and began to circle them.

Garudet and the others turned numb as their jubilation quickly faded. They were being circled by wild men. And where was Lance Briggs? The night suddenly turned a thousand times colder.

"Keep your guns handy," Garudet said to his men. He held his pistol at waist level, pointed at the circling bikers. Rokmer now made his move, going through the line of bikers, which stopped circling and surrounded the five men on all sides, their bikes pointed inward.

Rokmer stopped in front of Garudet, one leader recognizing the other almost by instinctive feel. "We've come here to help you," Rokmer lied easily and quickly.

"How did you know we were here and needed help?" Garudet asked, though he already knew the answer.

"Your man Lenny, or is it Lance, told us."

"Where's Lance?"

"Why, he's resting up," Rokmer said as the others laughed. "He's tired from all that walkin' he did."

Garudet knew he was lying. He also knew they were outnumbered four to one. But that didn't deter him. He was a professional who had U.S. Government property to protect and a mission to accomplish. Whether he died trying to do so in Siberia, or here, did not matter as long as he fulfilled the mission. Acting with that rare bravado desperate situations often call for, he stepped forward, grabbed Rokmer by the beard before the other man could make a move, and jammed the menacing Colt .45 to the side of his head.

"Where's Lieutenant Briggs?" he asked in a harsh voice.

Rokmer was stunned. No one had ever tried this with him. A murmur of confusion and indecision passed through The Bloodsuckers. This was a Mexican standoff.

"Where's Lieutenant Briggs?" Garudet repeated.

"He's sleepin'."

"You liar. You killed him!"

"No, man, no. He's alive," Rokmer swore, genuine fear in his heart now.

"Bring him to me. I'll hold you hostage and let your

people go so they can bring him here."

"They can't do that, man."

"Why?"

" 'Cause he escaped, man. We wuz holdin' him prisoner and he escaped. I dunno where he is."

"That the truth?"

"Yeah, man. He ain't dead."

Garudet looked sideways at Osseville. "This slug might be telling the truth, but I doubt it. I oughta kill you right here," he said, looking back at Rokmer.

"You kill me, my men kill you. I got more people than you do."

"And all their brains wouldn't fit the nearest piss pot." Garudet spit. He hesitated a second, then said, "I can't hold you monkeys. I'm going to let you go, but only if you leave your guns."

"No, man. No," Rokmer growled. "Without our guns you'll take us prisoner. We ain't goin' without our guns."

"If they don't drop their guns, I'll kill you."

Rokmer thought a second. "Don't drop your guns, men. If they kill me, kill them. We got the numbers. They're dead." He looked straight at Garudet. "You want us out of your hair, you let us go as we are. Guns an' all."

"What guarantee have I got you monkeys won't attack us after we let you go."

"You got none," Rokmer said with a savage grin. "What we got here is a Mexican standoff, which ain't gonna be one for long. If anything goes wrong and the shooting starts, you're dead. We've got the numbers and we've got you surrounded. So deal while the dealin's good, man."

"This bastard's got a point," Carbindell told Garudet.

"Okay," Garudet told Rokmer. "We'll do it like this. Your people leave in groups of five, drive down to the other end of the runway, turn around, and park with their headlights on so we can see they're far away instead of having gone just a few hundred yards to merge with the night. Then, when we're down to the last group, you and your people leave the same way. We'll keep our guns on you till you've joined your buddies. And if you decide to attack then, we'll be waiting and ready this time. Fair enough?"

"I don't know," Rokmer said, his mind confused. Trying to think while a gun was boring into the side of his head wasn't easy. "Okay," he finally said, trying to find an opening, as he had when he'd left Vista Royale and come back to attack it. He'd do the same to these scumbags. And what choice did he have in accepting Garudet's offer? There were possible dangers in the plan. But if things went on like this, it would end in a shooting and he'd certainly die. And that wouldn't be at all good.

"All right," Garudet said, pressing the gun harder against Rokmer's head, "pick five men and send them off." Rokmer nodded, and called out five names. Motorcycles were started and the quintet roared off down the runway. When they had reached the other end of the runway and turned around, their headlights on, Garudet forced Rokmer to send five more men off. They continued in that manner till they were down to the last five bikers.

"Okay, slug," Garudet said, "tell your four friends to go."

"Whaddya mean? I'm supposed to go with them."

"I've just changed my mind. If you stay with us they won't attack, will they?"

"You can't do that, man."

"Watch me. Remember, my gun's pointed at your head. Your gun isn't pointed at mine. Now tell these scumbags to move their asses and join their partners, or you're dog meat."

"I won't."

"That's no problem either. We've got equality in numbers. And if we fire first, some of us will survive and we'll win this round."

"If they go, that leaves me your prisoner."

"True. But being my prisoner alive is better than not being my prisoner dead. Which will it be, slug? Answer me quick. Time's running out."

Rokmer shuddered in fear and frustration. He held the upper hand coming in and now was under this man's thumb going out. It sure was a whole other ballgame fighting a professional military man.

"Well?"

"Boys, do as he says." They began to protest. "Just go. Black Donut's the platoon leader now. Let him do as he sees best. I'll survive. Don't fret. Just go." With some more grumbles they started their motorcycles and roared off.

Garudet looked at Carbindell. "Go lock up all access to the plane so no one can get in. Then come back here. And do it double quick."

As that was happening, he forced Rokmer off his bike. "That's a fancy piece of machinery, dude. I'd like to have one. Maybe I'll even take yours." As he was saying this, still holding onto Rokmer's beard, the other men were liberating Rokmer's weapons and ammunition and any weapons and ammunition on the motorcycle. Then, when Carbindell came back, Garudet and the others, dragging Rokmer along, left the runway for the darkness of the bushes alongside it.

"They won't be able to find us so easily among all this vegetation. And when they approach the bomber, we'll be able to see it and shoot them off their bikes."

Down at the other end of the runway The Bloodsuckers weren't taking this lying down. The Black Donut had been thinking and now called over the biker known as The Viking, who had helped kidnap Rayisa. "Zenthelm, I want you to leave your bike here. Walk up the runway to within a few hundred feet of the bomber—the dark will hide you—and scout out what's happening. Then come back and tell me."

"Why can't I ride?"

" 'Cause they'll hear you, even if you rode up with

the lights out so they wouldn't see you. And they'll notice one less pair of headlights here. I don't want 'em to know what we're doin'. Let 'em think we're still back here, frozen in indecision, while they're sittin' there like kings of the hill. We're goin' to break those bastards and crush their skulls and at the same time get back our man, San Quentin Sal." They all cheered that. The Black Donut then spoke to The Viking alone over on the side.

"It should take you twenty minutes or so to reach them if you walk fast and about the same time coming back. When you get there, squat down and just sit. Listen for voices, watch the terrain. You may not get anything at first, but then your senses will begin orienting you and you might pick up some interesting details. Understand?" The Viking nodded. "Go to it then."

It took The Viking a little longer than expected to get there. He stopped when he got to within 500 feet of the bomber, sat down, and listened. His eyes discerned no movement around the plane, but his ears oriented him to voices coming from bushes diagonally to his right 100 feet from the runway. He stayed a few minutes more, then headed back to where the others waited.

Willem looked at his watch again. They were less than 40 minutes' driving time from the valley. He nudged Stack, who was lost in his own thoughts. "Yeah, we there yet?" Stack asked.

"No. But we will be sooner than you think. This may all come out good in the end."

"I'll believe it when I'm standing atop a hill of bikers' carcasses with the vultures circling in the noonday sun. Right now we still haven't even entered the valley."

"You're a real pessimist."

"Look at the world around us," he said, making a brief sweep with his right hand. "Why shouldn't I be?"

"Each man to his own," Willem answered, and fell silent again.

One of the Bloodsuckers heard The Viking coming before the others saw him. Once he arrived they all crowded around as he told them what he had done and where the B-52 crew and Rokmer were hidden. "What's our next move?" he asked The Black Donut.

"We move out on foot, go off the runway when we get near the bomber, then approach from the flanks, blow their brains out, and free Rokmer. But shoot carefully. We don't want to kill San Quentin Sal."

"Right," a few of the bikers shouted. And then they started off. The walk, though not short, seemed longer to bikers used to riding from place to place. Those who had been in the military were used to much worse. Finally, they came to within 500 feet of the bomber, moved off the runway, and walked in three columns through grass, then bushes, stopping every minute or so on The Black Donut's silent hand signals so he could listen for sounds of conversation going on just off the runway.

Rokmer was arguing with Garudet somewhat loudly about why he wasn't being let go, and Garudet was saying come daylight he might do that. This continued till The Bloodsuckers moved to within 20 yards of where the bomber crew and their prisoner were concealed.

Raditsch was the first to hear the rustling in the bushes and pointed this out to Garudet. Everyone fell silent. "I think it's just the breeze," Garudet whispered after half a minute. "Maybe a small animal," Osseville added. After that, the talk started up again. The Bloodsuckers, who had frozen like statues, now began to move forward. But ten yards from the nearest crewman they were spotted.

"They're here," Stahl yelled and let off a shot.

Suddenly, the night erupted in a volley of shots. Slugs, flying forward on streaks of yellow, blue, red, and purple flame, cut through the bushes. Men yelled and fell down, firing wildly and blindly. Garudet thought he'd spotted a Bloodsucker, aimed his flare gun, and fired. The flare flew outward in a spasm of flame which temporarily lit the area before smashing into the midsection of the hooligan and exploding, sending sparkles of fire to all points as it badly burned the biker, who went down screaming.

Rokmer chose that moment to act. He smashed his fist as hard as he could into Gaurdet's head. The captain reeled to the side and Rokmer flew from the position, diving into nearby bushes as shots followed him and using the pandemonium of battle to crawl away while bullets whizzed around his head, cutting branches, sending torn leaves flying, filling the night with the stink of expended powder. But then the fire from the bikers, only 20 yards away, grew heavier, and the attention of the B-52 crewmen were drawn to them. Rokmer continued to crawl away. Let the others fight while he found safety. He could always take command later and lead the final attack in.

Back at the battle the level of firing died down. The combatants were running out of bullets. They stopped to reload and take account of what had been lost so far. Raditsch had been hit in the left shoulder and was in terrible pain. Stahl had taken a round in the abdomen and was bleeding badly. Among the bikers two were dead and two more were wounded, one of them having been burned by the flare gun and now, half in shock, mumbling for water.

"Shut that bastard up," The Black Donut said in a loud whisper as he peered into the darkness and tried to see where the enemy was.

"That's it," Willem said, pointing to the road ahead. "It'll take us down into the valley."

"It's about time," Stack told him.

"You certainly are impatient," Courtner exclaimed. Stack looked back for a second and saw the sickly look of fear on his face. He would rather have been someplace else right then. Stack tried to measure his own feelings. Fear was not among them, but tenseness was. He didn't feel afraid because his good work earlier on had given him the confidence he needed. And, unlike the others, he didn't need to hype himself for the battles to come. What had been done to Rayisa had prepared him more than enough. Animals like that were best removed from the earth.

The convoy moved more quickly now. Even when the paved road ran out they still maintained a good clip along rutted dirt roads, taking every curve skillfully as they moved over the crest and down into the valley. Looking down, they saw the pinpricks of light from the motorcycle headlights at the end of the runway.

"Those shouldn't be there," Stack told Willem.

"We'll find out what should and shouldn't be when we get down into the valley. For now, let's not draw any conclusions."

Back at the battle zone the fighting had slowed after the initial flurry. Garudet and his men were firing back sparingly. They were very low on ammunition and didn't know how long it would last. But at least they were holding off the more numerous bikers and keeping them from overrunning this position. But where the hell was their leader, Rokmer?

At that very moment he was moving, hunched over, through the bushes 100 yards away. He wanted to go far enough so that the darkness would cloak him and then make a run for the bomber to see if he could get inside. He decided to let his bikers take care of the crew. They were outnumbered four-to-one and in the end would lose. Meanwhile, Rokmer would proceed with his original objective. No reason to stop now. The fact that so many bikers had died made the objective that much more valuable. And, if he had the bomber, he had the power.

The convoy from Montieth had now come off the mountain road and started across the valley toward the pinpoints of light at the end of the runway. They drove fast, bumping up and down over undulating ground till they reached the runway, then drove onto it.

"Look, those are motorcycles," Stack yelled.

Willem drove with one hand and with the other extended his pistol out the window and began firing. Guns appeared from other car windows and began blasting away. Bike headlights were hit, glass shattered, metal was pierced, gasoline ran out on the runway, and several bikes ignited and began burning furiously, sending up five-foot orange-and-yellow, blue-tipped flames. And then the cars separated and, before some of the people in them knew it, rammed into, rode over, and crushed motorcycles under their tires, mangling those which hadn't been hit. Some of the bikes were caught under the cars and dragged screeching along the concrete, sending up sparks and chunks of flying debris. Then one of the cars came back and drove over those bikes which hadn't been damaged badly enough the first time.

The shooting, the cars, the flames were seen and heard by the bikers fighting in the bushes to destroy the handful of crewmen still holding out.

"Goddam," Tortellino shouted, "somebody's attackin' our bikes."

"Hell," The Black Donut screamed, "we've got to get back there." But then fire from the B-52 crew forced them to put their heads down and deal with the reality of what was going on where they were. No one was going anyplace while Garudet and his men had any say about it.

Back at the motorcycle graveyard, now a field of crushed rubble and flaming debris, the cars circled around looking for bikers. One of the drivers leaned out his window as Briggs yelled, "The bomber's at the other end of the runway." They looked and saw the flaming lines of tracers from the bushes off to the right, and raced full speed along the runway, headlights boring holes through the night as they headed toward the enemy objective.

"Listen," Stack told Willem, "guys like me, seated in the middle, can't really fight too well. Why not stop the cars near the bomber, let half the men out so we can make up a skirmish line, then you chase the bastards out of the bushes toward us."

"Good idea," he said, using the brake as the bomber loomed out of the darkness. He honked a few times to get the attention of the other drivers, who also began to slow down and came to a full stop when he did.

"Let half your people out," he yelled to them. "Have them form a skirmish line and we'll go into the bushes and drive the enemy out toward them."

They did that as Stack, Briggs, and Courtner got out to join a number of others. Then the four vehicles thundered off the road, headlights blazing, and into the bushes as if they were tanks.

The bikers saw them coming, pegged a number of shots their way, then began yelling in panic as the thundering beasts bore down on them and rose, those that weren't dead or wounded, and raced in every direction. But this exposed them to fire from the airmen, who blazed away. But there were so many targets now going in so many directions, and waving bushes were being mistaken for running men, and the flashing of the headlights, moving this way and that, sometimes blinded the shooters, so that often no one was hit.

The Black Donut began to run deeper into the bushes as he saw Sheriff Willem's cruiser coming straight at him. He leaped more than ran. But the car, jolted this way and that, ripping up bushes, grinding down others, moved relentlessly forward. It drove over a heavily wounded man Willem did not even see, crushing his chest and killing him. And then, finally, it reached The Black Donut, tapping him once or twice before it took on speed and rolled over him. He screamed as he was crushed underneath, then dragged along before his smashed, bleeding body was dropped into the grass and underbrush.

At the same time two vehicles moved toward the airmen, who rose, waving their arms to let the drivers know they weren't the enemy. The cars were almost on them before the drivers saw their uniforms, made 90-degree turns, and went looking for other fleeing bikers, now coming out of the bushes and racing toward the runway. There the skirmish line moved forward and began to fire away, streaks of flame cutting the night. Stack shot one biker and another right after that. Salamuth caught one in the legs and, when he went down, pumped more rounds into the body, watching it jump after each shot until it become still.

It was a scene straight out of hell as The Bloodsuckers were flushed from their positions like big game being driven straight toward the hunters by beaters. Rokmer, now under the bomber, looking for a way in, watched in horror, saying, "Fuckin' goddam bastards. If I had a bazooka, I'd blow them to bits." His men had been panicked and were either running away or not fighting back very effectively. But it was happening to *them. He* still had the shadows and the darkness. They did not know about him. Yet that did not matter, because there was no way he could see to get into the bomber. Deciding that retreat was the better part of valor, he moved out from under the bomber toward the woods on the other side of the runway.

Meanwhile, The Viking drew a bead and blew one of the skirmishers off his feet. But a second later, a car he had not seen shot from the darkness and rammed into him from behind, grinding him down until the screams which flew from his open mouth died away into bloody gurglings.

Elsewhere, some of the Bloodsuckers proved too quick and agile to be caught by the cars, and attempted to use the night to conceal themselves. But the bullets which flew from various vehicles caught some and wounded others. And they, in their frightened retreat, fired back, starring windows and wounding occupants. One of the bikers, the same Tortellino who had kidnapped Rayisa, fired and killed the driver of a blue '84 Chevy. The man fell dead as his front window starred and a spray of blood shot from his head. He fell to the side and lost control of the wheel, and his foot slipped from the gas pedal. The car went into a dip and stayed there, the motor going, the vehicle trembling with useless power. Doors flew open and men rushed out, firing at what they thought were other men and often were just bushes. One of them hit Brian Salamuth in the chest with a stray bullet. Stack moved out of the way and crouched down. There was a flurry of shots, and then the last bikers threw down their weapons and raised their hands in surrender. The battle for the B-52 was over.

It was time to count the dead and survey the booty of weaponry that had been taken. The cars came back to the runway. The vehicle which had lost a driver got another. One of the men even discovered the Kawasaki KDX which had been sitting on the runway near the bomber all this time. Rokmer's prize motorcycle was now theirs for the taking. Meanwhile, the force from Montieth laid out their dead, three men, with three wounded—one of them being Brain Salamuth, who was going fast. The airmen now came in from where they had fought their battle, bringing two wounded with them. One of them, Todd Stahl, was also dying. The bikers had taken fifteen dead. There were four prisoners, two of them wounded, and a dozen guns. Some weapons had been dropped in the bushes, and with all that darkness could not be found.

"Now let's question these bastards," Stack said, pointing to Tortellino first. "Let's find out about Vista Royale and what the setup is there. The force strength and so on. When we finish with that place, this whole thing will be over."

"I'll take care of that part," Willem said. He called Kudner and Kirtzler over. "I want you two to verify whatever these people tell me."

Faced with their defeat, menaced by the guns of the hard, angry men standing over them, sensing no choice but to talk, the bikers spilled their guts. They told where the people in Vista Royale were being held prisoner, how the defense structure around town was set up, and how many defenders were left.

"Where's your leader?" Willem wanted to know.

"He was their prisoner." Tortellino pointed to Garudet and his men.

"He fled from us when the shooting began," Garudet explained. "He may be dead or still out there."

"No need to look for him now," Stack said. "There'll be plenty of time for that come morning. The thing we have to do now is liberate Vista Royale and get medical attention for the wounded. My feeling is that we ought to leave a detail to guard the bomber, then send two men in one car with the badly wounded back to Montieth. After that, the doctor can come here to look at the less badly wounded. Meanwhile, the rest of us will pile into the remaining three cars and go to Vista Royale. Agreed?"

"Sounds good to me," Willem said. "You oughta be a general."

"If I survive this battle, you can promote me."

"You can count on it," Willem answered with a laugh.

17

They were out of the valley now, on the road to Vista Royale. Stack thought for a moment about the small force left guarding the plane. The three crewmen who hadn't been wounded and Briggs who joined them. Before they left, he and Briggs shook hands and said their good-byes, with Briggs thanking Stack for having saved his life. Stack had nodded without saying a word, half his mind on the battle ahead. With the two men who had taken the wounded to Montieth gone that left just nine men, one of whom had been slightly wounded.

As they drove toward Vista Royale, they made their plan of attack. Stack listened to a number of ideas, then said, "Look, we've got only nine people. The sheriff here, myself, Kudner, Kritzler, Courtner, the two people in his motorcycle club, and two guys from Montieth I'm not too sure about. In and around Vista Royale are a dozen Bloodsuckers, four of them women, who are not really trained combatants. They're spread out, which makes things a bit easier for us. The first thing we have to do is preserve the element of surprise. Now you and I know if we come to within half a mile of town the hidden sentry on either approach road will race out past us to give the alarm. What we do is send one car by with all the windows down, an armed man waiting at each window. And as soon as the sentry races past you give him a full volley and smear him all over the road. That eliminates their early warning system. Then, instead of going in like gangbusters, you drive off the road and wait. I want to go in like I did the last time, but with Kudner and Kritzler joining me, since they know the area. We go to the main concentration point where they have the most guards holding hostages and kill all the bikers there. It'll probably result in a firefight. The hostages will flee and more bikers will be drawn to the area. That will cut their strength everywhere else. At that point, when you hear the shooting, you race into town and blast the hell out of whatever is left of them. What do you think of the plan?"

"I couldn't have done better," Willem said. "You're definitely officer material."

"Thanks," Stack said with a grin.

Then they fell silent again as the miles ticked away. Suddenly, they spotted someone walking along the road ahead. As they approached and slowed down, the person, a young girl, looked back in fear and was about to race for the cover of the forest, but then saw the police cruiser and ran toward them. She was wet and dirty. Her face was scratched and her eyes were full of fear.

"Help me, help me," she cried out as she reached the police car and leaned down next to Willem's open window. She looked a mess and smelled of the forest.

"We'll help you," Willem said. "Where are you from?" He opened the door and got out of the car. The other cars had pulled to a stop behind Willem's car and now waited as Willem and those in the cruiser listened to Barbara Sidarsis tell her tale of woe and how she had been living in the forest, eating berries, drinking stream water, sleeping under bushes, walking through the woods and along the road, looking for a civilized place, but afraid to return to Vista Royale. She told about her beating and rape, painfully reminding Stack of what had happened to Rayisa, and of how she was supposed to be killed, but had been given her freedom by a biker. And then she related how she stayed a whole night and part of the next day in the woods, afraid even to come out because she might be spotted and picked up by some biker, which would result in her death—something the hoodlum who let her go had warned the girl about.

"Nobody's going to kill you," Willem said, putting an arm around her shoulder. "You're safe now. In fact, we're going to liberate Vista Royale in a short while. Soon you'll be home safe with your parents. So why don't you get in the car?"

"We can't take her with us now," Stack reminded him. "We're going into a dangerous, life-threatening situation. Why not ask her to wait here? When we're through liberating Vista Royale, assuming our attempt is a success, we'll come back for her. If she's stayed in the woods this long, she can stay a little longer. And if we're not successful in what we've set out to do, we'll still come back for the girl. What do you say?"

Willem looked at the girl for her reaction. "No need to explain, sir. I'll be glad to wait. I've seen more than enough action and don't want to witness anymore. Just bring me back when the place is free."

"You have my word on that." Willem got back in the cruiser and waved good-bye, then drove on. The occupants of the other cars also waved as they went past.

The tension began to build now. Vista Royale was less than ten minutes away. At the last minute Willem made a change in plans. He signaled a stop and told the people in the other cars that all of them would drive past with their windows down, and when the sentry rider raced from the woods they'd blast his guts all over the highway.

That decided on, they continued the journey, clasping their guns tightly as they came closer to Vista Royale. And then, without warning, they passed the first tripwire and the sentry rider shot from the woods. Only this time they were ready and let him have a stunning broadside as he came past, puncturing him in half a dozen places, sending him and his bike screeching across the highway as rider and motorcycle separated, both scraping along the road for perhaps 30 yards until they flew off into the woods. The cars pulled to a halt, swung around so their headlights could play into the woods, and saw the bike on its side on an incline, the wheels still rapidly turning. Nearby was the broken, bloodied body of the dead rider.

"Okay," Willem told Stack, "this is where you get out. We're not going any closer till we hear firing. Good luck, fella."

Stack nodded as he got out of the car, then went back to the second car in line and got Kudner and Kritzler. The three of them crossed the road, waved farewell to the others, then disappeared into the woods, Stack once again using his compass.

They found a trail, which they used part of the way, then went across virgin territory, walking where there were fewer bushes, almost going into a few potholes but generally making fairly rapid progress. After 40 minutes they were at the edge of the woods looking into a darkened yard.

"We go in this way," Stack whispered.

"Fine with me," Kudner whispered back, looking at Kritzler, who nodded his assent.

That decided, they moved from the woods into the yard, then across several yards, between two houses, and out the front way as they raced across the street to the next block, looking for the house with all the hostages and guards.

Once across the street, they raced up a driveway and between two houses to hide in the shadows. As they caught their breaths, they heard the sound of high heels coming. They moved deeper into the shadows for better concealment and waited. Ten seconds later a girl biker came by. She was wearing heels probably taken from some house and smoking a cigarette. In her other hand was a rifle. She was a potential adversary, so Stack moved out from his hiding place, one of his knives already unsheathed as he hurried out to the sidewalk, then rushed up behind the woman in a final run. One arm snaked around, cupping her mouth shut and pulling her head back, leaving her offered neck open to attack. She moaned in sudden fear, dropped the rifle, then brought her cigarette up and began to burn Stack's hand. "Arrgh," he groaned, gritting his teeth as he brought the blade up and in, plunging it into her chest just below the ribcage. The hand burning him with the cigarette fell away and the cigarette dropped to the sidewalk as he pulled the blade out and then plunged it in again. For good measure he pulled the blade out and sliced it across her neck.

He dropped the woman biker to the ground, where she bled to death as he looked around, then rushed back to where the others waited.

"Let's go. I had no choice in doing that. She had a gun and could have shot us later."

"Where's the gun?" Kritzler asked.

"Goddam, I forgot."

"No problem. I'll get it." Kritzler ran out, retrieved the rifle and came back. "Okay, follow me," he said. Stack and Kudner followed him across backyards, the three of them having to climb some fences. One or two times Stack winced audibly because of the burned place on his hand.

They moved between two houses and stopped, across the street from a house that was all lit up and from which the sounds of many voices came. "That's the house where the bikers told us most of the hostage-takers were concentrated," Kudner whispered.

"We'll try to kill them silently at first," Stack said. "But if shooting breaks out, let them have all you've got. Don't waste ammunition, but hold back nothing. This is the final assault. We either win it or they do. Just remember, victory is in our grasp."

The two men looked at him with burning eyes. They wanted victory even more than he did. This was their town. Their families and friends lived here and were suffering now under a terrible yoke.

Stack said nothing more as he moved out from

between the two houses, looked left and right, and then led them in a fast run across the street, between cars, across a sidewalk and lawn, and into the shadows between two houses, in one of which were the hostages and a good number of their captors.

The men stopped in the shadows to rest for a second, their hearts already beating too fast in anticipation. Stack then led them around to the rear of the house. He peeked into the kitchen, where some women were cooking under the watchful eye and ready gun of a female biker. With Kudner and Kritzler in tow, he circled the house, eyeballing the occupied first-floor rooms in one- or two-second peeks through the unshaded windows. Then he knelt down in the shadows and told them what he'd seen.

"It looks like fifty or sixty people are downstairs, male, female, all ages. I saw at least three bikers. There could be more upstairs. I don't think we're going to be able to take them out silently. We may have to go in shooting. So be it."

"There are almost three hundred people in Vista Royale. Where are the rest?" Kudner wanted to know.

"I saw fifty or sixty downstairs. There may be as many upstairs. Then there are other places where hostages are being kept, each with perhaps one or two biker guards."

"That's not important now," Kritzler said. "How do you plan on getting inside? The doors are locked. All the rooms are occupied. You can't slip in through an open window."

"Why don't we just do it the old-fashioned way?" Stack said. "We ring the front doorbell. And when they open up we blow their brains out if they don't drop their guns and put up their hands."

The other man laughed, nervously.

Stack led them around to the front of the house, then up the three steps to the door, and with them behind him, rang the bell. They waited 20 seconds and he rang it again. "Hold on, there. Coming, coming," a man's voice said from within.

The door came open, but instead of a biker an old man stood there. "That's Lane Graystock," Kudner exclaimed in surprise. "What're you doin' at the door, Lane?"

"They told me to open it, figuring, I guess, that it would be another biker. What're you doin' here?" he asked, looking over his shoulder.

"We've come to free you, old man," Stack said, moving forward and elbowing him aside as he rushed into the hallway, followed by the other two. A voice from the living room, obviously belonging to a biker, called out, "Who is it that rang the doorbell?"

Stack jumped into the living room, crowded with people. "Me, you scumbag," he snarled. When the biker went for the pistol in his belt, Stack waved the people aside. They fell to the floor, shrieking, as he pumped two rounds into the biker's chest. The big thug flew back, his arms flopping out as his white shirt turned bright red with the blood spurting from his jagged chest wounds.

As the sounds of shooting filled the house, the female biker came running from the kitchen. At the same time a male biker rushed from the downstairs bedroom, also filled with hostages. Kudner shot the woman who had rushed from the kitchen, but when he tried to hit the biker, his shots went wild, allowing the biker, also known as Ivan the Terrible, to skitter back into the bedroom. As this was happening, two bikers, a male and female, raced down from upstairs, guns drawn. Kudner and Kritzler shifted their fire to the steps as Stack rushed from the living room and let the female biker, racing down with a shotgun in her hands, have a slug in the side, preventing her from even using the weapon. She dropped it and began to tumble down the stairs. The male biker took a slug in the chest from either Kudner or Kritzler and fired back, striking Kritzler in the stomach before the hemorrhage inside him overflowed and blood began to spray across his chest and shirt. He fell to the steps as Ivan the Terrible peered out into the hall and fired a volley from his rifle. Bullets whizzed in every direction as Stack and Kudner went sideways into the living room and fought from there, popping in and out of sight.

Kritzler was on the floor now, bleeding all over the place, crying out, "I'm shot. Help me, help me." But no one could get to him while the biker in the bedroom kept on firing.

"Keep him busy," Stack told Kudner, then headed for the living room window, pulled it up, and dropped outside. Next he moved carefully along the side of the house till he was below the bedroom window, and peeked in. The biker was there, hunched against the door frame, looking out and firing into the hall as a lot of frightened people cowered on the bedroom floor.

Stack stood up, aimed his rifle, then between gritted teeth said, "Okay, you bastard. This one's for you." He pulled the trigger. The round howled in his ears as it left the rifle barrel, shattered the glass, and punched through the biker's back. He arched and tried to grab himself there, half-turning to see who had done this, then dropped to the floor as dead as any man can ever be.

Stack turned from the window, about to go back into the house as he ejected an empty clip from the rifle and put a new one in, when, without warning, a biker drove up in front of the house in response to the sounds of the shooting.

"Come and get it, you sonofabitch," Stack growled as he moved foward out of the shadows. The biker, going for his rifle, spotted Stack too late. Three shots winged his way, one missing but two others hitting their target. He dropped to the ground, moaning in pain, but not yet dead.

Stack didn't waste anymore bullets on him as he ran back inside and stopped to look at Kritzler, who was dying, his head being cradled by his niece, who had been a captive in the house. Stack then ran into the living room, which was filled with people coming down from upstairs and other rooms of the house. People crying, laughing, hugging Kudner and now Stack.

Kudner was being hugged especially hard by a white-haired woman. "My wife," he yelled over the sounds of joy, tears of happiness in his eyes.

"Come on, King," Stack said, calling him by his nickname. "There are still bikers out there. We've got to get them if we don't want these people to be taken captive again."

"Right," he said, tearing himself from his wife, telling the others there was still a job of liberation to be done. They cheered him on, some of them grabbing the weapons from the dead bikers and without asking joining their liberators so they too could help free Vista Royale.

The unruly mob rushed from there, Kudner giving Stack a thumbnail briefing about where the hostages were and the location of the other captors.

"I was told by the people here, before you came back in, that hostages are being held in one other house and the church. They also told me people were afraid to run away because of retaliation promised against their loved ones and because there were constant biker patrols so they couldn't get far enough without being caught. When the town first fell they ran to see to the safety of relatives and friends. By the time they were ready to leave, it was too late. They were all prisoners. You had to get out right away, like I did."

"But now they can be free."

Elsewhere in town, the biker guarding the hostages in the church and the one guarding them in a private house the next block over left their chattels and ran to find Zoyas. They knew their prisoners might escape, but didn't care. They'd heard the shooting and sensed the danger. Rokmer's men weren't back and they were being attacked. This was not good.

Zoyas, with Debbie at his side, was already out of the

HELL RIDE

house serving as his headquarters and getting onto his bike to go check what the trouble was when the two men came running.

"What the hell are you guys doing here?" he asked.

"We're being invaded," one of the wild-eyed bikers responded.

"Well, get back to your post. I'm going over to check what's happening right now," he told them as Debbie got on the bike behind Zoyas.

They nodded, unsure of themselves, and started slowly back to their posts while Zoyas drove his motorcycle away toward the house Stack and the others had already freed.

As he turned the corner and was about to enter the next street over, he saw the band of gunmen, led by Stack, coming his way. They lifted their weapons and began to fire. Zoyas made the sharpest U-turn of his life and raced away as bullets whizzed about his head, some of them thunking into the motorcycle.

Then he felt a sudden weakening of Debbie's grip around his waist. As he raced from the side street onto Main Street, Zoyas turned left, then stopped and looked back.

"Debbie?" he fearfully asked.

Her hands fell away. Her mouth was open, her breathing shallow, with pinkish bubbles forming at the sides of her mouth. And then she keeled over without warning and fell onto the asphalt. It was at that point he saw the jagged bullet holes in her back through the dark T-shirt she wore.

"Shit," he exclaimed, realizing she had been his shield, taking the bullets meant for him. He was about to lean over and try to pick Debbie up to see if she was conscious when he heard, then saw the three-car convoy come charging into town, the lead car a police cruiser, sirens wailing, colored lights flashing.

"Shit!" he again exclaimed as he turned his bike in the other direction, gunned the motor and roared away into the wind, leaving Debbie behind, lying on the asphalt.

The three-car convoy, firing shots into the air, warily eyeing every window, every corner, every doorway, saw nothing that would give them any trouble. But Willem spotted the fleeing biker.

He signaled a full stop, then ordered, "Go check the side streets," before he raced off in pursuit of the escaping hoodlum. Willem slowed down again as he detoured around the body on Main Street, then speeded up. Corpses he'd worry about later.

He made the effort to catch the biker despite the fact that Zoyas had a lead on him and was now racing away at better than 100 miles an hour, the wind blasting into his face, tearing at his eyes, and fluttering his beard. But Zoyas endured the elements, using every bit of skill he had learned on motorcycles to make it away and live. All was lost now. Only his life belonged to him, and no matter what, he'd protect that.

When Zoyas shot past the place where the other sentry was hidden, the biker in the woods wondered what the hell was going on, but made no move. Then Willem zoomed by in his wailing police car. Only then did the sentry realize Vista Royale had fallen. In response, he moved deeper into the greenery, waiting now for his chance to flee.

The two bikers who had been ordered back to their posts decided not to return to them, but to find their motorcycles and get the hell out of town. The posts themselves were being deserted by hostages, who were rushing out every exit, windows even, to hide behind bushes, in the shadows alongside houses, in yards, behind cars, even in the nearby woods.

The two cars Willem left behind took the first side street they came to and moved toward the sound of the shooting. On the way they passed a number of former hostages who cheered, seeing that help had arrived. The cars did not stop for them, but moved onto another side street. It was then they spotted the two bikers, now only a block away from their motorcycles. They never made it.

The cars roared past and volleys of fire flew from them. The bikers did not even have time to draw their guns and had barely begun to run when hot rounds chopped into them, arching their riddled, blood-spattered flesh before they crashed to the pavement like sides of slaughtered beef.

The men in the cars did not even look back as they turned into the next street and met the gunmen heading toward the church. They stopped to tell them about the freed hostages they had seen. Stack, Kudner, and the others then embraced Bay Courtner, Tom Grushin, Joe Angelicus, and a man from Montieth. Stack also asked where Willem was.

"He went chasing after a fleeing biker," Angelicus answered. "He'll be back soon."

Out on the road, Zoyas still raced the wind as he heard the wailing siren which told him the police car was no more than a mile behind. The beating of the wind on his exposed face—he had fled without his helmet and goggles—was no easier to bear, nor could he take the strain of going around curves at nearly 100 miles an hour forever. Sooner, rather than later, his luck would run out. Zoyas made a decision. He was coming to that logging road he and The Bloodsuckers went up the night when they had camped in the woods before the attack on Vista Royale. He had to grab at that straw, or die in the end when the police cruiser finally caught up with him. Having made that decision, he took the next curve, looked back, and began to slow down. When he saw the gap in the woods ahead, he turned right, and went off the road and across the rutted trail into the wilderness, riding the bike with all his skill to avoid losing his balance and being thrown. Then, after 200 yards, he slowed down and finally stopped, killing the lights and the engine. He sat there atop his bike, looking back over his shoulder at the darkness of the road, breathing much too hard, aware that his whole body was wet with perspiration and that his face felt numb now that the wind was no longer beating on it.

Half a minute later the police car shot by, wailing away into the night. Many minutes after it had gone and was no longer audible he still heard that wailing in his ears, and it made his heart beat like a crazed tom-tom.

Back in Vista Royale the celebrations and the tales of horror had already begun. The liberators were heroes. Thanks were being given in the church. Stack and the others were treated to an honorary breakfast. In the middle of all this Willem walked in. People patted him on the back, kissed him, and gave him their condolences over what had happened to his brother. Then he and Stack shook hands.

"Vista Royale is free," Stack told him.

"No one will ever be free of this nightmare. It's a new world out there. I hope you realize that."

Stack shook his head. "Did you get the guy you went chasing after?"

"No. But in the end I guess it doesn't matter. He's just one drop in the ocean."

"Maybe, maybe not. Time will tell."

"Look," Willem said, pointing to the window. "The sun's rising on a new day."

"Let's go out and watch it come up over the forest," Stack said.

"Yeah, I'd like that."

As they stepped outside, Stack asked, "When do you think we can get back to Montieth? I want to be there when Rayisa wakes up. She'll need me."

Willem patted him on the back. "A lot of people need you, good buddy. You came through for us when the chips were down. And now you can be sure we'll come through if you need help."

The two men fell silent and watched the edge of an

orange sun, like new fire, peek over the tops of the pines.

In the mountains above the valley where the B-52 sat in the light of a new day, Lyle Rokmer paused to look at the sun and the plane down below which for one fleeting portion of eternity had almost been his. To have gone so far and to have lost so much. He gritted his teeth. But at least he was alive.

He took one last look before continuing his climb and muttered to himself, "This isn't over yet. The world hasn't heard the last of Lyle Rokmer. People are going to pay for what happened in this place."

On the road leaving Vista Royale, the biker sentry, who had stayed hidden for hours, now emerged and raced off down the highway, away from the place where for a short while they had been kings. He was headed back to the coastal cities, where perhaps, among the ashes, he might find some old friends and join another gang. A bit earlier, farther up the road, Lance Zoyas had left his shelter and raced quickly away, looking for a road down from the mountains which had brought The Bloodsuckers to such heights and had thrust them down to such depths. He thought, as he raced along, of Debbie and Rokmer and Monster Man and The Black Donut and Ivan the Terrible. Strange, hard people. They had been his family, but now they were gone. And that filled him with a great sadness.

Make the Most of Your Leisure Time with
LEISURE BOOKS

Please send me the following titles:

Quantity	Book Number	Price
_____	_____	_____
_____	_____	_____
_____	_____	_____
_____	_____	_____
_____	_____	_____

If out of stock on any of the above titles, please send me the alternate title(s) listed below:

_____	_____	_____
_____	_____	_____
_____	_____	_____

Postage & Handling _____

Total Enclosed $ _____

☐ Please send me a free catalog.

NAME _____
(please print)

ADDRESS _____

CITY _____ STATE _____ ZIP _____

Please include $1.00 shipping and handling for the first book ordered and 25¢ for each book thereafter in the same order. All orders are shipped within approximately 4 weeks via postal service book rate. PAYMENT MUST ACCOMPANY ALL ORDERS.*

*Canadian orders must be paid in US dollars payable through a New York banking facility.

Mail coupon to: **Dorchester Publishing Co., Inc.**
6 East 39 Street, Suite 900
New York, NY 10016
Att: ORDER DEPT.